SOME TIME AROUND FOUR-THIRTY

SOME TIME AROUND
FOUR-THIRTY
A NOVEL

PHILIP P. GEBBIA

iUniverse, Inc.
New York   Bloomington

Some Time Around Four-Thirty
A Novel

iUniverse books may be ordered through booksellers or by contacting:

iUniverse
1663 Liberty Drive
Bloomington, IN 47403
www.iuniverse.com
1-800-Authors (1-800-288-4677)

ISBN: 978-1-4502-2546-5 (sc)
ISBN: 978-1-4502-2547-2 (ebk)

Library of Congress Control Number: 2010905161

Printed in the United States of America

iUniverse rev. date: 06/14/2010

In Memory Of

Paul P. Gebbia, Jr.
12/03/1948 - 02/10/2010

nothing is simple
and even less is easy
except death
(and you wouldn't
like it there, i think
the people are unfriendly
and the air is sticky
like a jersey summer)
but some things
sometimes
become strangely
and suddenly
clear

I would like to thank my family and friends for their patience and support in the writing of this book. I especially would like to thank my wife Julia and my friend Dr. John D. Wells for their creative assistance during the process of completing this project.

Chapter 1

"What the..." Wood woke from a deep sleep, nearly falling off his couch. Hungover from the night before, he tried to focus but was met with little success. He heard the voices first. Then the colors came, flooding the room in red and blue with various hues in between.

It was clearly a man's voice. "I just hit him once. He never got up." Other murky sounds soon followed in a blurred sensation. Wood continued to shake his head for clarity, and then, "I'm serious, just once." Slowly the voice became familiar. It was his neighbor, speaking with others just outside Wood's window. It was then he realized, that the sounds, as well as the lights, were not within but from somewhere outside his head.

Wood clumsily rolled off his couch and walked through a bath of purple haze to his front window. Outside, sat three patrol cars with lights flashing. A slightly overweight woman and, a tall balding male, were pulling a stretcher out from the back of an ambulance. On the street Jose, his neighbor, was cuffed and being led by two officers to one of the squad cars. It was Jose he had heard. The man he hit sprawled dead in the street, a sheet covering the corpse.

"Fuck him," Wood thought. "That bastard needs to be locked up." Seeing Jose arrested and taken in cuffs had become a common sight. He was a heavy drinker who often became violent. Kitty, his wife, was no different. The police, frequent visitors, were often called in to quell their drunken rages. The last time they were summoned, it was for Kitty. She was chasing Jose around their front yard, with a knife in her hand, threatening to cut off his "pencil dick."

As Jose was being placed in the backseat of the patrol car, Kitty, playing the faithful lover, ran over and grabbed an officer. She was crying and mumbling incoherently, trying to pull the policeman off her husband. She fought hard, ripping the sleeve on the officer's shirt. It took several of the other policemen to separate her from their colleague. Once apart, Kitty fell to the curb, sobbing, as the car drove off with Jose peering pitifully out the rear window.

The commotion outside did not help Wood's hangover. The longer he was awake the worse his headache became. He gave up long ago on aspirin. It didn't seem to give him much relief. There was a time when he tried some home remedies. These failed him as well. Besides, long before anything could have an effect, he would start drinking again. Wood decided to shower. The hot steam, followed by solid food and beer, he concluded, would help ease the agonizing pain.

By the time Wood showered and dressed, the pounding in his head showed signs of receding. He was ready to face the world, his first stop being Paci's, a local pub. With downcast eyes, he eased out of his doorway, hoping to avoid conversation with his neighbors who were still loitering outside of Kitty and Jose's home.

The walk to Paci's was short. Once there, Wood quickly took a seat at the bar, ordering a shot of vodka with a beer chaser. As the drinks were placed in front of him, Buffalo, a down and out war veteran, lifted his glass in a toast, "To your health."

"And to yours," replied Wood, downing his shot.

Ordering a second round, Wood stepped away from the barstool and headed toward the jukebox. Paci's was unusually quiet and Wood decided that it needed a little music. From a playlist, loaded with rhythm n' blues, and a healthy share of music from the fifties and sixties, he decided on cuts from Luther Allison, Johnny Ace, and the Rolling Stones.

A shaft of light from an opening door distracted Wood while he was making his final selection. Looking up, he spotted Four-Thirty, entering the pub to the beginning chords of the Rolling Stones' *Factory Girl*. Wood motioned her to the bar and the empty stool next to his. The bartender Jake, without hesitation, placed a glass of red wine in front of her.

"Hey Jake, put that on my tab." Wood instructed. Turning to Four-Thirty he continued. "Haven't seen you in a while, you okay?"

"Yea, everything's fine. You know, just been working."

The two had known each other since childhood. Four-Thirty became close to Wood's little sister Lucia when her family first moved into the neighborhood. Being Polish in an all Italian neighborhood wasn't easy. At first, Four-Thirty was quite shy around Wood, who had constantly teased her, and the other children. It was he who gave her the nickname "Four-Thirty" an apparent affront to the way her feet were twisted from paralysis. She remembered him as being exceptionally callous. It was only after her father's disappearance, that Wood began to treat her differently, almost like a big brother. The two were connected. Four-thirty could not shake the feeling that Wood knew something about her father. Yet, she never had the courage to ask.

"I just got back from a long weekend date in Atlantic City." Four-Thirty said, after taking a sip from her wine. At the ripe age of fourteen she began to prostitute in support of Deadeye, her boyfriend, and his heroin addiction. He left her when she became pregnant. Too young to be a mother, she made the difficult choice and gave her son up for adoption. Several years later Deadeye came back into her life, only to leave again, when she became pregnant a second time. Soon after the birth of her child Oria, Four-Thirty knew that she had to quit working the streets, or become cautiously selective of the johns she met. Feeling confident in her abilities to work the men at motel bars, she decided to focus her attention there. Over the years she established herself with several of them. It worked out well. As a result she was very capable of supporting herself and Oria.

"Want to take a table?' Wood asked, picking up his drink.

"Sure."

From the bar they moved to a secluded booth, away from the noise and activity near the pool table. Once seated, both looked at the menu, but decided to put off eating for the moment.

"Hear you had a little excitement this afternoon."

"Yea," Wood answered. "It seems like this time, that asshole Jose finally did it."

"From what I hear, he killed a homeless guy."

"I was sleeping and woke up sometime after the police came. I don't have a clue as to what happened. I must admit, it was a pleasure seeing that fool hauled off again."

"Mm, good wine," murmured Four-Thirty, licking her lips. "Anyway, I heard at the deli that the guy was picking through some garbage when Jose came out of his place. Apparently, he and Kitty were fighting and he took it out on the old man."

"It figures. There doesn't seem to be a day those two don't get into it."

Wood ordered another round. As the bartender brought the drinks to the table, Luscious and her lover Lady Cakes entered the bar. Walking past the booth, the two women nodded greetings to Wood and Four-Thirty. Lady Cakes headed straight to the pool table and began to set a rack for a game of Eight Ball while Luscious ordered two beers.

"You know," Four-Thirty continued. "This neighborhood sure has changed since we were kids. Don't you think there's too much stupid fuckin' violence?"

"I really don't think it's just the neighborhood. I mean, it's the times. But, I do have to admit, my block has seen more than its share of killings."

"You're right there, stupid cops and stupid killings."

"Yea, remember last Christmas?"

That day, as Wood remembered it, started out to be quiet and uneventful. His sister Lucia and her family had come into town, and arrangements had been made for all to meet at his cousin Joey's home, to celebrate the Christmas holiday. At the end of a day of exchanging gifts and a peaceful dinner, Joey offered to give Wood a ride home. During the drive, Joey spoke with Wood about moving out of the neighborhood. He stressed that it had changed and was becoming dangerous. Disagreeing with his cousin, Wood tried to explain how he enjoyed the mix of people within the community. "You know, not everyone makes tomato sauce," Wood joked.

The discussion abruptly came to an end. As they turned the corner onto Wood's street, they were blocked by several police cars and a crowd of spectators. Joey turned and gave him a looks as if to say "I told you so." Wood, in turn, thanked him for the ride and stepped out of the car, walking the rest of the way.

Moving through the gathering, Wood recognized the detainee in the backseat of one of the patrol cars. He did not know him by name, but he was sure he had seen the guy several times on the street.

"Would ya fuckin' believe," asked one of the bystanders.

"No way," said another, "and on fuckin' Christmas no less."

Looking around, Wood recognized a few of his neighbors. Approaching one he asked, "What happened?"

"Oh man," moaned Stella, the cashier from the corner deli. "The poor woman and her baby, he killed them."

Wood stared at the woman in disbelief. "What? Who?"

"You know that single mom living on the second floor, the Puerto Rican girl." Stella continued, pointing to the apartment building across the street. "Her boyfriend, he killed them."

"Yea," an old man in a ragged night shirt joined the conversation. "From what I hear she dumped him. Kicked him out, ya know, like today, on Christmas. I guess he was pissed, ya know, bustin' her head open with the kid's toy truck. Then he goes and freakin' drowns the kid."

"What a fuckin' mess." Stella said turning to Wood. "He dumped her body down by the tracks. They caught him coming back for the boy."

"You know, that boy be alive if the pigs didn't drag ass."

"Why's that?" Wood asked.

"Well," said the old man, reaching into his pocket for a cigarette, "the old lady across the hall called when she heard the screams, and then called again, when she heard the boyfriend yelling at the kid to shut up. Ya know, he was cryin' and all that. The cops came nearly an hour later. Like they really give a fuck, ya know."

Wood silently turned away and continued his walk home. He didn't want to think about it. He quickened his pace knowing that a twelve pack of beer waited for him. Into the isolation of his apartment he ran to close out the rest of the world, like a tired soldier weary of the battle.

―

"You know, if you think about it, we had to deal with a lot of shit growing up," Wood contemplated. "I mean, for example, my ole' man use to beat us all the time and yours, well you know. And, remember that bastard Corso and what he did to his wife?"

"Yea, I remember that." Four-Thirty answered. "He busted up her face pretty bad. That was really tragic."

"But unlike that shithead Jose, he only got away with it once." Wood hesitated, and then drained a shot of vodka. Wiping his mouth with the back of his hand, he continued. "I mean, I just think the neighborhood just dealt with it differently. When shit happened, we took care of each other. Now-a-days, people just fuckin' gossip and move on. There's no connection, you know, no togetherness."

"Yea, I guess you're right." Four-Thirty concurred.

It was strange that Wood had mentioned her father. It was true as Wood aptly put it, the neighborhood did take care of its own. Was this what happened to him? Did they "take care of" her father, and why? It was not that he had abandoned his family. If he did, then why would he leave all his clothes and belongings behind?

Four-Thirty remembered seeing her mother the morning after her father had gone out with several of the men from the block. She was sitting, crying at the kitchen table with Wood's mother, and a few of the older Italian women, all of them dressed in black. The women were consoling her. Wood's mother had her arm around Four-Thirty's mother's back, while another woman held her hand, speaking to the other women in their native tongue. Four-Thirty asked her mother if she was alright. Her mother, clutching Four-Thirty to her breast, began to rock.

"It's okay baby. He's gone." Four-thirty's mother whispered as they continued rocking.

"Who Mommy?"

"No more sweetheart it's over, no more."

Four-Thirty tried to speak but her mother hugged tighter, pushing the child's face deep into the comfort of her breasts. Although the scent of her mother was pleasing, Four-Thirty began to feel smothered, until one of the black clad women grasped her hand and led her to the living room where her brother Casey, eating buttered toast, was sitting in front of the TV. Once seated next to him, Four-Thirty was handed a plate of several slices of toast and a coffee cup filled with orange juice. For the remainder of the morning the two were left alone to watch cartoons.

—

Another round of drinks and a bowl of roasted nuts were brought by the bartender Jake. He, placing menus on the table, asked if they wanted lunch. Wood declined, indicating that they would order something later. As Jake walked back to the bar, the song *The Way You Look Tonight* by The Jaguars began to play.

"Nice tune," Wood spoke softly.

"Sure does bring back memories." Four-Thirty sat up, reaching across the table she grabbed Wood's arm. "Speaking of memories, you'll never guess who I ran into while I was in Atlantic City."

"Who?"

"Remember Laura, Deadeye's youngest sister?"

"You mean the short chubby one? Hell, I haven't seen her, let me think, it has to be since my last year in high school."

"Yea, that's the one." Four-Thirty answered. "She was down in Atlantic City, you know, one of those bus trips, with some other people we went to school with."

"What's she up to?" Wood asked.

"I could say three hundred pounds, but that would be tacky." Four-Thirty laughed. "But she did say she works at the Spenser's Bank. We didn't talk much. Still blames me for Deadeye overdosing."

"You weren't even with him when that shit went down."

"Yea, I know. But man, Laura's so bitter. She still won't accept Oria as her niece. Never mind that she also has a nephew out there somewhere. To her, I'm that slut who fucked up her brother's life."

One of the earliest memories Wood had of Deadeye was that of the two of them, barely five years old, stealing peaches off the stand out in front of Jennie's Market. They had been constant companions up into their teen years, when Deadeye lost sight in his left eye.

It was on a summer afternoon the two of them, with Ronnie C, Barrel, and Jo Jo, were strolling around the downtown stores of Passaic. They had just left The Rack of Relics, where they spun several forty-fives in the record booth, when Ronnie C announced that he had to head home to avoid being late for dinner.

It was Barrel who suggested they take a short cut down Third Street to the Monroe Street Bridge. The guys were less than two blocks from the river when they approached a small gathering standing outside an old tenement building. They were wearing gang colors.

"Oh shit," Jo Jo spoke. "I think we got trouble."

"No, no, let's just keep walking. We'll be okay." Wood instructed.

"I'm glad you think so." Barrel added.

The five of them walked briskly past the stoop where several members of The Dragons, a small Puerto Rican gang, were milling around. Just as they passed the building, a member, barely twelve years old, stepped out from an alley, blocking their path. Barrel, looking into his eyes, snickered and walked around him. The others followed.

"Hey man," one of the older Dragons called out. "Where ya punks think ya goin'?"

Wood and Deadeye turned to answer. It was Deadeye who spoke. "We're just going home. That's all."

"Oh, but this is Dragon territory, ya know."

Deadeye, trying to keep the peace, spoke calmly. "No disrespect, man. Just two blocks and we're across the bridge."

"You have permiss'?"

"Fuck this." Barrel mumbled. "I'm going."

"Easy," Wood whispered to him, but it was too late.

"What you say?" The smallest of the Dragons asked, as he stepped up to Barrel.

Outweighing his challenger by at least fifty pounds, Barrel stared fiercely into his eyes and spat out, "Fuck you, I'm going."

"Fuck me? No man, fuck you." As Barrel turned to walk away, the Dragon pulled a screwdriver from his pocket. Deadeye alertly stepped between them. "No, wait. We don't need..."

Aiming for Barrel's shoulder, the warrior lunged forward, planting his weapon into Deadeye face instead. Overcome by excruciating pain, Deadeye froze, blood gushing from his eye, like water from a broken pipe. Everyone scattered as panic stricken, except for Barrel who, after throwing his foe to the ground, began to stomp him into unconsciousness. And Wood, sitting on the stoop, his arms wrapped around his injured friend.

—

It was after Deadeye's release from the hospital when Four-Thirty, barely thirteen, began to hang out with him. She felt sorry for him. Having lost sight in his eye, he became despondent and withdrawn. Deadeye avoided Wood and his other friends, often secluding himself in his room. Four-Thirty concluded he needed a companion. Besides, with his eye patch, she thought he looked cool, like a storybook pirate.

At first, Deadeye was annoyed by Four-Thirty's constant presence. He didn't want her, or any of his friends, to witness his suffering. Yet, she stuck around, eventually melting into his routine.

Initially, Deadeye suffered a lot of pain. Taking his medication would often put him to sleep. Awake, it left him numb, unable to leave his bed. His mind wandered, and within those landscapes he would often get lost. He started to double his dose, pushing himself further into his new world seeking newer visions.

Eventually the medicine began to run out. His doctor, sensing the teenager's growing dependency, refused to write another prescription. The doctor was convinced, expressing to the family that their son should not be experiencing any pain. "It's all in his head." The physician would tell Deadeye's parents. "Just give him aspirin."

Unable to face the cold slap of reality, Deadeye sought out alternatives. Marijuana was easily obtainable, but it was not much more effective than the aspirin. Besides, it was too sociable of a drug, something you shared. Yet, he would often smoke with Four-Thirty, who remained his silent companion. Once high, they would climb into his bed. There he would lay with his arms wrapped around Four-Thirty as he drifted into his fantasies and illusions. She would just sleep. They rarely talked. He kept her on the fringe, outside his world, an uninvolved participant. She was too young Deadeye rationalized. Four-Thirty was not yet in high school, whereas he was a junior. She would never understand.

It wasn't long before Deadeye graduated from marijuana to heroin. He had made the transition through one of his dealers, and soon began to roam the shooting galleries, with a naïve Four-Thirty in tow. Very often, he would buy several bags of the drug, and then find a spot in one of the rooms where he would fix. There he would nod into oblivion as Four-Thirty cuddled him like a child until he was ready to move on.

It was an early autumn afternoon when the two had cut school, and gone to a desolate tenement building on Alabama Avenue in Paterson. There, in a second floor apartment, Fatman ran a shooting gallery and managed a stable of prostitutes. As they walked through the door, Deadeye and Four-Thirty encountered Fatman sitting in an overstuff chair. On the arm perched Kenyatta, one of Fatman's girls.

"Got anything for me?" Deadeye asked, wiping his running nose with the back of his hand.

"I got a ten-pack for forty-five." Fatman said.

"Is it good shit?" Deadeye asked, sitting with Four-Thirty on an old couch across from the dealer. It was obvious he was hurting and needed to fix. He began to rock unsteadily.

"Don't ya insult me man." Fatman replied angrily, "I ain't never given ya any bad shit."

"No, I guess not." Deadeye started to show his impatience. Unconsciously, he scratched the invisible bugs under his skin. "I only have thirty-five. Front me the rest?"

"Again, don't insult me motha' fucker. Besides, ya owe me for two dimes from the last you was here."

"Man, you know I'm good for it," appealed Deadeye, sitting on the edge of the couch.

Four-Thirty began to shift nervously. If Deadeye didn't get his drugs, her cutting school would be the least of her problems. She had been there before. He nursed a continuous flow of bitterness with the potential for violence. She had often been his victim when it suddenly erupted.

From her seat, Kenyatta picked up on Four-Thirty's uneasiness. She gave a shy smile as to reassure Four-Thirty that she would be alright.

"All ya fuckin' junkies," Fatman began, "ya'll want to be fronted. Ya'll think you are good for it. Look at me. I ain't no social service here. If you want welfare then get ya ass downtown."

"But…"

"No, no, I ain't listening to ya shit." Turning toward Kenyatta, he placed his right hand on her leg. With the other, he wiped the sweat off his brow, looking toward Four-Thirty. Pressing against Deadeye, she could feel Fatman undressing her with his dark eyes. She nudged Deadeye to leave, but he remained cold and unresponsive.

"I'll tell ya what," Fatman continued. "I'll give ya that freakin' ten-pack for thirty-five and let ya slide for what you owe. But..." Snickering, he hesitated.

"But what?" Deadeye asked.

Fatman leaned forward and nodded toward Four-Thirty. "Ya girl over there, she and me, in the back. She do me a turn."

"What da fuck?" Kenyatta screamed as she bolted off the arm of the chair. "Look at her. She's just a baby!"

"Well, maybe it's time to grow up."

Kenyatta, standing in front of Fatman, pleaded. "Com' on nigga', don't do it."

"Shut up bitch." He said, pushing her aside. Turning to Deadeye, he asked. "Deal?"

"Nigga' I'm out of here. Don't want no part of this shit." The woman spoke as she walked toward the door. Turning to Four-Thirty she added, "Child, ya com' with me. He ain't gonna stop ya."

Four-Thirty was unable to move, frozen by the icy stare of Fatman. As Kenyatta closed the door behind her, Fatman tossed the ten-pack on the table.

Leaning forward, Deadeye snatched up the package and answered. "Yea, it's a deal."

—

"Hey, are you okay?" Wood startled Four-Thirty.

"Ah," she hesitated, "yea, I'm fine."

"I don't know, seems like you were drifting off or something."

Four-Thirty took a sip from her wine, composing herself before answering. "Well yea, I kinda did for a moment. I was thinking about Deadeye."

"Are you sure, seems you look a little pale." Wood observed.

"Yea, yea, I'm okay." She drank a little more of the wine before continuing. "Did you know the guy they called The Fatman? You know, he was one of Deadeye's connections."

"Can't say that I did."

"Well," Feeling a little edgy, Four-Thirty began twisting a napkin around her finger. "I use to go to his place in P-town with Deadeye, when he needed to score. Was first guy Deadeye have me do, you know."

"Sorry."

"No, no don't be. Believe me, it was really nothing. Nothing like it could have been. Believe me."

"Well," said Wood, "I really didn't know much about what you guys were up to back then."

"You know, it was really quite funny, now I'm thinking back on it." Four-Thirty smiled. "I mean, here I was with this guy, Fatman. He had to be at least three, three hundred fifty pounds. And there he was, sitting on the side of the bed, with his big black gut hanging over these tight white briefs. I remember he had stretch marks, kinda like a road map running down that huge belly of his. Anyway, he dropped his draws and there it was."

"Yea, what, there was what?"

"Did you know Deadeye swapped me to this guy for a few nickel bags? Isn't that something? Just so he could get high, fucker." For a brief moment she withdrew again, reflecting on her relationship with Deadeye. Turning back to Wood, she continued. "Anyway here was this huge gut, and just below it was the smallest penis I have ever seen. The guy was a freak."

"Are you serious?"

Four-Thirty continued, "I remember thinking my baby brother was bigger than him. So Fatman points down to it, like he wants me to suck him. Keep in mind, I'm scared shitless. One, because this guy was a mean looking bastard and two, I was just about to burst out laughing, 'cause he was too big to be so small. Know what I mean? Man, I was afraid he was gonna kill me."

"So what did you do?" Wood asked.

Finishing the last of her wine, Four-Thirty placed her glass on the table. "Well, he motioned me over and then pushed me down between his legs. I think he said 'suck me' or 'eat me', you know, something like that. Anyway, thinking I had no choice, I grab him between my thumb and finger, he was that small. Next thing I know this guy is shooting all over himself."

Wood laughed. "You're kidding me, really?"

"No seriously, all I did, I mean, I just touched him." She chuckled. "Man, Fatman was so embarrassed that he started yelling at me like it was my fault. And then to top that, when we walk out of the room he tells Deadeye, who's sitting there nodding oblivious to the world, that I was the best piece of ass he ever had. Imagine."

"That's funny, that's sick, man." Wood laughed. "Did you ever go back after that?"

"Yea, we went back several times. You know, Deadeye had to have his dope. But Fatman, I don't think he could ever look me in the eye again. Like he knew I had something on him."

"I guess you did." Wood added.

"Yea, I guess I did," Four-Thirty replied. "I also learned something that day, you know. I learned that men are weak. The Fatman had his weaknesses, Deadeye had his for dope. You got yours, no offense, for whatever reason. Yea, men are weak. For the most part I had to learn how to exploit that. And I think I did. At least, to have survived all these years doing what I do."

—

Jake had announced last call and began to clean up behind the bar. Exchanging her cue stick for a broom, Luscious started sweeping out the dining room, while Lady Cakes waited patiently for her to finish. Buffalo slowly hobbled out the front door, leaving his drinking buddy No Hope alone, dozing at the bar.

"Well," Wood said, downing the last of his beer. "I guess I'll head on home."

"Looks like we don't have much of a choice," Four-Thirty replied. "I might as well do the same."

"You gonna be around tomorrow?" Wood asked, scratching at his three day old beard.

"I had planned to go out to the mall, you know, do a little shopping," answered Four-Thirty, reaching for her purse. "I was also thinking about spending some time with my daughter. You, any plans?"

"Nothing really, might stay home and do a little reading."

Briefly looking at the check, Four-Thirty pulled two ten dollar bills from her wallet and placed the money on the table. Leaning back in her seat, she let out a soft sigh. "Have you been doing any writing lately?"

"Nah," Wood shook his head. "That part of my life has long passed."

"That's sad." Four-Thirty said. She had briefly followed his literary career and, unbeknownst to Wood, traveled to Virginia to listen to him read from his last novel. "It would be nice to see another book by you, or even a short story."

"Like I said, that part of my life is long gone."

"What about teaching?" Four-Thirty asked. "I'm sure you can do that again. You might be able to teach a class or two at the community college."

"That too, is in my past."

Snapping her wallet shut, she placed it back in her purse. Looking across the table, she gave Wood a cold, hard stare. He, unable to make eye contact, turned away from her.

"I guess if you're here, I might see you tomorrow." Wood said, putting on his jacket. He started to leave, stopped, and shrugged his shoulders. Turning back to Four-Thirty, he conceded, "Listen Kiddo, I'll figure something out. But, writing or teaching I just don't see it."

Chapter 2

Returning home after a long day shopping at the mall, Four-Thirty was welcomed by the sounds of Oria, her daughter, in the kitchen. On a small table next to the entrance, she placed her packages and hastily hung her jacket and scarf on a hook next to the table. Catching a glimpse in the hall mirror, she stopped briefly to face her image. Dark rings encircled her tired eyes and her graying hair was slightly skewed from the mild wind. "My God," softly speaking to no one. "I look so worn. Definitely need some time off."

Her frown upturned into a smile as she entered the kitchen. "Hey baby, wha'ya got cooking? It smells really good in here."

Oria leaned over and gave her mom a slight hug and kissed her gently on the cheek. "Nothing special, just some roasted chicken. And, as an added touch, I thought that you might like some of Nanny's stuffed artichoke."

"Oh Sweetie you don't know how much that will make my day." Four-Thirty said, peering into the oven.

"Hey, I just opened this Riesling. Would you like some?" Oria asked, reaching for a glass from the cabinet above the counter.

"Sure, that would be nice."

Upon taking the wine from Oria, mother and daughter lightly touched their glasses together. Smiling, Four-Thirty took a seat at the table as Oria returned to her cooking. She was quite proud of her child. Oria had graduated from college with honors and worked her way through graduate school, receiving a master's degree in Human Resource Management. Neither the circumstances surrounding Four-Thirty when she first became pregnant, nor the difficult choices she was force to make, were causes to prevent her daughter Oria from doing well.

—

It was several years after Four-Thirty had given up her first child for adoption, when Deadeye, the baby's father, reentered her life. It was on a May afternoon. She was helping her mother with some spring cleaning when she heard knocking at their door. Upon answering, there was Deadeye on her stoop, shocking Four-Thirty by his presence. She never thought she would ever see him again. He had been gone for more than three years. Rumors had circulated that he either had entered a rehab program or landed in jail. Four-Thirty could not have cared less where he went. At that time she had convinced herself she didn't want him back in her life. Now, seeing him standing there, like a prodigal son, with a pack hanging off his shoulder and a slight hint of a smile, she wasn't so sure.

It didn't take much prodding from Deadeye to persuade Four-Thirty to live with him. They soon found a small basement apartment which they furnished by exploring second hand shops. At first, the two of them seemed to be doing well. Four-Thirty took a job at a local dress shop, and Deadeye agreed to go out daily looking for work.

Contrary to the promise he had made to Four-Thirty, Deadeye rarely ventured out of the home. Employment was the least of his concerns. In addition, he avoided his old friends, often referring to Wood as a pseudo-intellectual hippie and the others as just plain useless.

As it is with most honeymoons, the bliss of their reunion was short lived. It soon became apparent, Deadeye, not only was he still using drugs, his lust for heroin had intensified. As before, to support his addiction, he once again pushed Four-Thirty into prostitution. Only this time, he did so with severe brutality.

Living with Deadeye had become a frightening situation. He would occasionally beat her without reason, constantly accusing her of stealing from him, and forcing her into situations that were dangerous. It was during a time when the streets were dry, and Deadeye was unable to feed his hunger, he put Four-Thirty in the hospital.

She has just returned from Dr. Cante, her physician, only to find Deadeye home pacing the floor. For more than a week he had difficulties making a connection, and what drugs he did find didn't satisfy his needs. Knowing that Four-Thirty was meeting with her doctor, Deadeye was confident that she, one way or another, would convince the doctor to write a prescription. Seeing her come in, he quickly grabbed her purse, and rifled through it.

"Where is it?" He anxiously asked. "Didn't Cante give you anything, a script?"

Four-Thirty watched, fearing the worst, as he dumped the contents of her bag on the table. "No, I didn't ask."

"What the fuck," yelled Deadeye, throwing the purse at Four-Thirty. Avoiding being hit, she ducked as the handbag buzzed passed her. "Why didn't you?"

She had witnessed his rage before. It has become commonplace and all too often, she was his victim. Sensing the danger, Four-Thirty moved around to the opposite side of the table, out of his reach. "I just, I…"

"Don't give me any excuses." Deadeye screamed. "You know fuckin' well that there's nothing out there. I'm hurting, don't you fuckin' care?"

"Well, I…" she didn't know how to tell him. She was pregnant again. She remembered how he walked out on her the last time without looking back. She wanted this child, she wanted a family. She was frightened that he would abandon her again. "Well, I had…"

"Well what? Spit it out bitch."

"I didn't ask, 'cause I had to see him about me. And, oh damn, if I did ask, he wouldn't have given it to me anyway."

Deadeye hesitated long enough to light a cigarette. "What do you mean he wouldn't give it to you? Fuck, he's the candy man. He gives shit to high school kids."

"Well," Four-Thirty took a deep breath before continuing, "I'm late about six weeks. I'm pregnant."

"No, no. no," Deadeye paced nervously across the floor. Stopping directly across the table from Four-Thirty, he looked piercingly into her eyes. His fury quickly reached a crescendo. "Fuckin' no, you are not pregnant."

Answering softly, "Yes I am."

Rushing around the table, Deadeye pushed Four-Thirty up against the wall. He began to scream, a shower of spittle burst off the tip of his tongue. "I know what you're doing. You're doing this so that you won't have to trick anymore. You're doing this to get back at me. Well, fuck you!"

"Get real for once in your life." Underneath the fear, her anger began to intensify. Four-Thirty spewed back, "I'm pregnant. It just happened, that's all. It's not about you." She tried to move from under Deadeye's weight but was unable to do so.

"Well you're right there. It's not about me 'cause it ain't my fuckin' kid. No fuckin' way."

"What?"

"You heard me. It ain't mine. You know, it's one of those guys."

"Listen to you, you little bastard." Four-Thirty said, building up courage. "Don't you get it? I suck cock for you. I suck cock. That's why we only get five or ten dollars. And if I did let someone else stick his dick inside of me, you damn well know we did it with a rubber. The baby is yours, I'm sure of it, the baby is yours."

Turning away from Four-Thirty, he picked up another cigarette and lit it. He took a drag, slowly exhaling a long cloud of blue smoke. No longer screaming he added, "Well for one thing, we're not keeping it."

"No," she responded, raising her voice, "you're not making me give up this baby. I'm not doing that again. I swear."

With a back handed fist, Deadeye punched Four-Thirty, blood spurting from a cut above her right eye. A wooden chair crumbled beneath her as she fell to the floor. "We're either going to give this kid away or abort it, even if I have to do it myself. We're not keeping it."

"Fuck you!" Four-Thirty screamed at him. "It's my baby. And I'm keeping it with you or without you!"

He hit her again. She felt the knuckles of his fist crack against her forehead. Deadeye began yelling, but in her daze, Four-Thirty was unable to hear him. With a kick to her right side, she started to lose consciousness. Watching Deadeye's foot rise slowly for a second kick, she tried to brace herself against the impact but passed out before it landed.

Blinded by rage, Deadeye beat her ferociously. Only, after seeing her lying there in a pool of blood, he stopped. Fearing that she was dead, he bolted out the door. Four-Thirty never saw him again. She and Oria, her baby, survived.

—

"Hey mom, Dinner is about ready." Oria announced, breaking Four-Thirty's thought process. "Would you like some more wine?"

"Sure sweetheart. Can I do anything? Set the table? Make a salad?" Four-Thirty asked as her daughter refreshed their drinks.

"Yea, there is something." Oria answered. "I'll set the table mom if you promise to make that kale and white raisin salad you're famous for."

"I don't know about famous, but your wish is my command." Four-Thirty giggled, getting up from the table.

The recipe was a variation of one that was handed down from her maternal grandmother. It was quite simple. Four-Thirty chopped a fair amount of fresh kale leaves, which she placed into a medium sized bowl. Added to that was a handful of white raisins. She then carefully measured out a quarter cup of feta cheese which was then mixed with the greens and raisins.

It was in how she made the dressing, which Four-Thirty's recipe differed from her grandmother's. The elderly woman generally stuck by tradition using basic vinegar and oil. Instead, Four-Thirty concocted a balsamic vinaigrette with crushed garlic and nutmeg. This she poured on top of her salad and tossed.

The table was set. The roasted chicken was taken from the oven and placed on a hot plate near the artichokes. As she took her seat, Four-Thirty added her salad to the mix. She smiled as Oria took her place across from her, and as if on cue, both lifted their glasses and clicking them together. "Another great meal fit for queens."

"Oh mom, wait." Oria said, scooping up an artichoke and placing it on her mother plate. "Try this first. I know you will love it, I'm sure."

Leaning over the serving, Four-Thirty, with a cupped hand, fanned the steam from the vegetable as to blanket her senses with its aroma. Smiling approval, she pulled out a leaf near its center. With her upper teeth, she softly scrapped off its tender morsel. Before swallowing, she slowly savored the essence of the artichoke and its cheese flavored stuffing. "Wow that is heavenly!"

"I knew you would like it." Oria expressed her satisfaction. "And I think Nanny would be most proud."

"Yea, she taught you well."

"You both did."

"I could accept that." Four -thirty chuckled. "Yea, I really can."

"You know," Oria spoke tentatively, "This artichoke that we both dearly love, somehow I get the feeling that it's not something handed down from great grandma to Nanny to you. That it really isn't a long kept family recipe of Nanny's."

"Why's that?" Four-Thirty said, restraining a laugh. She knew that her daughter was right.

"Well, you know, she was first generation Polish," Oria said while looking toward her mother for affirmation, "and, you know, she never did learn to speak English, right?"

"And?"

"Mom, think about it." Oria tried to explain, "You have garlic, parmesan cheese, and olive oil. That ain't exactly Polish, right?"

"Yea, you're right." Four-Thirty laughed.

"So how is it that grandma got to make this and all those other Italian dishes?" Oria quizzed her mother.

"Oh Baby, that's easy to explain."Four-Thirty answered. "It all started around the time when my dad, your grandfather, left."

Oria gave her mother a quizzical look. She wasn't sure how the two were connected. "Okay, so..."

"Don't ask how or why we moved there, I really don't know, but we were the only Polish family in an Italian neighborhood. Back then, things were different. People tended to live near their own kind. You know, like, near people from the same village or town, back in the old country."

Oria ate her meal slowly as she considerately listened to her mom. It was rare for Four-Thirty to speak freely about her childhood. Oria often felt that her mom had been too secretive, was hiding something. Much of what she knew about her family came from either her grandmother or her uncle Casey.

Before continuing, Four-Thirty pulled a piece of white meat from the breast of the chicken. She took a bite and chewed leisurely. "Your uncle and I, we were okay. We had made some friends. But my mom, at first, she was really isolated. She had no family. They were all still in Poland. And the women on the street, well, they kinda ignored her. She wasn't one of them, you know."

"That's sad."

"Yea, it was." Four-Thirty answered. "But then, my dad left, and that next morning they were there, you know, all these Italian women, in our house, as if we were one big family. Next thing you know, they were cooking for us, helping mom with the cleaning, and things like that."

"I don't understand." Oria stated.

"It was kinda confusing at first but, like they adopted us or something. We became part of the neighborhood." Four-Thirty continued. "I mean, here's your grandmother, she barely could speak English, never mind Italian, and she's treated like she was from the old country, you know, Sicily. Next thing you know, she's cooking like them."

"What about grandpa? What happened to him?"

"I don't know." Four-Thirty answered. "I really don't know. We never saw or heard from him again."

"Someone has to know."

"Yea, I'm sure. I have my suspicions." Four-Thirty said, redirecting the attention back to the dinner. "That's how Nanny learned to make such a wonderful dish as these artichokes, and how you and I got to eat such great meals."

"Kinda like honorary Italians," laughed Oria.

"Well, at least I am, honorary that is." Four-Thirty laughed in return. "Thanks to your dad, you're half Italian."

—

The two women continued with their meal. Neither of them was bashful about taking second helpings. After the meal, Oria set up a pot of coffee as her mother brought out a bowl of fruit for dessert. Four-Thirty remembered, while shopping she had purchased some Italian pastries from Aloia's Bakery. She placed several on a plate and put it on the table with the fruit.

"Any luck job hunting?" Four-Thirty asked, as Oria finished pouring the coffee.

It was a little less than a year since Oria had completed her degree program. She was having some difficulty finding employment within her field. While she was studying for her Master of Arts degree, she had taken a job as a substitute teacher in the local school system. After graduating, she continued working, with the hope that she would find something in management. Oria was unable to find acceptable employment. The only opportunities available seem to be limited to the fast food industry. She wasn't prepared to flip hamburgers.

"I don't know mom, seems like there really isn't much out there." Oria sighed.

"Sorry to hear that."

"I really don't want to substitute teach the rest of my life. Know what I mean?"

"I guess." Four-Thirty said, after taking a sip from her coffee. "I wouldn't want to deal with second graders for any length of time either."

"I don't mind the kids, really don't." Oria responded. "But, they're not the population I thought I would be managing when I went for my degree."

"Have you looked into any employment agencies or head hunters?" Four-Thirty asked.

"Yea, but most seem to offer these trainee positions in places like Jiffy Burger, or some other fast food place. I'm not sure I want to go from managing six and seven year olds to pimply face teenagers."

"Yea, I see what you mean." Four-Thirty took a small bite off a chocolate covered cookie before she continued. "Have you thought about an alternative?"

"Well, Joanie and I have been talking about relocating, perhaps L.A. or Seattle."

As best friends since grade school, Joanie and Oria had been inseparable. Oria had always been the calm reserved one. Whereas, Joanie the outspoken, outgoing, and, as Four-Thirty often labeled her, the flaky one. She liked her, but knew that Joanie wasn't very dependable. She often acted on impulse, quickly losing interest, then moving onto something else. For Oria's sake, Four-Thirty secretly hoped this wasn't one of those moments. Yet, she had faith in her daughter. In the end Oria would take care of herself.

"That might be nice." Four-Thirty reluctantly replied. "A change might do you some good."

"Maybe, but I can't go if I don't have the money, and I can't get the money unless I get a decent job that pays."

"You know, I might be able to help you." Four-Thirty offered. She immediately thought of Dennis Slovinski. Although she knew him since high school, their relationship was more recent. He was a client who paid her well for small talk and straight sex. Often, he would brag about his position in county government, adding that if she ever needed a favor he could deliver.

"How so?"

"Well, I know this guy. He and I have been friends for a long time and he's a county supervisor." Four-Thirty explained.

"A boyfriend," Oria joked.

"No, no," laughed Four-Thirty, "just a friend. Anyway, I think he might know of something. I mean, there might be something in one of the county departments, or something with a company that does business with the government. Who knows?"

"Do you think he might, you know?" Oria didn't want to get her hopes up.

"Let's see what I can do. You know the old saying. 'Nothing ventured…'"

"Mom, you know you really don't…"

"Shh," Four-Thirty said, putting her finger to Oria's lips. "For my baby there's no 'you don't have to'. You know that."

Chapter 3

The rain has been steady for the past three days. Wood could no longer take being homebound and was developing cabin fever. Having drank his last beer the night before, he decided to head out to Paci's. Not owning an umbrella, he grabbed an old sweatshirt and baseball cap to help keep him dry. Once outside, he pulled the cap low over his eyes and swiftly walked the few blocks to the neighborhood hangout.

His choice of weather gear proved to be a failure. Upon entering Paci's he was soaked through to his underwear. With squeaking shoes, he made his way to a back booth where Four-Thirty sat, sipping her favorite wine and reading the newspaper. "Only fuckin' ducks," Wood muttered.

"Yea, only fuckin' ducks should be out in this shit." Four-Thirty responded without looking up from the paper. "So why are we here?"

"Hey Jake," Wood called out to the bartender, "the usual." Turning to Four-Thirty, "Hey, just couldn't take the four walls much longer. They were, like, crowding me, and I was beginning to feel like I wanted to punch holes in them."

"Sounds like you're a little on edge."

"Yea, feels like it." Wood said, squirming in his seat. "Don't know why. Maybe the weather, maybe not, just don't know."

The bartender placed a shot and beer on the table. Wood quickly downed the vodka. "Bring another shot." He instructed Jake before taking a sip from the beer. "Got to get the blood flowing again, you think?"

"Know something," Four-Thirty said putting down the paper, "you really don't look too good."

"Hell, I'm just sitting here in a puddle, drenched to the bone, shivering because the air in here is turned way up and you think I don't look too good?" Wood sneered. "Shit, I wonder why."

Four-Thirty took a sip from her drink and smiled, "I guess you got something there."

The second shot of vodka was brought to the table. Wood downed that as quickly as the first. Looking into the empty glass, he decided to hold off awhile before ordering a third.

Considering how bad the weather had been the last few days, Wood was quite surprised as to how many people were in Paci's. Of course Buffalo and No Hope would be there. The bar was their only true refuge. And, as usual, Luscious and Lady Cakes were in the back shooting pool. A few of the other regular patrons were either playing pinball or sitting at the bar watching the local news. Wood had guessed, like himself, after staying home through several days of heavy rains, they also had to get out, avoiding cabin fever.

The bartender walked over to Wood with a sweatshirt and overalls in his hand. "Had these hangin' in the back, from when I painted the upstairs apartment, should help keep you warm some."

"Thanks."

"Hell, I thought, tho' you ain't a fixture here like one of those guys," nodding toward Buffalo and No Hope, "you are one of the regulars. It ain't right letting you sit here this way."

"Hey, if I ever become one of them, just shoot me."

"I got the ammo ready. Don't give me a reason to use it."

All three of them laughed as Wood slid off the seat and headed toward the men's room. The bartender called to him, "Hang your stuff on the hook back there. You can retrieve it later."

"Thanks again, Jake."

Upon his return, and wearing the dry clothing, Wood saw that another round of drinks was left at the table. He looked up at Jake, who nodded and said, "It's on the house." Wood nodded back in gratitude.

"So, how are you really feeling?" Four-Thirty asked, believing that she had reason to be concerned. He didn't look healthy. He appeared thin, his skin tone was quite pale, and he had developed some dark rings around his eyes that made them appear to be phantom like. She was more concern about his breathing. That appeared to be labored.

"Fine, I guess. Why?" He wasn't being honest. Although he had quit his two packs a day habit more than fifteen years ago, lately he has found himself to have difficulties walking stairs. Even the few blocks walk to Paci's had become a slight challenge.

"Oh, I don't know. I haven't seen you in a couple days and it looks like you lost some weight. It's just too damn noticeable."

"Maybe so, but I feel fine. No complaints." Wood really didn't know when the last time was that he really felt well. He didn't think that he was actually ill, but that his body wasn't functioning as it had been. Mornings have been difficult. He had been waking up tired and spending the day fatigued. Then there were those aches and pains that seem to steadily get worse. "I'm just getting old," Wood thought, and with that, all medical opinions were invalidated.

Four-Thirty gave Wood a smile and asked, "Are you eating right?"

"You know what they say about that," Wood laughed. "A hotdog a day keeps that ole' doctor away."

"Don't tell me you're still going to The Hut."

"No, no, God no," Wood chuckled. The Hut had been a high school hangout when Four-Thirty and Wood were teenagers. It was a place to meet, show off your car and, occasionally, a place where fights between rival towns would break out. Unlike other hotdog joints that were known for the *Texas*, a boiled frankfurter covered with raw onions and chili, The Hut staked its reputation on one that was deep fried and smothered in their secret mustard relish. Back in Wood's day, they were three for a dollar or a buck and a quarter with fries.

Four-Thirty gave Wood a concerning look. "I hope not."

"Sweetheart, have you seen that place lately?" He asked. "It's nothing more than a den for junkies and crackheads. I mean, the place was never high class. You know what I mean. But now, it's really the pits."

"Changes," she responded to Wood. "You know, everything changes."

"Yea and you know, not always for the good. Lately, seems like nothing has been for the good."

Four-Thirty wondered what Wood was implying by that last statement. Yet, she wasn't ready to inquire. "Do you remember that night we were up at The Hut in that old beat-up junker your uncle gave you?"

Wood smiled as he thought of the old fifty-one Ford he briefly had as a teenager. His dad's oldest brother originally owned the car. For years, Wood and his family would visit his uncle, the highlight being Wood, playing in the old car, and his uncle Johnny promising to give it to him when he passed his driving tests. Sure enough, the morning after the road test, his uncle had the coupe towed over. The way Uncle Johnny saw it he was getting rid of an eyesore. To Wood, he was rescuing a classic from becoming a planter for ragweed. The car was kept in old man Pacifico's lot until Wood got it running. Once it started, Wood reminisced, the old Ford purred like a kitten.

Wood turned to Four-Thirty, "We were up there in that ole' thing lots."

"Boy, the first night I ever set foot in that heap," Four-Thirty recollected, "I remember that the back seat had no floorboards. Rusted right through, you could see the road below you. I was always afraid of falling through to the pavement while we were cruising around town."

"Well yea, but it was dependable. It got us to The Hut many nights."

"You remember the night I'm sure, the four of us, you, me, Deadeye and Ronnie C. It was when you and your brother got into it. I mean, I was really afraid you were going to kill him." Four-Thirty momentarily hesitated then continued, "That was scary with the cops and all. Two brothers, you would never…"

"I was really pissed." Wood cut her short.

"What was it with you two?" Four-Thirty asked, not expecting an answer.

Wood and his brother Phillie Wheels had been estranged at a very young age. Although he could not remember exactly why they had fought that particular night, he knew that there had been an accumulation of events and issues that led up to it. He did remember his rage. Wood firmly believed that at that moment, he had wanted to kill his brother, and perhaps would have, if the police had not stepped in. Thinking back, Wood felt embarrassment by his actions and all else that caused the split between them. In spite of his indignity, he still felt a twinge of anger toward Phillie Wheels.

Distracted, Wood's eyes followed Luscious as she walked toward the jukebox. She dropped in a few coins after which she selected several songs. As Luscious started to walk back to the pool table, the Fabulous Thunderbirds' version of *Scratch My Back* began to play.

His eyes drifted back to Four-Thirty. "You know, I'm not sure what happened that night. Between him and me, it could have been anything. Yea, I would say anything. I'm sorry to say that I probably did want to kill him."

Four-Thirty signaled to the bartender for another glass of red wine. "That's sad."

"Yea, it is sad, ain't it?" Wood said softly. "That night capped off a lot for me. My dad was so pissed, he left me sitting in jail. Then when I got out, he beat my ass so bad I was bruised for days."

"Didn't you leave home after that?"

"Well, it was more like he put me out. Kinda like once removed." Wood answered. "I thought that I had no choice but to leave. I knew he would put me out. So I moved in with my aunt. My dad, that bastard, even took my car. He sold the Ford to Billy Monte. Remember him?

Anyway, the old man kept the money. He and I barely spoke after that."

"I didn't know that." Four-Thirty appeared to be surprised. "I knew you and Phillie Wheels parted ways, but I thought you and your dad had patched things up when you left for school."

"Nah, not really," Wood answered. "I never really understood him. Seems like, he was always making excuses for my brother. Always blaming me for what he did. I guess he thought he had his reasons. It didn't make sense to me."

—

The music selections made by Luscious played out and the barroom remained relatively quiet. Other than the occasional cracking of the cue ball hitting another and the nearly inaudible hum of the refrigerator cooling various brands of beer, the only sound heard was of the TV.

From within the pub it was difficult to know if the rain had let up. The windows sat high along the walls and were covered with various beer signs, making it nearly impossible to look out. Like the other patrons, Wood wasn't too concerned about any change in the weather. He looked around the room. All appeared to be oblivious to what was going on outside. It didn't matter if it was raining, sleeting or if a major blizzard had stuck. They were inside unaffected, content.

Apparently, Buffalo had fallen asleep at the bar. His head laid peacefully on its surface with his arms dangling at his side. His partner in drink Eddie Hope, often referred to as Bob Hope's illegitimate brother No Hope, continued to nurse a glass of straight whiskey. Occasionally he would prod his buddy in an attempt to wake him. Buffalo would fail to stir, leaving No Hope to continue drinking alone.

Lady Cakes, taking a break from the pool table, walked over to the jukebox. She dropped in several coins, browsed the list, and made a few selections. She paused for a moment while she continued to review the playlist. Unable to choose, she looked up and turned toward the booth where Four-Thirty and Wood sat. "Hey Rain Man," she called out to Wood, "any suggestions?"

"Yea," Wood responded. "How about some Clapton, old Clapton?"

Lady Cakes looked at the playlist and quickly made a selection. As she walked back toward the pool table she announced, "I guess it's *Bell Bottom Blues*."

Wood perked up in his seat. Somehow he felt obligated and decided that he had to do something in return. He signaled and got the bartender's attention, "Hey Jake, a round for the house."

"No problem," remarked Jake. A gracious acknowledgement erupted throughout the room. Drinks were poured and bottles were being opened. One was placed near Buffalo's head. To No Hope's surprise and disappointment, thinking he would down his friend's drink, Buffalo woke to the sound of glass striking the table. Seeing all were served, Wood raised his shot and said, "To the Paci's family, may we always be."

"Right on!" shouted Luscious from the back.

"*Saluti*," a voice came from the bar.

Downing his drink, Wood looked at Four-Thirty. She grinned. "Nice touch, my man."

"Well, whatever."

"No seriously, that was nice." Four-Thirty continued, "It was also a little surprising. You showed a little generosity and compassion."

"What?"

"Hey, we both know that you're tight with your money. The compassion thing, that's a side you never show."

Shaking his head Wood retorted, "Maybe it's the weather, who knows?"

"Yea, maybe so," Four-Thirty answered. "But you can't blame the weather for everything. Maybe, you let loose a little and you were just being yourself."

Embarrassed, Wood attempted to redirect the conversation. What came to mind was food. "Had any thoughts about eating?"

The kitchen at Paci's remained open in spite of the rain. Although Jake and his crew had not expected their usual number, a few diners came in and were sitting in the back room being served. Both Four-Thirty and Wood decided that they were hungry. Instead of moving to the dining area, they opted to remain in their booth where they felt more comfortable.

The order was taken and the food was quickly served. As an appetizer, Wood ordered a plate of mussels smothered in a spicy red sauce, with fresh Italian bread for dipping. Wood, always a meat and potatoes man, ordered a half-pound cheeseburger made of ground sirloin, with steak fries on the side. A house salad made with locally grown vegetables, as advertised, was selected by Four-Thirty. That was topped with a homemade sun-dried tomato dressing.

⁓

Finishing her meal, Four-Thirty set her plate to the side. She was eager to continue the conversation they were having about Wood's brother. She was most anxious about gaining an understanding about the split between the two. Yet, she wasn't sure how to approach Wood about the subject, thinking that it may be difficult for him to address. Her curiosity, nursing its own hunger, sought satisfaction. Treading lightly, she said. "Your brother, you know, I've heard stories but really don't know what happened. Like, I heard he was dead. Some other people told me he took off for California."

"Well for one," Wood answered, "he is dead, but not like people think."

"Oh."

It had long been speculated in the neighborhood that Phillie Wheels had died either from an overdose or by the mob. Shortly after finishing high school, he had begun to hang out with a group of mafia wannabes at the Garibaldi Avenue Social Club. At first, he was nothing more than an errand boy, working his way up the criminal ladder. Eventually he was running a small crew and making decent money doing strong arm work, hijacking trucks, and drug distribution.

Being around bookies and narcotics, in many ways, wasn't very healthy for Phillie Wheels. He soon developed gambling and heroin addictions. In support of both of these habits, he became heavily indebted to the local boss. Then one day he just disappeared. Wood and his father initially believed Phillie Wheels had skipped town. At first, several ex-football players turned enforcers would show up at their home, demanding Phillie Wheels' return. Once they stopped coming around, Wood and his father assumed that he was dead, that the mob, or the drugs, finally got to him.

"You know," Wood continued. "Good thing my mom wasn't alive when all that shit came down about Phillie's drug use and the shit about the mob. But, on the other hand, it was sad that she wasn't around, nor my dad, when I found out what really happened."

Curiosity perked, Four-Thirty gave Wood a quizzical look. She, like many others, thought Phillie Wheels had met his demise through a mob hit.

"Hell, seems like my brother was a lot smarter than what he was given credit."

"What are you talking about?" Four-Thirty asked, quite anxious to hear the story.

Wood, finishing the last of his steak fries, pushed his plate to the side. After taking a gulp from his beer, Wood answered. "About four or five years ago a woman and her two teenage daughters came looking for me. Said she was my brother's wife and..."

"His wife," Four-Thirty interrupted. "You're kidding me?"

"Nope," Wood laughed. "She said she was his wife and his two daughters were with her. Could you imagine? It had been ages since I gave my bother up for dead and then, out of nowhere, comes his wife and my two nieces."

"That's crazy."

"Yep, sure the hell is." Wood added. "That ain't the least of it. Seems like Phillie, after leaving here, ended up living in St. Joseph, Missouri. Once there, he bought himself a piece of land and started a farm." Wood hesitated long enough to down the rest of his beer before continuing. "Now, get this. Rosie, that's my sister-in-law's name, tells me that not only was Phillie a successful farmer, raising cattle and stuff like that, she met him at a church gathering."

"I don't get it," Four-Thirty remarked. "When he disappeared he was strung out and being hunted. I mean didn't he owe the mob?"

"Well, I can't imagine, my brother successful at anything and going to church to boot. Anyway, she had a letter from my brother. Something Phillie wrote just before he died."

"I still can't imagine Wheels married with kids." Four-Thirty commented. "It's not like him, not at all. If I heard it from anyone else, I just wouldn't believe it."

"Yea, I'm with you on that one, but let me continue. So, I ask Rosie what was up with Phillie. She gets all solemn, and tells me that my brother died of cancer of the liver. Rosie then tells me that she never knew that he had family. Like, he never spoke about living here in Jersey and how he got to Missouri, none of that stuff. Then, just before he dies, like the day before I'm told, he tells her about having a family back East."

Hearing a sound behind him, Wood turned to observe someone new walking into the bar. From his vantage point he was able to see that the rain had finally let up and the sun was attempting to break through the clouds. Wood, facing Four-Thirty again, commented, "Looks like the rain has finally eased up."

"Yea, it does." Four-Thirty answered. "We could use a break in the weather."

Wood nodded his head in agreement then continued with the story of his brother. "So here you got Phillie dying, and his wife is standing there losing a husband, and finds out she has a brother-in-law somewhere in New Jersey, and God knows what else. So, the day before he dies, he makes her promise to look me up. Talking about stress and trauma, but, you got to give her credit. She must have really loved my brother because within a week of burying him here she was, with my two nieces, knocking at my door."

"That is totally amazing." Four-Thirty said, leaning against the side of the booth. "So, what's she like? Has she kept in touch?"

"She's really nice." Wood answered. "She's really a sweet person. Nothing like anyone you would think would hook up with Phillie. And her daughters, Allie and Giuseppina, named after my mom, are really sweet as well. We've kept in touch. In fact, I'm planning on going to Allie's wedding."

"That's great, that's really great. I'm glad for you. But, I must tell you," Four-Thirty's demeanor changed. Her body stiffened. Turning to Wood, she sternly said, "I'm really pissed at you. I can't fuckin'…"

"What?"

"I can't fuckin' believe you." Four-Thirty felt her anger building. "After all these years you've known about Phillie Wheels, and to top that, you have met and remain in contact with his wife and kids, but not one word."

"I don't know what to say."

"Don't say anything. You'll dig a deeper hole, ass."

The two sat in the booth for several long minutes. Four-Thirty's posture communicated that her anger and disappointment would linger. She couldn't imagine how, she being Wood's closest friend, he would be so secretive about his brother's family. She couldn't figure him out. Sometimes she felt so close to him. Other times he was just an ass. Was it a man's thing or was he really that insensitive? She had hoped not.

To break the ice, Four-Thirty finally asked, "What about the letter?"

"Oh that, well," Wood said, running his fingers through his hair. "He wanted to apologize."

"Apologize?"

Wood shifted in his seat to face Four-Thirty before responding. "Yea, I guess that he realized that he was responsible for my horrid relationship with my father, probably wanted a clean slate before he died."

"Phillie thought he was responsible, in what way?"

Easing back into the booth, he told Four-Thirty about how it was a day not much different than the day they were sitting in Paci's. It had been raining. Wood, at the time was in the sixth grade, and Phillie Wheels, who had just started high school, were home from school for the afternoon. Both of their parents were still at work. Unable to play outside, Wood and Phillie Wheels remained indoors, entertaining themselves in their bedroom.

Sitting at a desk, pieced together with cinderblocks and an old door, Wood was building a model of a Corvette Stingray. Phillie Wheels, on the other hand, sought his pleasure in harassing his younger brother. Wood tried to ignore him but was without success. "Leave me alone" and attempts to push Phillie Wheels away were only met with more teasing and tickling. Eventually, they got into a pushing match and ended up wrestling on the floor.

Bigger and much stronger than his little brother, Phillie Wheels easily dominated Wood. On the other hand, Wood fought as well as he could and actually thought at times, he would overtake Phillie Wheels. Yet, each little triumph was met by the older brother's strength. In the end Phillie Wheels had successfully immobilized Wood, wrapping and locking his legs around his brother's arms and torso.

"Com' on fuckin' let go. I want to finish my car." Wood remembered telling his brother. No longer resisting, he hoped that Phillie Wheels would release him. Instead the grip became tighter as his brother began to unzip his pants. "What the fuck?" Wood said squirming, trying to break the hold. Phillie Wheels held tighter and began to push Wood's head into his crotch. "Suck it, suck on it," he demanded as he continued to push Wood's head down.

"Oh my God," Four-Thirty exclaimed. "Did he, did you..."

"No" Wood answered. "You see, that's when my dad walked in, and things just got worse."

"How?" she asked.

"I didn't hear or see my dad come in. I mean, my face was, well, you know. When Phillie let go, I sat up and was nearly crying when I saw my dad. Next thing I hear was 'you fuckin' little faggot' with my dad punching the shit out of me. I mean, he was really beating me, fiercely. The bastard broke my nose with the first punch, and he didn't give a shit. He just kept yelling, and calling me names, as he beat me into the ground. Meanwhile, Phillie just sat there, not saying a word. I guessed he feared being next. Instead, when my dad was done with me, he turned to Phillie and told him to get out of the room. Both just walked out leaving me there bleeding."

"I'm so sorry. I would have never imagined things were like that in your home. It does explain why you and Phillie Wheels were always at odds." Four-Thirty reached for his hand and added, "I'm really sorry."

"My dad really made it hard on me after that. I guess, in his mind he was just trying to make his queer son straight."

"Did you ever talk to him about it?" Four-Thirty asked. "Did you ever forgive him?"

"My dad, I tried to talk with him before he died, but by that time he was too senile. Forgive him? No I will never forgive that bastard, never."

"What about Phillie? Did, would you forgive him?"

"I don't know." Wood answered. "I really don't know."

Chapter 4

The phone rang incessantly on the now bare desk. Dr. Lap stared at the phone emotionlessly, believing that Dean Trudy was calling. He didn't want to speak with the dean knowing, that he had nothing to say, and Dean Trudy wasn't going to tell him anything he wanted to hear. Besides, the college had already spoken. His services were no longer needed. Christopher H. Lap, PhD had been fired.

One of the longest tenured professors at the college, Dr. Lap was hired as an instructor prior to the completion of his doctorate program. At the time, a profession in teaching seemed remote. He had been on probation for a drug charge and was considering leaving school. But Dr. Lap had a guardian angel, someone on the inside pulling for him, his old college roommate, Wood. Having been promoted to an assistant professor position, Wood recommended that the school hire Dr. Lap to backfill his instructor position. At first, the college was reluctant, but on the promise that he would remain clean, Dr. Lap was hired.

His run as a professor had come to an abrupt end. Placing the last memento of that career in a box, Dr. Lap patiently browsed around the empty shell of what was once his office. Picking up the carton, he slowly turned toward the door and exited.

Outside in the reception area sat Mayda, the secretary who had served him faithfully during his years at the college. "Dean Trudy has been calling. He wants to speak with you." She said softly.

"I know." He whispered back as he continued to walk out toward the elevator.

"What should I tell him when he calls again?"

"I left."

Mayda looked down. Shaking her head, she said. "Damn you Doc."

"Yea, I know." Dr. Lap snickered. "That's what most people think now-a-days."

"No, no, you know."

"That's okay, I'm sorry." He replied, stopping at the elevator door. "Just tell him I'm gone. You didn't see me go."

"Please take care of yourself." Mayda said as Dr. Lap reached to press the down button.

He looked up and saw in Mayda's eye a tear. They both knew, this was the last they would see of each other. She was more than his secretary, Mayda was a friend. Among all he had encountered at the college, it was she who was most affected by his misadventures. He, standing next to the elevator door, stared into her eyes. It became painfully clear. He no longer deserved her respect and she was reluctant offering it.

As the elevator door opened, he stepped in and answered unconvincingly, "I will."

Leaving the Riker's Building, Dr. Lap felt an unusual stillness. The campus was too quiet. Deciding to ignore it, he continued his walk to the post office, turning up his collar to the slight chill of the autumn air.

Turning left at Hays Hall, the original college building built in 1803, he entered the main pathway. Tall oaks, like ancient soldiers, line the cobblestone walkway. Their autumn colors were fading and slowly falling to the ground, anticipating the coming of the cold winter weather. At the end of the path was Katrina Hall, a Civil War era brick building. In its basement, the post office was housed.

He entered the building and walked to the window for his last package of mail. A few students were milling around prior to their ten o'clock class. Although several had looked his way, none made eye contact or spoke. Nursing a mild state of paranoia, Dr. Lap sensed that they were avoiding him.

Just a few days ago, Dr. Lap was doing very much the same as these students. He would have been mingling with them, with coffee in hand, discussing his *Social Principles* class or something as mundane as the weather. This was all new to him. He was never dismissed before. Much worse, he was fired within the first week of the new term. Not sure what to make of it, he felt quite lost.

Dr. Lap left his change of address card, forwarding all his mail to his home address, at the post office front window. Feeling vulnerable, he began to panic. Anxiously, he turned away from the window, forgetting to pick up his last bit of mail. He needed an escape. He had nowhere to go, but home. Dr. Lap walked swiftly to his car, placed the box of books on the passenger seat, and jump behind the steering wheel. He sat for a few minutes until his shakes began to disappear.

Sitting in the driver's seat, Dr. Lap nervously surveyed the sprawling campus. Most students were in their morning classes and others were just getting up for the next period. It was when Agnes Hall, the woman's residence, came into his vision the long overdue fear finally overcame him. He was lost, in all his years he never felt so alone. He had no one at the school to turn to, burning those bridges with his recent antics. His colleagues simply turned their backs to him.

Starting the car, he quickly drove out of the parking area. Pulling onto the roadway, he nearly hit an oncoming pickup. Oblivious to the driver screaming and giving him the finger, Dr. Lap swerved onto the shoulder to avoid the collision. There he sat, fists clenching the steering wheel, until his knuckles turned white.

Taking a deep breath he quickly surveyed the oncoming traffic. Not far down the road he focused on a tractor trailer, heading in his direction. Resolved in what he was about to do, he planted his left foot firmly on the brake pedal and his right on the gas. He watched as the truck sped toward him. Anticipating the right moment to release the brake, he began to press down with his right foot. Through the steering wheel he could feel the motor accelerating, building power for the lunge. The truck kept coming closer. Behind its wheel sat the driver, humming to a Willie Nelson tune playing on his radio, oblivious to the fate waiting for his arrival. Dr. Lap's arms stiffened, but as the truck rushed pass, he eased off the pedal, letting the engine retreat into a quiet idle. "Fuck," Dr. Lap cried. "Can't I do anything right?"

Chapter 5

Starting the new day wasn't easy for Four-Thirty. She had gotten home quite late from another of her weekend dates, not getting much sleep. From the bed, she limped quietly into the bathroom. The throbbing in her leg pulsated up into her lower back. A hot bath, she thought, would ease the pain. Turning on the water, Four-Thirty quickly added bubble bath and a capful of lavender bath oil, her favorite. Sitting on the edge of the tub she softly smiled, reflecting on the weekend. "I think I'm gonna miss him." She whispered to no one.

She had been with Jerrod, an electrical contractor, whom she had been seeing for more than twelve years. The arrangement that they had made was virtually unchanged. Once a month he would send a car for Four-Thirty, which would deliver her to a motel where Jerrod was waiting. The two would then travel to Atlantic City, spending the weekend at one of its many casinos. For her time and services Four-Thirty was paid well, in addition to receiving the occasional small but expensive gift.

It was a business arrangement. If Four-Thirty had forgotten that fact, she was sorely reminded when Jerrod had requested to renegotiate. From the very beginning, she had convinced herself that a relationship, initiated solely on the basis of sex, had become a friendship. Instead, she was a sexual commodity, and Jerrod was now looking for a newer model. Her services were no longer desired. Jerrod was now asking

Four-Thirty to set him up with a woman who was younger and, as he emphasized, someone who was not deformed.

It saddened Four-Thirty knowing that her relationship with Jerrod was to end. She had enjoyed going on these trips. Jerrod would give her sufficient money to play the slots or to gamble at the table of her choosing, while he was off elsewhere, playing for higher stakes. Lacking an interest in gambling and being uncomfortable among crowds, Four-Thirty often sought out other forms of amusement. It would have not been unusual to find her exploring the boutiques and souvenir shops surrounding the casinos. What she enjoyed most was her time spent on a bench, contentedly overlooking the beach.

Although troubled by Jerrod's proposition taking away these little pleasures, Four-Thirty was very professional in making the transition. The two discussed locating her replacement and developed a verbal contract, outlining services and expectations. He accepted what she proposed to be a fair finder's fee. They had also decided as to what amount was to be paid to the new girl. As a result, Four-Thirty believed she was defining for herself a new role in the sex trade. As management, or as an agent, she was taking the steps in ensuring a small income from a commission she was to collect from her soon to be employee.

A young single mother recently started to solicit in Paci's. It was she whom Four-Thirty thought she could set up with Jerrod. Four-Thirty had watched her hustle the patrons at the bar. It was obvious she was uncomfortable playing the sex game. It was also obvious, she needed the money. Through the grapevine, Four-Thirty learned that the woman had a child, similar in age to that of Oria, when Four-Thirty decided to quit solicitation on the streets. The little girl's father died of an overdose leaving them penniless. Four-Thirty decided that when she next saw the young mother, she would approach her with the proposal. Four-Thirty knew that the woman, without hesitation, would take the offer.

Having finished her bath, Four-Thirty stepped out from the tub and stood naked in front of the full length mirror. Like writings on the outhouse wall, it spoke to her. She didn't like what was said in the familiarity of the image looking back. It reminded her of her mother, just before she died. Like her mother's body, the firmness of her own escaped her. Her breast sagged over the soft tissue of her drooping stomach, her butt now nonexistent. With her finger she gently traced a fading scar along her abdomen. A faint reminder of the son she has never known.

There was no use for her to look at her leg. It disgusted her as it always had. In fact, she contoured her body in such a way, the bones and loose flesh of the limb would not be visible in the mirror. Still, she was not satisfied with the image staring back at her. As to why men have been attracted to her, with her body so twisted and disgusting, she was confused. They seemed to enjoy being with her. Yet, in her heart, she knew she was cheating them. They didn't deserve what she had to offer. Thus, she did her best to disguise her deformity, and then do whatever it would take to satisfy them.

—

It was at the Horizon, a motel bar near Newark Airport, where she first met Jerrod. She was working its pub for several weekends with little success. Having conceded that she needed a new location, she decided to spend her last night sipping red wine, hoping to make one more score.

On the opposite side of the bar sat Jerrod, dressed in a light grey suit with a blue plaid tie. Fingering the rim of his drink he would occasionally look toward Four-Thirty. Catching his glance she replied with a coy smile. Jerrod took another sip from his drink, before heading toward Four-Thirty on the other end of the bar. She followed him, with downcast eyes, as he confidently loosened his tie and unbuttoned the collar of his shirt.

"You know, I was sitting there," slipping onto the stool next to Four-Thirty, "admiring you from afar and thought it was time to admire you from a near."

Almost spitting into her glass, Four-Thirty blurted out, "What?!"

Confidence began to drain as from an open spigot. "Sorry," he said, sliding off the seat.

"No, wait. Don't go." Four-Thirty giggled. "It's just that, that's the lamest fuckin' line I've ever heard."

"Sorry, but you're right. It is weak. I guess I need to do better."

"Well, one thing is for sure." Four-Thirty said, laughing. "It can't get any worse."

"Oh my God, I hope not. I mean look at you and I," Jerrod began to stumble and stutter on his words. After taking a deep breath, he continued. "Maybe I should just extract this foot from my mouth and keep it shut."

"I don't know about that. You do have a sweet voice."

Jerrod smiled, "Thanks."

Another round was ordered after which introductions were made. Conversation was kept light as they slowly finished their drinks. It didn't take long for Jerrod to invite her to his room. Four-Thirty quietly accepted. Jerrod, when charging the bar bill to his account, asked that a bottle of red wine be sent to his suite.

They rode the elevator to the top floor where Jerrod had a three room suite. By the time they had arrived, the bottle of wine had been set up on a table in the lounge area. Four-Thirty sat on the sofa as Jerrod opened the bottle and poured two glasses.

"To a new friendship," he toasted as he tapped his glass to hers.

Conversation came easy to Four-Thirty when meeting with a john. To avoid unnecessary guilt, she knew how to steer the discussion away from wives and families. Instead, she made them feel special by focusing on their interests and work. She had them believing she was impressed, by asking the right questions at the right time, and praising them for being extraordinary. She was good at it and she knew it. Thus, when the time came to discuss her fee, she easily got what she asked for and sometimes more.

As she expected, Jerrod was no different. Four-Thirty soon learned that he worked for an electrical contracting firm out of Washington,

D.C. He headed their Northeast Division, overseeing major projects in New York City, Boston, and Northern New Jersey. He spent most of his time in the New York/New Jersey area, often taking time to visit the casinos in Atlantic City. As he spoke, she would touch or brush against him. Each time he would become more animate and vocal about his work as she pulled him into her grasp. Eventually, there was a lull during which Four-Thirty took the lead.

"Why don't you go into the bathroom and change into something more comfortable," Four-Thirty instructed Jerrod. "I'll keep the bed warm."

"Okay," Jerrod said, placing a kiss gently on her forehead.

Waiting in bed was safe for Four-Thirty. Keeping the customer's focus away from her leg made the encounter go smoothly. She didn't need anything to change the mood. Much less, she didn't need for a john to lose interest and walk away from her. It has happened before with unpleasant consequences, the least being called a freak, and the worse, a beating. These dates had to be all about the john, not about her. This she knew better than others, having it imprinted in her mind from early childhood, long before she met Deadeye, long before her father leaving the home.

Only a few minutes had passed before Jerrod, dressed in satin pajamas, returned from the bathroom. The light yellow garment stood boldly against his tan skin. Yet, he appeared shy, and somewhat childlike, standing above Four-Thirty, reclining in the bed.

"You look quite handsome in those jammies," Four-Thirty complimenting Jerrod, as she pulled back the bedding for him. "Too bad they have to come off."

Comfortably lying next to Four-Thirty, Jerrod gently stroked her face and hair. He was quite confident as he continued to softly caress her. She quickly realized he was not like other johns, whose only concern was a prompt ejaculation. He was much more caring, more sincere, and seemed to be intent on pleasing her. As his kisses went from her breast to her belly, Four-Thirty, in anticipation, spread open her legs. Without hesitation, he took her cue, slipping his head between her thighs.

Four-Thirty surprised herself. She had never allowed this before, not with a paying customer. She broke one of her own rules. In doing so, Four-Thirty had surrendered to his every touch, to his every kiss. He had taken her completely under his spell.

"Tell me something," Four-Thirty later asked.

"Yes," Jerrod answered through passive eyes.

"When we were downstairs, you know, in the bar." She spoke hesitantly. "Did you think, did you think that I was a…"

"No, not at all," Jerrod said, wrapping his arms around her.

"Oh, now that you know, are you disappointed?"

"Are you kidding me?" He replied without hesitation. "Right now, will I ever see you again, is the only thing I can think of."

Four-Thirty pulled herself closer to Jerrod and smiled, "Yea, I think so."

"Boy, how things change." Four-Thirty thought, as she transitioned from her memory to the moment. "Was I, am I really that naive?" In retrospect, what started out as an affectionate relationship, albeit a professional one, deteriorated into her becoming nothing more than his Atlantic City sex toy. She was no longer his companion, often left alone while he gambled at the poker table or some other card game. When they did meet, it was for dinner and then sex. That became their routine as Jerrod mutated into a regular john.

Chapter 6

Not far from the County Psychiatric Hospital, near the intersection of Ramapo and Euclid Avenues, just past the tracks for the NJ Transit Lines, sat an aging Victorian home. Its front porch, partially hidden behind an outgrowth of weeds and shrubs, sent a message of desolation. The house appeared to be empty, soon to be swallowed by the brush wildly encroaching it perimeter. Yet, in its driveway, a hint of life, sat a state van with the words "Jefferson House" printed on its sides.

It was here when Jordan, being placed by his mother, first learned that he was adopted. He was only eight. His father had died the week before and his mother decided that she either could not, or would not, continue to care for him. For her it was easy. She really never wanted to adopt a child. It was her husband's idea. Throughout their marriage she was unable to bear any children. He so desperately wanted a son. When Jordan became available through the local affiliate of Christian Charities, her husband was elated.

She, on the other hand, felt that she was getting too old to be a mother. At her age many women were becoming grandmothers. She didn't want to spend her senior years bringing up a child. Adoption was an uneasy concession. From the moment Jordan came into her home, she felt displaced and she resented it. The closer Jordan and his father grew, the more she despised him and cursed the day Jordan entered her life. Now, with her husband's death, she no longer felt the commitment.

The ties were cut coldly. Instead of saying goodbye, she informed Jordan that she wasn't his real mother. He did have many questions about who his mother was and where she may be. All he got was a simple "I don't know". With that, she walked away, intending never to see him again. There was no doubt that he felt the pain of being abandoned. Yet, even at eight, this was not a shocking revelation. It just gave some meaning to the chill he had always felt around her, the distance in her eyes.

Jordan became convinced that he would eventually find his real mother. He thought that he knew how, something his father had taught him. It was only a few days before his father had died. They were outside their home talking to a neighbor. As the neighbor walked away, Jordan's father turned to him and whispered, "I don't trust that man."

"Why?" Jordan asked.

"I could see it in his eyes. There was something in his eyes, yea, I could see it."

"Oh." Jordan responded.

"Listen son," his father turned to face him, "people's eyes don't lie. If you really want to know someone, it's in their eyes. They don't lie."

That was the last he and his father had spoken. Jordan remembered seeing sadness in his father's eyes that day. He knew he was dying. Jordan saw it, but didn't understand. Later that evening, his father was rushed to the hospital. Within the week, he died without seeing his son again.

Thinking of his father and that last day they were together, Jordan was sure this was how he would find his biological mother. Thus, Jordan vowed to himself and his mother, someday they would be reunited. All he would have to do, as his father told him, was to look into her eyes and he would know. It was that simple.

———

Mr. Philips, a counselor at Jefferson House, and Jordan, standing on the front stoop, watched as Jordan's adoptive mother's car pull away. With his tears welling, he began to hope that she would turn back and tell him that it was all a mistake, his father was still alive, waiting at home to take Jordan to a promised baseball game. The least he hoped for was for her to look back and wave goodbye. These hopes, as well as others, were lost at the moment the Chevy turned the corner, never to be seen again.

"Com' on son, let me show you your room." Mr. Philips said, picking up Jordan's bag and leading him into the home. They had entered into the kitchen through a side door. From there they went through a large combination dining area and living room to the stairwell. Once on the second floor, Jordan and Mr. Philips entered the last room on the right. The room had a faded green rug partially covering a worn hardwood floor. Across from the entrance were two desks, each under an opened but barred window. Bunk beds were situated on the opposite side of the room. Mr. Philips placed Jordan's bag on the lower bunk.

"This here is your bed." Then, pointing to an old dresser, he added, "You can put your stuff there."

"Okay." Jordan said, holding back the tears.

"Eric, he's your roommate." Mr. Philips continued, "He and the other boys will be home soon. They're in school."

"Okay."

Mr. Philips took a blanket and bed sheets off the top of the dresser and handed them to Jordan. "Why don't you make up your bed? When you're done come on down, you can help me with dinner. Okay?"

"Yea," Jordan was noncommittal.

Before leaving him alone, Mr. Philips placed his hand on Jordan's shoulder. "Don't worry boy. You'll be alright."

The door softly closed behind Mr. Phillips isolating Jordan in a strange new world. No longer able to hold it in, Jordan fell to the floor bawling. He cried for the father who he last saw lying lifeless in a copper colored coffin. He cried knowing that they will never take another trip together, play catch, take walks to the park, visit the zoo, or take a Sunday drive to the shore. He cried for the mother who had left him standing at a strange house, unwilling to say goodbye. He cried for another mother who he has never known. He cried because he was now alone among strangers. With his tears becoming uncontrollable, Jordan climbed onto the bunk and wrapped himself around his pillow. The harder he cried, the harder he would bite into the cushion to muffle the sound. In time, he cried himself to sleep.

—

A shuffling sound, and the door opening against the dresser, woke Jordan. Coming into the room was a casually dressed teenager. He placed several books on the dresser and turned to Jordan sitting on the bed.

"Hi, I'm Eric your roomie." The teenager said. He then turned to two boys who had followed him into the room, introducing them as Dennis and Jessie. Eric climbed onto the top bunk and the others sat at the desks. Soon they were locked in conversation about school and some of the girls in their classes. During a lull Jessie, a pimply face boy of fourteen, asked Jordan as to why he was placed in Jefferson House.

With eyes welling with tears, Jordan whispered, "I don't know."

The three others broke out in laughter. Confused and hurt, Jordan cried. He called out for someone to take him, wishing that he died along with his father.

"Hey, wait a minute, it's okay," Dennis chimed in. "I, we, mean what did you do to have them lock you up in here?"

Sniffing, Jordan tried to hold back his tears. With the back of his hand, he wiped away a trickle, dripping off his nose. Desperately, he tried to think of a reason to give to them. Unsure, he offered, "My dad died."

The boys, confused, looked at him, thinking that there had to be more. Dennis took the lead. He told Jordan about how his mother was a drug addict, who had been jailed for leaving Dennis and his sister alone without food. He explained that his sister, who was only four, was placed in a foster home. He was at Jefferson House because social services couldn't find a home for him.

"Ah hell that ain't nothin'," Jessie interrupted, "I killed my sister, that's why I'm here."

The room became very still, the three boys watching Jordan, anxiously waiting for his reaction. Jordan froze, unsure of what to make of the announcement. His fear of the home grew deeper.

"Yea," Jessie continued. "She was only a few months old. You know, she was always crying and my mom didn't do shit to stop it. So, to shut her up, I stuffed cotton in her nose and mouth and then I stabbed her, about twenty times. I don't know, maybe more." Coldly, he added. "Want me to show you how I did it?"

"No." Jordan shuddered, pushing himself against the wall.

Jessie got up from his chair and started to move toward Jordan on the bed. Jordan pushed harder against the wall. "Stay away from…" he yelled, triggering laughter from Eric and the others.

"Easy man, he's just fuckin' with you." Eric snickered. "That asshole is here because he keeps getting caught stealing candy from the same store. So his mom put him out."

"I guess my mom put me out too." Jordan said, trying to comprehend his own predicament. He began to feel a little more at ease with the other residents as he spoke of his dad dying. He drew some sympathy from them when speaking about how he learned that he was adopted, and how his mom drove away without saying goodbye.

"That sucks." Eric said. The others agreed.

The conversation among them eventually migrated onto several other lighter topics. They continued to laugh and kid each other, often involving Jordan in their dialogue. As the camaraderie grew, Jordan slowly eased himself away from the wall, integrating himself into the group. The interaction continued until they were called down for dinner.

Dennis and Jessie were first to exit the room, Eric and Jordan followed closely behind. Eric wrapped his arm around Jordan's shoulder as they walked out together. Jordan felt the weight of Eric's arm. It reminded him of how his dad held him. He missed his dad, knowing that his young life will never be the same without him. Thus, he relished that little security in Eric's touch.

"Here we're family. The only family you will need to know." Eric reassured Jordan as they entered the dining area. "You're my little brother now. I'll take care of you."

The other residents of Jefferson House, introduced as Jeff and Craig, and a second counselor named Janice, were serving dinner. Jordan was led to a seat next to Mr. Philips and across from Eric. The meal consisted of pork chops, various vegetables, bread, milk and juice. Each resident served himself. Observing the others, Jordan followed suit. Jordan waited for someone to say a prayer of thanksgiving, as was customary in his home. There was none, instead, everyone began to eat. Uncomfortable with not giving thanks, Jordan briefly bowing his head, prayed quietly before taking his first bite.

Unlike meals at home where each sat stoic, silently eating their meal, at Jefferson House commotion ruled the day. Conversation was chaotic, people talking over each other, neither listening to the other. At times, one of the two counselors would attempt to create some sense of civility. That was often short lived.

During a lull, Craig made a comment about Eric getting a bitch. Janice angrily slammed her hand flat against the table, giving Craig an icy stare. Craig, unable to maintain eye contact, looked apologetic and said something about how he was only joking. Although he did not understand, Jordan knew it was derogatory, and possibly a reference to him.

After the dinner, Jordan aided the other residents with their household chores. When these were completed, Eric and Jessie retreated to watch TV, while Dennis, Craig, and Jeff went to their rooms. Jordan journeyed out to sit on the porch to watch and to wait. He watched the early evening traffic and he watched the skies waiting for a sign. Although the sky offered no hope, there were a few moments when, sitting on the edge of his seat, he watched as a familiar looking Chevy pulled toward the house. The closer the vehicle approached the driveway, the taller he sat, until it drove pass without acknowledgement, leaving Jordan to sink further back into his chair. Exhausted, Jordan returned to his room as the evening dissolved into an empty night.

Chapter 7

A warn ray of sunshine broke through an opening between the pale green curtains that framed large living room windows. The brilliant beam of light gently fell on Wood, sitting in an overstuffed brown chair, digesting the early news. To his left, a narrow table held a half empty cup of coffee, cooling in the chilled morning air. Unread sections of newspaper laid folded, beside a partially eaten bagel seated on a paper plate of yellow, red, and blue birthday balloons.

Wood, turning the page, quickly sat upright. A small photograph with the caption *Storm Downs Ancient Willow Tree* caught his attention. He tried reading the article, but his eyes kept drifting toward the image of a small island with a lone tree lying on its side, its branches reaching into the water. It was Belmont Lake, a place he has frequently visited, to people watch, or to spend an afternoon reading. Yet, there was something in the photo that sent chills throughout his body. There was something about how the angle of the picture was taken, something about the bench along the water's edge.

"Becca," Wood whispered as he dropped the newspaper onto the arm of the chair. Swiftly he walked into his bedroom. He swung open the door of a small walk-in closet. Falling to his knees, Wood rummaged through several scattered boxes and piles of clothing. First thrown to the side, was a pair of western boots, purchased during a road trip to the mountains of East Tennessee. "Damn," Wood thought, "these are at least thirty years old." Next, he pulled out a dust covered brown fedora. It was his concert hat, last worn at a Grateful Dead show, when Jerry Garcia was still alive. Crawling deeper, he finally found what he was looking for.

At the edge of his bed Wood sat, cradling a small cardboard box. Taking a deep breath he hesitated before peeling off the yellowed scotch tape sealing its top. Pulling back the flaps, he delved through the collection of photographs, postcards, letters, and other personal items.

—

Wood first met Becca in the beginning of his third year teaching at the college. He, Dr. Lap, and several other faculty members, were at a local pub, celebrating the end of the first week of classes. Dr. Lap and another instructor, David Jensen, were comparing notes on the incoming coeds. Dr. Lap set his eyes on a petite blonde who registered for his *General Principles* class. Not far from the bar where Wood and his colleagues were stationed, she and several other new students gathered in a booth near the entrance. It was obvious from her posture she was interested in a boy sitting to her left. He, overdressed in a tan suit and bright blue tie, appeared to be oblivious to her overtures. Instead, he directed his attention to another. She, a brunette dressed in a college tee-shirt and jeans, showed no interest at all.

"Oh man, look at those little titties." Dr. Lap said, speaking to Jensen. "Don't you think she looks pretty in pink?"

"I don't know. I mean, she's cute but…"

"But what," Dr. Lap questioned. "Wouldn't you want those soft white thighs wrapped around your head? And your tongue, boy I can taste it now."

Jensen turned to face the group of students. Leaning back, resting his elbows on top of the bar, he answered. "Yea, but she's flat. I want some breast I could wrap my hands around."

"Well maybe, but you do know what they say about a mouthful."

"Yea, Yea, anything over is wasted." Jensen giggled.

Shaking his head, Wood could only laugh. "You guys are sick. They're just kids."

"Maybe so," Jensen said, turning to Wood, "but, if they're old enough to…"

"Fuck you Jensen." Wood interrupted. "Tell you this much, If that was my kid, I would cut your dick off to the point where you couldn't fuck an insect."

Jensen turned, slamming his drink on the bar. Pushing past Dr. Lap, he stationed himself in front of Wood, puffing out his chest. He was about to speak when Wood, noticing that Jensen's ballpoint pen had leaked through his breast pocket, laughed. The image of Jensen with his ink stained shirt, hitting on a coed, was quite hilarious.

"What the," Jensen's anger escalated. He, stuttering uncontrollably, pressed his finger into Wood's chest. "Wh … who do you th … think your laughing at?"

Jensen's hand, shaking feverously, did not go unnoticed. He had made a mistake challenging Wood. Jensen knew that Wood was not a fighter, would not get physical. But Wood, the perennial cynic, would definitely cause him to lose face among his students and colleagues. "Look at you, trying to be a tough guy but you're shivering like a dog. Like I said Jensen, you're fuckin' sick."

"Now ladies," Dr. Lap said, stepping between them, ensuring that Jensen avoided a final verbal blow, "let's be civil."

"Yea, I know peace." Wood, turning away from Jensen, waved toward the barmaid. Drawing two drafts of beer, she placed these in front of a couple at the far end of the bar and then, quickly walked over to Wood. Motioning to Dr. Lap, Jensen, and the others, Wood said, "I know you really should cut these guys off but before you do, let me buy another round."

"That's for the five of you?"

"Yea and," leaning over the bar, Wood chuckled as he pointed to

Jensen. "That man over there, tell him he might want to change his shirt. I mean, don't you think he looks like he's been shot and is bleeding blue?"

The barmaid, smiling, nodded in agreement. Moving toward Jensen, she tapped him slightly on his shoulder. As Jensen turned, she reached over the bar and whispered into his ear. First looking down at his shirt, and then glancing at Wood with disdain, Jensen placed his hand across his chest and briskly walked out of the pub.

"I guess that's four now." The barmaid called to Wood.

"Yea, I guess so." He smiled.

—

Inconspicuously, Wood scanned the pub through a smoke colored mirror, situated behind the mahogany bar. From his vantage point, he observed the petite blonde, no longer showing interest in the suit, to be in a conversation with an upperclassman, dressed in a dark blue football jersey and pressed khakis. The brunette, seeking her niche, left to join several sorority sisters, circling a large table. They, in association colors of white and kelly green, traded Kamikaze shots with several of their pledges.

It was in the lower left corner of the mirror, behind the second shelf of liquor, between bottles of *Absolut* and *Smirnoff* vodka, where Wood first caught a glimpse of Becca. She, dressed in a light tan peasant blouse and faded jeans, stood out among several of the new faculty, who had just entered the pub. Wood couldn't help but notice how her longish brown hair, with a thin braid neatly tucked behind her left ear, swept across her shoulders as she surveyed the crowd before her. Recognizing someone in Wood's group, she and her companions quickly moved toward the bar.

"Who is that?" Wood whispered to Dr. Lap.

"Oh, just another new freshman," Dr. Lap answered without taking his eyes off of the petite blonde sitting in the booth.

"No, not her you idiot," Wood responded, realizing that his colleague had not stopped eying the coed. "Who's the brunette coming our way?"

Turning his attention away from his fantasy, Dr. Lap looked toward the group approaching them. "Oh yes, I'm not sure of her name but she's the new literature instructor."

As they approached, one of the new faculty members, dressed in a green sports coat, began to introduce himself and the others to Wood's party. Becca, slightly uncomfortable in the surroundings, remained in the back of the group. In making eye contact with Wood, she gave a shy smile, causing a dimple to emerge on her right cheek. At that moment, Wood knew he was falling in love.

"Here," Wood nervously rose from his stool and waved her over, "have a seat. I mean, I need to stand anyway, been sitting too long."

"Thanks," she replied, walking toward the bar. "I'm Becca. I'm new in the English and Literature Department."

"Yes, I know. I mean, ah, that you're in the English Department, not your name. The English Department, I knew, not Becca your name, the English, shit." Wood felt the cloak of embarrassment slowly rise as he stumbled with his words. He was becoming uneasy, failing miserably in making a good impression. "Sorry, I'm Wood. That's what they call me."

"Oh, I heard about you." Becca smiled, softly biting her lower lip. Again, Wood was swept away by an emerging dimple.

"Huh?" Wood responded.

"Actually, we were warned about you."

"What? Warned?" Any semblance of self-confidence quickly waned.

"Yes," Becca's smile grew, drawing Wood's attention to her dark eyes. There, a radiance of innocence and compassion, the likeness of which Wood was convinced he has never seen before, eased his wavering composure. "In the parking lot this guy..."

"Jensen?" Wood interjected. "This guy, did he have an ink stain down his shirt?"

"Yes, yes, that's the guy." Becca laughed. "We had just gotten out of our car when he came up to us, mumbling about you being an ass. He actually said you were dangerous and we should avoid you."

Turning away briefly, Becca ordered a glass of the house's red wine. She reached into a tan leather bag, retrieving a twenty dollar bill, placing it on the bar. Not wanting Becca to think he was being too forward, Wood decided against buying her drink. Yet, he promised himself that he would pick up the tab for her next one.

"It was quite funny," Becca continued. "I saw this guy coming toward us, with his hand over his chest, mumbling to himself. At first, I thought the stain was blood, that he was cut, stabbed, or something. Imagine that. As he came closer, I realized that it wasn't blood but ink. I guess the way he was holding his pen kind of tipped me off. Anyway, someone, I'm not sure who, remembered him from the Math Department and tried to talk with him. But he just walked by and kept mumbling about you being crazy and all."

Wood smiled, shaking his head in disbelief. He, reaching around Becca, picked up his beer. "You know, I find that hilarious. He is saying that I'm dangerous, that I'm crazy. Especially after the exchange we just had. That's funny."

A glass of red wine was placed on a coaster by Becca. The barmaid winked at Wood as she picked up the twenty dollar bill and, in its place, left several smaller bills in change. Lifting her glass, Becca turned back to Wood, gently tapping his drink with hers in a toast, "To Jensen."

"Yes, to Jensen," Wood laughed.

"So what is it with you two guys?" Becca asked, placing her wine back on the bar.

"I'm not sure that there's something between us. I mean, we did have a disagreement, but something between us, I don't think so."

"You guys talking about Jensen?" Dr. Lap joined the conversation, briefly turning his attention away from the coed. "It's no secret. I mean, the guy is really a jerk."

"Do you remember those guys in high school?" Wood asked, turning to Becca. "You know, those pimply faced guys that everyone picked on? The ones that always tried to fit in, to be one of the 'in-crowd', but things seem to never go their way? Well, Jensen is one of them."

"I think I know what you mean."

"Well," Wood continued, "here he was eying the new freshman women, trying to play the stud. He and my buddy over here," pointing to Dr. Lap, "were discussing their fantasies. The whole time Jensen, striking his best Bogart pose in his ink stained shirt, trying to catch the eye of any coed who dared to look his way."

"So why is he so pissed at you?"

"Mr. Nice Guy over here," Dr. Lap once again, redirecting his attention, "called him an ass, never mind threatening to castrate him."

"Well, not really, I just kinda pointed out the absurdity of the whole situation."

As they continued talking, another round of drinks was placed on the bar. Singling out one of the new faculty members, the barmaid indicated that it was he who bought the round. Wood recognized him from the morning's faculty meeting, where he was introduced as a new member of the Art Department. Although unable to recollect his name, he remembered that his area of expertise was pottery. "He plays with mud," Wood laughingly whispered to Dr. Lap during the instructor's introduction.

Picking up his drink, Wood turned to his colleague and tipped his glass in a silent toast.

Nodding, the artist acknowledged Wood's gesture.

"So you guys come here to hit on the coeds." Becca joked, resuming the conversation.

"No," Wood became defensive. "Not me, but yes, that's what was going on. I mean, these guys, like Jensen, never grow up. They never left college. I mean, yea, they crossed that aisle and are now teachers, but they're still students socially. They never made that transition. I guess it's because they never really left campus life."

"Yes, I think I can see that." Becca said contemplating. "Believe me. I, unfortunately, dated guys like that."

"It's like," Wood continued. "They have always been students, I guess, since the age of five. They never got away from it. So it's their reality."

"So, what about you," Becca asked, "are you one of them?"

"Well, I got away from the whole thing for a while. You know, worked as a community activist in the southern mountains. Did some stuff with coal miners, you know, I got to see life differently. Beside, why would I be interested in a child like that," stated Wood, pointing to a coed walking pass the bar, "when I have someone like you sitting beside me?"

Blushing, Becca turned her head away to hide her embarrassment. It was quite obvious, he was interested in her. She, feeling her own little spark for him, didn't know how to respond. Fortunately, Dr. Lap directed their attention elsewhere. "Hey you two, we decided to go to my place for some music and whatever. Join us?"

"Uh, I don't know. Yea, I guess so, if my ride is going." Becca responded.

"Hey, you can ride with me." Wood was quick to reply. "I mean, if it's okay with you."

"Sure," Becca smiled. "It's fine by me."

—

That, was three years prior to the photograph, which Wood held in his hand, had been taken on the bank of Belmont Lake. Wood smiled, his fingers gently caressed the image of him and Becca, standing by the water.

The photograph was taken on a bright, cloudless day. Becca dressed warmly, in a tan overcoat and navy blue scarf hanging loosely from her neck. Wood, in a pea coat with the collar turned up, was standing beside her, with one arm draped over her shoulder, the other inching into the opening of her coat, resting his hand on her belly. Wood was quite surprised by how happy he looked. There he was, his head held high, chest puffed out, and a smiled that stretched from wall to wall.

Traveling north with Becca to attend his sister Lucia's wedding, Wood decide to take some extra time off, to give Becca the grand tour of his childhood. Not far removed from his hippie days, he took her first to Belmont Lake where he and many of his fellow freaks spent days playing music and tripping on LSD. From the lake, Wood led Becca down the trail along the railroad tracks to the abandoned chemical factory. It was there, after places like The Hut would close, he and his friends gathered, getting high and listening to music blaring from their car radios. Pointing to crumbling loading platform, he bragged it was there, where he had smoked his first joint. Yet, Wood dared not tell Becca that it was also there, at the ripe age of fifteen, he had his first sexual adventure, Laura, his best friend's thirteen year old sister.

To Wood's dismay, the factory complex was completely surrounded by barb wire fencing. Every few feet along the perimeter, the EPA posted signs, signifying the area as hazardous. Beyond the barrier, several buildings remained standing in various stages of deterioration. Wood briefly considered climbing the fence but was dissuaded in doing so by the razor sharp barbs. Looking for an alternate entrance, he was once again discouraged, this time by Becca, who felt an icy discomfort in the dead silence of the ghostly concrete shells.

"This place is creepy," Becca said, shivering. "Let's go back to the lake."

"Yea, okay," Wood took Becca by the hand as they quietly walked away. He was quite shaken by the hazard warnings. The factory had been abandoned after a suspicious fire destroyed several of its warehouses. The closure was assured by the firemen, who allowed the blaze to spread to several buildings within the complex. Once the factory was vacant, any risk posed to the community was gone, a belief held by many. Afterward, no one thought about any of the residual effect of chemicals left behind, or any that may have seeped into the soil.

While Wood was completing his graduate studies, a number of his hometown schoolmates had died, among them Ronnie C and Barrel, within a few weeks of each other, of a rare form of cancer. As to the cause, no one had any answers. The dots between the factory and the deaths were never connected, at least not publicly. Looking back toward the complex, Wood shuddered thinking that it was there, within the factory walls, the disease that took his friends might have been born.

Feeling his hand tighten around hers, Becca asked, "Are you okay?"

"Yea, I think so." He lied.

Becca quietly led him to a bench alongside the lake. Climbing on, Wood positioned himself on its top railing as Becca sat below him. She leaned over, wrapped her arms around his legs, and laid her head against his knee. There they sat in silence. The thoughts of his friends' battle with cancer, and the possible cause of those deaths, continued to haunt Wood.

Lifting her face to the sky, Becca absorbed the warm rays of the sun. Although it was early March, they were being teased by a period of mild weather. Across from them, on its own island, a willow tree softly waved its branches in the slight breeze. Tiny snow drifts gently rippled across the frozen lake, sending mirrors of light back into the sky. Enjoying the break from the harsh winter, a number of skaters dotted the ice, while others lazily strolled along the lake's paths. At the far end, a makeshift game of hockey was being played out by several high school students.

After a time, Wood slipped off of the bench's back railing onto its seat, pressing closer to Becca. With eyes peering across the lake, he unconsciously began to finger the end of Becca's scarf. "See the island over there?"

"Yes."

"When we were kids we would come here to skate or hang out. This place would get mobbed. Anyway, instead of that flag up there," Wood pointed to a flagpole on the island, "they had this piece of plywood painted white, a huge red ball in its center. It would be set up against that tree, and like that flag, it would let us know when it was safe to skate. There was a time, over a period of several years, we couldn't skate. Winter would come, cold as ever, but the lake just wouldn't freeze, if it did, the ice was uncharacteristically too thin."

"That doesn't sound right."

"Seriously, we would pass by looking for that red ball, but it was never there. Eventually, we stopped coming altogether."

"What happened?" Becca questioned. "I mean, obviously the lake had begun to freeze again."

"You wouldn't believe this." Wood put his arm around Becca, gently pulling her head onto his shoulder before continuing. "There was this high school senior, a real nerd, who lived in that house over there." Wood pointed across the road to a lone, white two-family home, surrounded by an empty parking lot. "Anyway, as a project for a chemistry class, he took some samples of the water and had the samples tested in his school lab. As he had expected, the lake was polluted. But get this. He was able to trace the chemicals back to that abandoned factory. Near it, there's a stream feeding into the lake and those bastards were dumping their waste into it."

"That's amazing." Becca remarked, snuggling closer to Wood.

"Imagine, a freakin' high school student, not some scientist from the state, not the EPA, but this nerd of a student figured out why the lake wasn't freezing. Hell, I'm not even sure they really cared. Anyway, this kid gets into all the papers. People then started to make a big stink about how the lake wasn't freezing, and how all these fish were dying, you know, jumping on his bandwagon."

"And," Becca sat up curious to hear more of the tale.

Turning to face Becca, Wood continued. "After a while this kid, and a few of his neighbors, form a committee and sued both the city and the chemical factory. In the end the factory settled. They were forced to clean up their waste disposal and paid a fine, while the city had to dredge the lake. It's my understanding the fine was to cover the cost of the dredging. Imagine they almost killed a lake." Thinking again about Barrel and Ronnie C, he added, "We'll never know how many people they poisoned."

Sensing an uneasiness radiating from Wood, Becca attempted to redirect his attention, "This is a wonderful park. I understand why you like coming here."

"Yea, it is a pretty place. When I was a little kid we use to come here all the time. You know, we fish, have picnics, ice skate."

"A lot of family stuff?"

"Yea, kinda," Wood answered. "Especially when I was younger, but you know, as you get older, you kinda break away from the family."

"I was the same way. It's nature." Becca giggled.

"I remember one year, my old man sold hot chocolate to the skaters. He would have my mother heat up this huge tub of water at home. Then, my brother Phillie Wheels and I would load it in the trunk of my dad's car. Mom would drive the car up here, praying the whole damn time that it wouldn't spill. Sometimes, when his business was doing well, the old man made us carry the tub from the house while mom heated up another. Imagine, I was like nine or ten and Phillie was just a few years older. We'd carry that thing for blocks."

"You're kidding?"

"Seriously," Wood laughed. "Once we got it up here, the old man would dump a box of cocoa in it and sell the hot chocolate for a dime. The cheap bastard would even charge Phillie and me."

"That's funny."

"Yea, looking back on it I guess it was."

"What about Lucia?" Becca was quite curious about Wood's sister, having just met her at the wedding. "What was she like?"

"*Mia Lucia bella*, she could do no wrong." Wood got up from the park bench. Turning toward Becca, he placed his closed fingertips on his lips, kissed them and then, thrusting his hand toward the sky, he opened his fingers, as if to send the kiss to the gods. "She was my father's favorite, definitely spoiled by him. It's so sad he and my mom weren't alive to see their daughter get married, so sad."

"Yes," Becca agreed. "She was so beautiful in your mother's dress, and it was a wonderful ceremony."

Lucia had decided to take her vows in The Church of Our Lady the Virgin Mother. It was the church where Wood, and his siblings, were baptized and received their First Holy Communion. Although a predominately Sicilian parish, the pastor had always been Irish. The last that Wood remembered, was an overweight alcoholic, who often financed his newest Cadillac with the parishioners' money. Yet, the community didn't seem to mind, as long the other priests were Italian, who honored and allowed them to practice their traditions.

The newlyweds kept the ceremony simple. Lucia's dress, worn by her mother more than twenty-five years prior, sparkled in its unadorned elegance. Forgoing a veil, she wore a white hat trimmed with champagne colored baby roses. Escorting Lucia up the aisle, Wood radiated in his pride, and love, for his little sister. Once at the altar, they were met by the groom Vincent, and the current pastor, to Wood's surprise an Asian, who performed the service. Vinnie stood tall in a charcoal grey pinstripe suit, a red rose on his lapel. He, having just completing his doctorate program at the state university, had taken a position with a firm in Massachusetts and planned to relocate with his bride to the Boston area. Following the wedding, as a gift to the newlyweds, Wood catered a small party at the Garibaldi Avenue Social Club.

"I'm so happy for Lucia. I really think she and Vinnie would do well." Wood said, again sitting on the bench next to Becca. Turning to face her, Wood somberly asked, "Do you ever think about getting married?"

"Yes, I have thought about it some." The tinge of seriousness in Wood's voice sparked Becca's curiosity. "Why do you ask?"

"Well, it's that I can't see you or me for that matter, getting married in a church. I often thought that when we do it, we'd marry in a park or something."

"Wait a minute," Becca shot up in her seat. "Did I hear you right? Did you say 'when we do it' I mean," She paused, leaning against the back of the bench. "Yea, you did say it."

"I guess I did, but…"

"So tell me," Becca cut him off, "was that a proposal or are you so damn confident that I want to marry you?"

Wood began to blush. "Well, I guess a little bit of both. I had thoughts of us getting married and was thinking about asking you. But, this wasn't my plan. I mean, this wasn't how I thought I would do it."

Becca turning, wrapped her arms around Wood's neck. Her teary eyes glistened. "Yes!"

"You mean…"

"Yes, yes, yes."

Surrounded by the park sounds, they sat drenched in their shared pleasure. They had been living together for nearly three years. Neither had known a happier time. They had move to a small farm, isolating themselves from campus politics. There Wood, following in his grandfather's footsteps, planted several fruit trees and absorbed himself into an organic vegetable garden.

Professionally, Wood and Becca fed off each other. Prolific writers, both enjoyed success, he with literary and academic publications, and she was in the final preparations of her second novel, scheduled to be released in the spring. Marriage, Wood thought, was the frame that would make their union a perfect picture.

A young mother and her child of about four walked past the two lovers. The little boy looked up to Becca and, as he brushed his blond churls from his eyes, gave her a sunny smile.

"Damn," Becca whispered, pulling away from Wood. "There is something I need to tell you."

"Okay."

Looking down at her hands, she took in a deep breath, avoiding eye contact with Wood. "I, damn, I had wanted to talk with you before we left to come here. But, I just wasn't sure how you'd take it. I was afraid I might ruin the wedding for you. I just…"

"Becca," Wood, placing his hand under her chin, gently guided her head, looking into her eyes. "Please Becca, you couldn't ruin a thing. What is it? Are you alright?"

"It's that I wasn't sure." Becca smiled. Reaching for Wood's hand, she continued, "Now that we're going to get married, I'm sure, I know, it will be okay." She paused. "Wood, I'm pregnant."

Wood snapped up from the bench. "You're what? That is great! You mean I'm going to be a father? That is so freakin' great. Boy, do I love you."

"Do you mean it?"

"Hell yes, I mean it!"

Wood looked toward the lake where an elderly gentleman, dressed in a dark blue overcoat and grey fedora, was standing with his wife. Watching the skaters, she would occasionally point out one, apparently her grandchild, as he circled the island. Turning back to Becca, Wood asked. "Do you have your camera with you?"

Becca reached into her purse and pulled out a small instamatic. Taking it from her hand, Wood walked over to the couple and tapped the gentleman on his shoulder. As he turned, Wood lifted the camera toward him and asked, "Mind taking a picture of us?"

An image flashed in the gentleman's mind. Although he thought he recognized the young man with the camera, he wasn't sure. "I no mind. I take picture for a you. "

Wood walked over to Becca. Taking her hand, he led her to the back of the bench. Setting her against the rail, he framed the photograph with the willow tree behind them.

Lifting the camera to his eye, the old man's memory came into focus. "I know'a you, you the boy who fix'a old car in my lot."

"Mr. Pacifico? Oh my, you look so good. So sorry I didn't recognize you."

"Mama, looka here," Mr. Pacifico called to his wife. "It'sa Giuseppina's boy."

"*Dio mio!*" Mrs. Pacifico exclaimed. She walked over and gently pinched Wood on his cheeks. "*È diventato così grande.* You'a mamma be proud, such a man now."

Wood introduced Becca to the Pacificos as his fiancé. Wishing them both well, Mrs. Pacifico affectionately hugged Becca and placed a soft kiss on her brow. Stepping back, she stood next to her husband, both broadly smiling.

"So you wanna picture."

"Yes, of the three of us."

"*Tre?*" Mr. Pacifico quizzed.

"Yes, three," Wood answered with a glowing smile as he slipped his hand into Becca's coat and placing it on her abdomen.

Four days later Becca was dead.

Chapter 8

S itting at the bar, Wood was watching the Giants vs. Dallas football
game. With the first half coming to an end, the game was still
scoreless. Behind Wood, the dreamy sounds of the Flamingo's *I Only
Have Eyes for You* drifted from the jukebox. As usual, Buffalo was at an
end stool sleeping. He, Wood, and a young couple sitting in a corner
booth were the only customers in Paci's.

At the two minute warning the game broke to a commercial. A man,
dressed in jeans and a blue flannel shirt, appeared on the TV screen,
selling a new line of trucks. As he spoke of the ruggedness of the four
wheel drive model, a hand gently touched the shoulder of Wood. He
turned to look into the crystal blue eyes of Four-Thirty. She smiled and
nodded toward a booth. Grabbing his beer, Wood quietly followed.

"It's such a beautiful day out there. Isn't it?" Four-Thirty said as
Wood slid onto the bench seat.

"Yea, it is." Wood acknowledged. For October, the day was unusually
warm. A spell of mild weather seemed to have crept in, a direct contrast
to the chilling frost that blanketed the last week of September.

"Let's get out of here." Four-Thirty urged. "Come on."

"Well," he hesitated.

"No seriously, let's get out of here. Walk with me to the park.
Besides, you look like you could use some sun."

In spite of the clear skies and a gentle sun, Wood had spent most

71

of his time indoors either at home or in Paci's. His pale skin betrayed him, allowing Four-Thirty to insist on a stroll to the park. Not interested in going, Wood, frustrated, downed his beer. Feigning a smile, he conceded. "Okay, I'm game."

Their walk to Belmont Park was lively. The beautiful autumn weather energized the neighborhood. People were gathered into groups entrenched in conversation, enjoying the warmth of the sun. Young children played under the watchful eyes of their mothers, while older siblings huddled around stoops, listening to music blaring from radios. Occasionally, someone would wave a friendly hello.

The park was just as cheerful. Observing the action, the two leisurely strolled around the lake to a park bench, where they could fully appreciate the sun's offerings. Wood sat with his arm around Four-Thirty's shoulder. She, taking his lead, rested her head against his chest. Wood, closing his eyes, took in a deep breath of air. She, on the other hand, watched as children engaged in various forms of play.

Across from the bench, a laughing three year old was entertaining herself by feeding a small flock of ducks. From her mother's outstretched hand she'd snatch a piece of bread. Then, with blonde Orphan Annie curls bouncing off her shoulders, she'd race to the water's edge. Halting to a stop the child, nearly tipping over, would toss the bread to the ducks, barely reaching the shoreline. Giggling, the child rushed back to mom for another round.

"Isn't she sweet?"

Wood, uninterested, watched as the little girl, once again, returned the ducks with bread in hand. "Yea, she really is," He admitted.

"That's such a wonderful age," Four-Thirty sighed. "I remember when Oria was about five, the summer after she started school. She was so cute and I had so much fun with her. Boy did she enjoy the park. She had a little play group we would frequently meet. I, and the other moms, would bring lunches which we shared as the children played. It was such a wonderful time."

"You know," Wood said, kicking his foot into the gravel beneath the bench. "I kinda wish that I had been a father."

"You really don't know what you've missed." Four-Thirty said, looking up to Wood.

"Well, in a way I think I do." He had never told Four-Thirty about Becca or her pregnancy, nor was he willing to do so. "Yea, I think I do."

—

The two sat quietly watching the little girl, until her young mother decided it was time to leave. The child and her mother walked around the lake, occasionally pausing to watch other children at play. Wood kept them within his view, until they reached their car. After strapping the little girl in her seat, the young mother entered the driver's side. Once they drove off, Wood redirected his attention to Four-Thirty. "Do you remember when you were that young?"

"Sure," Four-Thirty answered, turning toward Wood. "I was a happy little kid, at least, before the accident, before I fell and injured my back and leg."

"Sorry, I didn't know you..."

"Yea," Four-thirty interjected. "I fell, that's how I fucked up my leg, a simple, stupid fall."

It had been some time since she last thought about that horrific day. Other than family, she spoke with no one about the event that caused her paralysis. In reliving the incident, she explained to Wood that was the last day she remembered being truly happy. She admitted to having some fleeting moments, but none like those she felt before she was injured.

Four-Thirty was only four when her life changed. It was a bright summer day. She and her family had gone to the country to visit her grandfather's farm. She had anticipated the trip for days, knowing that she would meet up with her friend Jessie. During the ride, Four-Thirty and her brother Casey, to make the long drive bearable, entertained themselves with songs and games. Once they were on the dirt road leading to the farm, Four-Thirty stood up on the backseat with her face pressed against the window. Soon, the image of her father's parents, waiting in their driveway, came into view. Her smile grew as Jessie, standing behind them, became visible, frantically waving as the car approached.

Four-Thirty, anxiously waited for her father to park the car, before jumping out and running to hug Jessie. Jessie, who had just turned five, had with him a puppy his parents gave to him for his birthday. The two children quickly ran into the field, the dog following close behind.

"You know something," Four-Thirty turned toward Wood. "I don't think we were there for more than an hour before it happened."

Unsure of what to say Wood remained silent. He reassuringly squeezed Four-Thirty's shoulder, understanding that it was a difficult story to tell.

Four-Thirty continued, explaining how she and Jessie had gone to the creek. The puppy was playing along the creek's edge when Casey, on the other side, began throwing stones, wanting to splash his sister. Four-Thirty, trying to avoid getting wet, climbed up along a small waterfall. Reaching the top, she grabbed hold of a moss covered rock. Unable to maintain her grip, Four-Thirty fell backwards onto a pile of rocks. Laughing, Four-Thirty tried to get up but her legs, twisted underneath her, wouldn't move.

"Damn, that's scary. What happened next?"

"I guess I passed out." Four-Thirty answered. "I mean, the next thing I remembered, I was in a hospital bed, in a body cast. I had fallen against a jagged edge of slate, crushing a vertebra, damaging some nerves. That's why my leg is so screwed up."

"And you were just four. That's something."

Four-Thirty, running her hand through her hair, leaned back against the bench. "After that, things at home were different."

"Do you mean they treated you different because of what happened?" Wood asked.

"I don't really know. It seems like, we weren't happy anymore. I don't know if it was because I wasn't happy or it had always been that way and I was just noticing it more. Like, my parents seemed to be always fighting and yelling, blaming each other for what had happened." Sighing, Four-Thirty continued. "Then my father, he changed. He started to do things to me and made me do things to him."

The image of Four-Thirty's father quickly came to mind. Wood was only a young boy when his father, grandfather, and several other men from the neighborhood confronted him before he left town. "Your father, I remember…"

"No," Four-Thirty stopped Wood. "I really don't want to talk about him now, please."

"Okay," Wood understood. "That's fine by me."

—

Thinking about her father was too painful. Over the years she had blamed herself for his abuse. At one time, she was his shining star, pure, untouchable, then to be tainted by paralysis. Only if she had stayed away from that stream, only if she had followed her parents into her grandfather's home, only if she had done something different, she would have not have been tempted to climb those rocks, and then maybe the fighting between her parents wouldn't have started and he would have left her alone. Yet, she couldn't blame him. It was she who was the one damaged, it was she who had changed. Four-Thirty couldn't overcome the uneasy feeling that she had become a disappointment, especially for her father.

It was unknown to Four-Thirty as to what Wood knew. She had her suspicions, nothing that she could confirm. When her father disappeared, she began to notice how Wood treated her differently. Before, he was mean and teased her a lot. Afterwards, Wood was gentler, friendlier. At times he acted as a protector. He accepted her in the group. She always suspected that the change in his demeanor, and her father leaving, were somehow connected. Yet, she was too afraid to ask.

It was Wood's sister who first drew attention to Four-Thirty and her father. Lucia, three years younger than Wood, was the same age as Four-Thirty. It was she who had initially befriended the new girl and her brother Casey, when they moved into the neighborhood. The three immediately became friends and were often inseparable.

One night at the dinner table, Lucia was complaining to her parents about how Wood was teasing her and her friends. Although he was chastised by their parents, Lucia wasn't quite satisfied. Expressing her contempt, she turned to Wood and said, "Well, I know something you don't know."

"Yea, so what," He replied.

"Casey tells me things."

"Think I care. He's a cry baby."

"He says," Lucia continued, "he says to me, Four-Thirty, her daddy makes her do things with her daddy's pee pee. Her daddy makes her he says."

Wood's father reached out, gently grabbing Lucia's by her arm, "Look at me Lulu." Softly speaking, he continued, "Are you making up a story? Did he tell you this?"

"That's what he tells me Daddy. I'm no lie."

"No one thinks you're telling lies baby." Their mother joined the conversation. Getting up from her chair, she directed Lucia away from the dinner table. "Come with me honey. Let's go to your room and talk."

"Okay," Lucia said, climbing off her seat.

Leaving the kitchen, Lucia and their mother walked into Lucia's bedroom. Just before closing the door, their mother turned to the table and said firmly, "You tell no one about this. I mean no one." Although she did not address any one in particular, Wood knew she was speaking to him.

Whatever Lucia disclosed to her mother that day, was quite concerning. During the night, after going to bed, Wood laid awake listening to the sounds of his parents in determined conversation. Unable to discern through his closed door what was being said, he was sure it was about his sister and Casey's secret. By the intensity of his parents' voices, he sensed that Four-Thirty was being harmed. Wanting to know more, Wood considered sneaking into the living room. He was dissuaded when the discussion abruptly ended, with the sound of his father leaving through the front door.

Unable to explain to Four-Thirty what he knew, Wood sat quietly. Stretching out his arms, he quickly yawned. Then, standing up, he reached down clutching Four-Thirty's hand. "Com' on, let's walk around the lake."

Their stroll along the shoreline was captivating. Blankets of yellow and orange dominated the fall foliage. With an occasional splash of red, the trees brighten up the park, giving it a festive look. Fallen leaves, fueled by a slight wind, swirled along the pathway, in a gentle dance of color.

Reaching the play area, Four-Thirty stopped to watch several young children amusing themselves in a sandbox. She gently nudged Wood, "Look at the chubby one. Isn't he cute?"

There in the box a toddler, looking like a bowling ball in green bib overalls, sat shoveling sand into a blue pail. Without warning he turned to another, dressed in tan shorts and a strap tee shirt, dumping the contents over the child's head.

"Don't do that," called an anonymous mother from the bench. "Play nice."

The two boys continued, oblivious to the empty directive. The young mother turned back to her latest issue of a Hollywood gossip magazine, and day dreams of a tryst with the week's buff centerfold. Again, a pail was turned over the second boy's head. This time, he turned to the butterball, smacking him with a red shovel, causing the toddler to whimper. Looking up briefly from her magazine, the wannabe starlet issued a firm demand. "Stop it!"

"Look at that one in the guinea tee," Wood laughed. "With that shirt, and greasing back his hair, he'd fit right into Phillie Wheels' crew."

"A gangster in the making," Four-Thirty retorted, grabbing Wood's arm and redirecting him back down the path along the lake.

Chapter 9

Stretched out on his recliner, Wood was reading Jack Kerouac's *The Town and the City*. Deep into the third chapter, he was startled by a loud knock at his front door. Placing the book on an end table, next to yesterday's partially eaten chicken, he hurriedly looked around for anything suspicious, anything compromising. Realizing that such precautions were unnecessary, he shook his head, surprised by the depth of his paranoia.

"Hey, old man," the familiar voice of Dr. Lap echoed in the hall.

"Chris, what in hell are you doing here?" Wood asked, leading his friend into the apartment.

Declining to answer, Dr. Lap, wearing a drab brown overcoat, entered and surveyed the room. It was sparsely furnished but cluttered. Aside from a small TV and radio, there was an old coffee table, a small sofa, and two chairs, one of which was covered with books. In the far corner, piles of newspapers sat on top an overflowing trash can. "Looks like the maid's day off."

"Yea, I guess," Wood responded. "Anyway, I kinda expected that you would show up here."

"Yea, how's that? A little bird told you?" Dr. Lap answered, setting his suitcase near the door.

"You can say that. One named Dean Trudy."

"Oh, did he say anything?"

"No, just that if you showed up, you were to call him. Is everything okay?" Dean Trudy's call perked up Wood's suspicion. It was uncharacteristic. Wood knew that Dr. Lap was a dedicated educator, a little quirky, but dedicated nonetheless. Classes, Wood estimated, started a little more than a week ago. Abandoning his students, he understood, was not in Dr. Lap's nature. Sometime was wrong.

"Believe me, nothing is going on, I'll give him a call."

"Haven't classes started?" The evasiveness of Dr. Lap stroked Wood's curiosity.

"Hey everything is okay. I have it under control." Dr. Lap, a little edgy, answered. "I'm sure Dean Trudy just wants to verify my coverage."

"Chris, you really amaze me. Why in hell did you list me as next of kin?" Sensing Dr. Lap's discomfort, Wood laughed, redirecting the conversation. "Don't you have any family? I mean I did meet them."

"Well, if you met them, then you should know why the college has you as next of kin. Would you want my father, my brother involved in your life?"

Wood silently agreed. Both of Dr. Lap's parents, quite wealthy, were self absorbed. His father traveled a lot for his business, often with his new girlfriend and, as usual, one younger than his sons. Meanwhile, his mother was content, socializing at afternoon teas, getting quite drunk before evening. His only sibling, an older brother, was serving time in a federal prison for embezzlement. No, Wood wouldn't want them in his life either.

"Yea, I guess you're right. But what makes you think I want to be involved in your fuckin' life?"

"Hey, have you ever turned me away, or I you? I mean, here we are, right?"

"Well..."

Not waiting for an answer, Dr. Lap continued, "Then, I rest my case."

Wood knew it was useless to argue. Instead, he turned to the book covered chair, moving the pile to another resting area. Offering a seat to Dr. Lap, Wood went into the kitchen returning with two bottles of beer. The two sat quietly for a few moments. Lap continued to survey the room and was dismayed by his friend's lack of housekeeping skills. For as long as he has known Wood, he has never seen his home as cluttered as he was now witnessing.

"Did you get lazy or something?" Dr. Lap asked.

"What?"

"I don't know. I mean, you never kept your place like this."

Wood looked around and agreed. "Well, you're right. I just didn't have the motivation, so things just got out of hand."

"Looks like something more than motivation that's lacking. When's pickup around here."

The criticism irritated Wood. He shot back, "Listen, I don't need..."

"No, wait a minute," he was cut off by Dr. Lap. "I didn't mean anything by it. I just thought that I'll give you a hand taking it out. I mean, if I'm sticking around for a few days I need some floor space to sleep on."

"Floor space, my ass, you're sleeping on the sofa." Wood replied. "Besides, have you ever slept on the floor in my place?"

—

The two had been friends since their college days. Whenever Dr. Lap thought of that first meeting, it brought a warm smile to his face. He had just enrolled in his third school, in less than a year, when they first met. They were to be roommates.

Dr. Lap was assigned a corner room, on the top floor of the men's residence. Upon entering, he observed military style bunk beds to his right. The top bunk held a bare mattress with linen neatly folded by the pillow. The lower one had nothing but springs and a thin plywood bed board. Dr. Lap had been informed that he would be sharing the room but, seeing the empty bunk bed, he hoped that the front office was wrong. It wasn't. Someone else had moved into the room, evident by clothing scattered on a chair and a stereo on top of one of the two dressers.

Dr. Lap though it was odd. From the stereo, a long cord looped over an arm of the chair, snaking under the closet door. Curious, he opened the door slowly. To his amazement, the missing mattress sprawled across the closet floor. On it, Wood, eyes closed, humming to the sound emanating from his headphones.

"What in hell are you doing?" Dr. Lap asked.

Lifting his left earpiece, Wood responded, "Listening to the Mothers." Reaching up, he pulled the door closed, shutting Dr. Lap out of his solitude.

Dr. Lap had no idea as to who the Mothers or the Mothers of Invention were. His concept of music was shaped by main stream AM radio, with the likes of the Temptations, Four Tops and the Righteous Brothers. Seeing an album cover on the dresser, he picked it up and curiously examined the colored distorted photo of a group of long haired men, and the title, *Freak Out*.

The song list was just as intriguing. "Who the fuck would write a song with a title like *Wowie Zowie*?" he questioned. Little did Dr. Lap know his concepts of melody and rhythm would soon be shattered. He too began to listen to the Mothers and other groups, such as The Fugs and David Peel and the Lower Eastside. An introduction, by Wood, to marijuana and other psychedelics drugs, facilitated his evolution. In the end it made college life bearable.

—

Picking up Wood's copy of *The Town and the City*, Dr. Lap began to leaf through its pages. Stopping to briefly read a passage, he turned toward Wood, "Haven't you read this before?"

"Yea, several times," Wood answered. "I think it's the best thing he's ever written."

"That's interesting," Dr. Lap noted, continuing to flip through the pages. "Seems like the critics think Kerouac's best work came later, with *On the Road* and his spontaneous prose."

"Well, you know how I feel about critics. You know those, who can, write and those who can't yadda, yadda, yadda, kinda like teachers. Besides, I think much of that stuff had more to do with him being a cultural icon, you know the beatnik shit, than his actual writing style."

"Well, maybe so," Dr. Lap replied, placing the book on the end table, "but this, it's so, so conventional."

"Conventional, you mean like James Joyce, Thomas Wolfe?" Wood sarcastically replied. "I don't see that as conventional. It's a classic man, pure genus. His other stuff, well, I'm not so sure?"

"So you don't think he was a great writer, he didn't push American literature into a new direction, that all these experts are wrong?"

"Look Chris," Wood began after a short hesitation, "you know that I don't buy into all that ivory tower, academic bullshit. But, to answer your question, do I think that *The Town and the City* is great, yea. Do I think he was a great writer, no, good, very good but, not great. As for a new direction in American literature, I give that credit to people like William Carlos Williams, Ginsburg, and Burroughs."

"I don't get it. I mean, hundreds of books have been written about him, all that fame, and you think…"

"And where did all that get him?" Wood asked, interrupting Dr. Lap. "He died angry, drunk, and still in love with his mother."

"Man, you are harsh."

"Maybe so," Wood answered before downing the rest of his beer. "Besides, what the fuck do I know about literature? Hell, I'm just an old broken down sociologist."

"Yea, fuck, that's two of us." Dr. Lap nervously laughed, ending the conversation.

Apprehensive, Dr. Lap moved toward the front window. Outside, the weather continued to be dismal. It was gray, as a light rain had been falling all day. A young girl dressed in a light jacket, carrying a blue umbrella, came into his view. He watched as she crossed the street, entering one of the row houses across from Wood's apartment. His mind drifted to thoughts of the coeds on campus. Shaken, he tried to refocus on the rain. But one name, Susanne, continued to haunt him.

"Hey," Dr. Lap said, turning to Wood. "Is that bar still opened? You know, the one with the great mussels."

"You mean Paci's?"

"That's the one." Dr. Lap answered recognizing the name.

"Yea, it's still opened. It's just around the block."

"Great, let's go get something to eat." Dr. Lap grabbed his overcoat, heading toward the door before Wood could answer. "I'm freakin' famished."

"Sure, that sounds good." Wood agreed.

Chapter 10

While serving a three-year stretch at The Central State Correctional Facility, Jordan encountered Eric for a second time. It was in general population. Jordan had been playing basketball with several other inmates, when he caught a glimpse of Eric, mingling with a group of skinheads. The sight froze Jordan long enough for him to miss a block, his opponent scoring a basket. Distracted, Jordan left the game.

Nearly fifteen years had passed since they last crossed paths. Jordan had to be sure. Eric, obviously older, was much taller and heavier than the picture Jordan had engraved into his memory. Walking through the group of skinheads, Jordan intentionally bumped into Eric. Their eyes locked but Eric showed no sign of recognition. Jordan, only a runt of an eight year-old when they last met, didn't expect that he would.

The fire deep in Jordan's chest began to burn. Seeing Eric again only stoked it higher. Jordan would never forget what Eric took from him that first night at Jefferson House. It was that next morning, when Eric was being taken away, Jordan vowed his revenge.

—

Jefferson House, a group home for emotionally disturbed adolescents, was where Jordan's adoptive mother abandoned him. His father had died a few days before, and his mother, just prior to leaving him forever, saw fit to tell Jordan he was adopted. With a child's understanding that he was not who he thought he was, compounded by the feelings of isolation, Jordan was overcome with the greatest emotional pain he had ever know. Later that night, Eric his assigned roommate, amplified that terror.

At Jefferson House lights out, or bedtime, was at ten. Although accustomed to going to bed much earlier, Jordan was unable to sleep, spending much of the night curled around his pillow. His eight year old mind could not comprehend his feelings of the separation and loss. Nor was Jordan able to understand the lack of compassion exhibited by his mother. The sounds of the city, creeping in from the outside, didn't help either. Yet, perhaps out of complete exhaustion, he started to drift off to sleep.

It was at a moment near sleep when Jordan, weary eyed, felt Eric slide into his bed. At first, he was startled. Although he habitually slept alone, there were times Jordan had slept with one or both of his parents. Those moments he cherished. This was different. He was in an unfamiliar bed and Eric was a stranger. Yet, the warm body against his brought to mind feelings of comfort and security.

Feeling at ease, Jordan slowly drifted back to sleep. Taking advantage of the child, Eric placed his hand on Jordan's genitals. Initially, Jordan, believing that Eric had fallen asleep, thought that his arm slipping was just an accident. When Eric reached down, pulling off his underwear, Jordan began to protest. Eric's breath brushed past Jordan's ear as he whispered "It's alright." Jordan, scared and uncomfortable, wasn't sure. He tried to push the intruder off, but he was strongly resisted.

Eric entered Jordan harshly from behind. With a jolt, Jordan's body burst into excruciating pain. Jordan tried to let out a scream, but was muffled, his face pushed into the pillow. The torment and pain caused by his mother soon became secondary. Deep in the core of his being, every cell screamed out in anguish. Each thrust made it more unbearable. Yet, for a brief moment he found himself numbly floating above, observing a young, fragile child being brutally raped. Realizing it was he who was being savagely attacked, his soul, like a rubber band, snapped back into the shell, which once was Jordan.

Mr. Philips came in the next morning to wake Jordan and to prepare him for his school enrollment. Jordan did not respond but remained fetal, whimpering. Jokingly, Mr. Philips partially pulled back the covers from the child's aching body. He stepped back, startled, as he saw the paleness of Jordan's skin against blood stained sheets.

"Oh my God, what happened?!" Mr. Philips exclaimed, knowing that Eric was responsible. He called down to Janice to come to his aid. Entering the room, Janice gasped at the sight of Jordan, naked on the contaminated sheets. She immediately called the police.

It was while Jordan was being placed in the ambulance he witnessed Eric being taken away in handcuffs. An attendant closed the ambulance door, shutting out the view of Eric in the backseat of a police car. Jordan knew what he had to do and who was to suffer like he did.

Jefferson House, and Eric's initiation of Jordan into the system, was just the beginning of a series of placements, from foster homes to group homes, and through various levels of residential programs. With his innocence shattered, he was most unwilling to adapt to the ever changing environments. At each step in the series of placements, Jordan grew more distant, more oppositional and eventually numb. At the ripe are of fourteen Jordan, after a series of home burglaries, became involved in the criminal justice system, his first stint in a youth detention program. Jordan abandoned all hope. He knew that he was nothing more than a penny on a railroad track, waiting for the train.

—

Jordan floated through numerous placements, patiently waiting for the moment that he and Eric were housed in the same facility. He was quite surprised that it has taken so long for it to happen. Considering both were products of the child welfare system, he had expected that they would have met at one of the group homes, or a juvenile center.

Whenever he entered a new program or facility, Jordan would seek Eric out, only to learn that he had moved on to another. At Yardtown, a mental health facility for incarcerated juveniles, they had missed each other by one day. Maintaining an established pattern, Eric had brutally attacked another resident. For this, he was transferred out of Yardtown to a maximum security facility, in the southern part of the state. The next day, Jordan was transferred in.

At the Central State Correctional Facility, Eric quickly stepped into the inner circle of the Aryan Brotherhood. After the incident at Yardtown, the skinheads recruited Eric as an enforcer. He did not disappoint them as he relished in his viciousness. He swiftly moved up their ranks, establishing himself as a leader, more due to his reputation as a cold heartless killer, than to his leadership abilities. Throughout his incarceration, he deeply entrenched himself among the most brutal. Within the correctional environment, there were very few who were more feared that Eric.

It wasn't long after his arrival that Eric began to notice Jordan. It was intentional. Jordan appeared wherever Eric went. Jordan wanted to be seen. Eric began to realize that these occurrences were far too many to be coincidental. It seemed, whenever he was in the yard with the Brotherhood, Jordan was a few feet away, playing basketball. Whenever he was in the cafeteria, Jordan was standing, watching from the chow line. Whenever he was in the library, Jordan was in the next stack over. Not sure that they had ever crossed paths before, Eric could not understand what attracted this stranger. Jordan kept up the pressure. He wanted Eric to know he was being followed, that he was being stalked. It was working. Eric was becoming uncomfortable.

Others in the Brotherhood began to notice as well. Not knowing who Jordan was, they were also curious as to why he was stalking Eric. One thing they did know, if Jordan was indeed following Eric, then he was nothing more than a chicken about to be plucked. They were out for his blood. Soon they began to taunt Eric, pointing out Jordan. Eric just shrugged these off. Yet, he knew that he had to act soon, or he would lose his standing among the skinheads. Jordan knew this as well. He couldn't afford a confrontation, one that he could not control. Somehow he had to maintain an upper hand. Like Eric, he had to act soon. If he didn't Jordan would surely die.

—

It was at a noon meal, when Eric, leaving early, told his brothers he was tired and was heading back to his cell. Generally, they were the last to leave the cafeteria. They had deals to make, shipments to monitor, tasks to delegate. For Eric to leave, without overseeing brotherhood business, was unprecedented. Thus, they didn't believe him. It was a consensus. Something was about to happen. They watched Jordan, taking bets on how his last day would end. He did not disappoint. Smelling blood, they anxiously watched Jordan get up from his table and follow Eric through the cafeteria doors.

Eric, not wanting to lose face among his gang members, finally decided to challenge Jordan. To him, Jordan was nothing more than a skinny little punk, one as annoying as a fly buzzing around the cell late at night. He had his reputation to preserve and wasn't willing to let this insect tarnish it. Feeling confident, Eric knew that Jordan would follow him. Anticipating a confrontation, he slipped under the stairwell between the cellblocks and waited.

Eric considered his options. He could make this punk into his bitch and pimp him out to the other inmates. That would be easy. On the other hand, He knew that he could have any new fish at anytime. It would be just as easy to swat the fly.

Hearing someone descending down the stairs, Eric took a deep breath. His prey was approaching. Like a hunter waiting in his blind, he stood motionless anticipating his kill.

—

Walking swiftly to the exit Jordan lost sight of Eric. In the stairwell he panicked, not knowing which way Eric had gone. Taking a chance, he decided to go down the stairs, hoping that Eric was heading toward his cell. At the bottom, he sensed that he was no longer alone. A hand reached out, pulling him under the steps. It was Eric.

"Who are…?" Eric demand.

Jordan putting his finger across Eric's lips, whispered, "Shhh." Looking into his eyes, Jordan saw nothing but darkness. There was no emotion. He was soulless. Jordan now knew he had no choice, but to continue. Jordan knew one of them had to die. Petrified, he wasn't sure it wouldn't be him.

Gently, Jordan grabbed Eric's arm and slowly pulled him deeper under the stairwell. Again, Eric tried to speak but as before, Jordan stopped him. Without a word Jordan, slipped to his knees. Looking up into the coldness of Eric's eyes, he casually unbuckled and unzipped Eric's jeans. Eric watched, as Jordan gradually wrapped his mouth around his penis. Eric, letting down his guard, began to relax, his organ growing stiff in Jordan's mouth.

Sensing Eric was about to ejaculate Jordan, with a palmed razor, slashed deeply into Eric's scrotum. After the initial sharp pain, Eric began to feel a numbness overcome his groin. Unsure of what had just happened, he reached down only to feel the blood quickly flow into his hand. He slipped weakly to his knees. Pain and confusion began to set in. All he could do was mumble a simple "Why?" With a second stroke as swiftly as the first, Jordan cut deeply along the side of Eric's throat. Fading into unconsciousness he heard Jordan answer "Jefferson House".

Scared and unsure of what he had done, Jordan ran back toward the cafeteria. On his way up, he passed three skinheads, going down. All four froze on the stairs, staring at each other. He was not the one they had expected to return. Seeing the blood covering Jordan, they continued down to seek out Eric.

Jordan, searching for a place to hide, scurried into the shower room.

Looking into the mirror, he was horrified by the sight of Eric's blood, covering his face and shirt. He, tearing off his shirt, began to cleanse himself of Eric. Fear was beginning to overcome him. He had placed a target on his back. Everyone from the Brotherhood will be out for his skin. To take down someone like Eric was significant. He was a major player among the Aryans. Now, skinheads throughout the facility will be jockeying for his position. Taking out Jordan will definitely give another an edge in replacing Eric.

Contemplating his next more, Jordan stood in front of the mirror. Chi Chi, leader of the Latin Kings, and several other Latino inmates entering the shower room, approached Jordan. Holding tightly onto the sink, he readied himself for a defense. Through the mirror, Jordan and the Latinos exchanged glances.

"Hey man, ya okay?" Chi Chi broke the silence.

Jordan, speaking to Chi Chi's reflection in the mirror, answered, "Yea, I guess so."

"They're goin' to want your blood man, you know."

Jordan nodded, "Yea, I guess." He looked around at the Kings, standing their ground behind him. He no longer felt threatened. He kept focused on the mirror, where all remained in view. "Word gets around fast."

"Well you know, the telegraph," said Chi Chi, walking toward Jordan's right side. "Besides man, everyone saw it comin'. It was in your eyes whenever ya two were near."

"Yea," Jordan responded.

"It's just, man," Chi Chi hesitated, "no one though ya be the one to walk away. Ya know what I mean?" He reached down, taking the bloodied shirt from Jordan's hand and passed it to one of the Kings. "Man, we'll get rid of this for ya," he said firmly.

Jordan continued to look into the mirror. He nodded his acknowledgement to Chi Chi. With that, they walked out the door, leaving Jordan alone. Before exiting, one of Chi Chi's lieutenants turned to Jordan, "Hey man, don't worry much, okay. We got your back."

Chapter 11

"Have you ever thought of suicide?" Dr. Lap asked, almost sheepishly.

The thought of a shotgun in his mouth came immediately to Wood's mind. He clearly remembered sitting at his office desk, with both barrels in his mouth and his finger on a trigger. It was shortly after Becca died. Giving up on a façade of normality, he had walked out of his class, promising that he would never go back. The shotgun was to make it easy. Yet, there was a bottle of vodka, sitting on a pile of test papers he had failed to grade. Looking at those papers, and the bottle on top, he decided to kill the vodka instead. After that, not much else was clear. Wood thought about telling Dr. Lap about the shotgun incident, but "No" was all he said.

"Do you remember the guy they called Milkshake?"

"Yea," Wood answered. "He's that guy who lived above the bookstore, across from the campus."

"That's the one. You know, he's still around." Dr. Lap hesitated. Picking up his beer, he took a long gulp. Then, shifting in his seat to face Wood, he continued, "Would you want to be him? Would you trade your life for his? I mean, he's the fuckin' poster boy for failed suicides. A gun to the head, pop, and the fucker misses." Leaning back in his seat, Dr. Lap took another swig before concluding, "Man, all he did was fuck up his life forever."

Milkshake, after being charged with armed robbery, tried to kill himself. Feeding a heroin habit he, flashing a toy gun, pulled off a string of gas station robberies. He was caught when one attendant, noticing that the gun was plastic, jumped over the counter and smacked Milkshake with tire iron. Afraid of prison, or perhaps, unable to withdraw from his smack habit, he decided to just take himself out. Milkshake missed, lodging a small caliber bullet in his brain.

He survived, but not without consequences. Losing any semblance of motor control, he was left in a constant state of twitches and spasms. It was most evident when walking, his arms wildly flapped, like a baby bird, trying to take flight. The irony of it all, his court appointed lawyer got him off on a technicality. He would have never served a day and probably continued in a state of drug induced bliss.

"The Swede," Dr. Lap continued, "he's another one."

"But he died." Wood responded.

The Swede, a long time friend of both Wood and Dr. Lap, experiencing severe pain, suffered through a long period of illness. Doctors were unable to help him. Weakened, he could no longer take the extreme and continuous pain. Thus, like Milkshake, The Swede put a small caliber pistol to his head. He missed, shooting out his eye. At the hospital, the doctors frantically tried to stabilize him and stop the bleeding. They did. He, conscious of his failure, died a few days later, from an undiagnosed kidney infection.

"That's true." Dr. Lap replied. "But he died, knowing he blew it. He knew he failed."

"I guess you're right, but…"

"No, just listen," Dr. Lap leaned forward, placing his beer on the table. "If you're going to do it, then you need to do it right. Not like these fuckers. I'm going to do it right. Yea, if you're going to do it, then do it right."

Wood, unsure of Dr. Lap's insinuation, asked, "Chris, did I just hear you say that you are going to kill yourself?"

"Nay, I don't have any plans. I mean, I don't have any intent to do so.

But, haven't you thought about killing yourself?" Dr. Lap, remembering the condition Wood was in after Becca died, continued. "You can't tell me that when things were really rough on you, you didn't think about packing it in. Don't tell me, that sometimes, you just don't want to get out of bed. Wishing it was all over."

"I'm sure I have," Wood responded, "but that's not suicide."

"Yea, I guess maybe you can say that." Retreating from the conversation, Dr. Lap leaned back in his seat, downing the last of his beer. Resting his head against the wall, he closed his eyes and softly sang to the Rascals' *It's a Beautiful Morning*, flowing from the juke box.

Watching him, Wood wasn't convinced. The unwelcomed image of Dr. Lap, possibly hanging himself from the shower head in Wood's bathroom, haunted him. He didn't want any part of that agenda. Wood didn't want the hassles, the dealing with police and speaking to Dr. Lap's family. Missing his solitude, Wood's only desire was for Dr. Lap to return to the college.

—

Dr. Lap, after ordering another round of drinks, sat back quietly surveying the pub. Luscious and Lady Cakes, sitting in a back booth, patiently waited on another couple to finish their game of pool. Buffalo and No Hope remained at the bar, slowly nursing shots of whiskey. Every now and then, someone would drop a few quarters into the jukebox. The music played continuously, a healthy mix of fifties doo-wop, blues, and sixties rock. The bar remained relatively at peace, until an altercation erupted between Buffalo and No Hope.

Buffalo and No Hope were inseparable. But, when it came to his alcohol, Buffalo was cautious around No Hope. He didn't trust him. Momentarily forgetting this, Buffalo got up to go to the bathroom. Heading toward the restroom Buffalo, suspicious of No Hope, turned back to finish his whiskey. As suspected, No Hope swiped the drink and downed it. Angrily, Buffalo grabbed No Hope by his sleeve, yanking him off the barstool. The two swung at each other wildly, neither landing any punches. Jake jumping over the bar, as he had done so many times before, subdued the combatants. It was quickly over, as Jake grabbing both, pushed them out the door.

"Hell," Dr. Lap laughed. "If they were out in the alley, he would have pissed in his pants before leaving a drink with that loser."

Ignoring Dr. Lap's comment, Wood, feeling slightly intoxicated, said. "Chris, as you know, we're slowly committing suicide anyway."

Confused, Dr. Lap stiffened. "What?" he asked.

"Yea," Wood answered. "Life, as far as I'm concerned, is nothing more than a slow painful form of suicide. We do what we do to ease that pain. So, we slowing kill ourselves by becoming workaholics, or drinking ourselves to death. Others quicken it by blowing their fuckin' heads off."

Dr. Lap, curiously looking at Wood, asked. "Okay Mr. Philosopher. What the fuck are you talking about?"

"Damn, we all have pain, and we're killing ourselves to get rid of it. You have yours, you know, and I have mine, whatever it is." Wood continued. "Take a look at some of these businessmen. They get so highly competitive, working twelve, fifteen hour days. They don't eat right, smoke, whatever, and then it all catches up, a fuckin' heart attack at fifty. Why, someone was making more money than them, a fucked up marriage?"

"Go on," Dr. Lap said, "humor me."

"Those two guys that were thrown out," Wood began.

"Yea?"

"The first guy, the one we call No Hope, I talked with him not too long ago. You wouldn't know it, but he was in Special Forces during the war, a trained assassin. He was telling me that he couldn't remember how many kills he had, but every morning when he wakes up, like ghosts, they're all around him. So he drinks, trying to erase them."

"You're kidding me, him, Special Forces?" Dr. Lap bewildered scratched his head.

Wood first chugged a shot of vodka then answered. "No, seriously, he was. Then, after the war he did some Special Ops, you know, CIA type of shit."

"Him?"

"Yea, him," Wood snickered. "One time, he said he was dropped off in Central America, in one of the Latin American countries. He was to escort an oppositional leader and his wife out. When they met up, this guy had his wife as planned, but also brought his daughter and her child. No Hope tried to explain, it would be too dangerous to take all four, but they insisted."

"Wait a minute," Dr. Lap interrupted. Feeling warm, he rolled up the sleeves of his shirt. "Is he for real?"

"Well, I don't know." Wood answered. "It's what he told me. Anyway, according to No Hope, they were traveling at night through the jungle, when they happened upon some guerrillas. He had the family hide in the brush. Then, as the patrol came closer, the baby began to whimper. Afraid of getting caught, afraid of failing his mission, he took the baby from the mother and held his hand over its mouth to keep it quiet."

"What happened?" Dr. Lap impatiently asked.

"As he said, his mission was to get this politico to safety. That was most important. So, there he was trying to keep this baby quiet, you know, trying to complete his mission. As the guerrilla patrol kept getting closer, No Hope kept squeezing tighter to keep the baby from crying. Just as the patrol passed the brush where they were hiding, the baby fell limp."

"He killed the baby?" Dr. Lap exclaimed. "Unbelievable!"

"Yea, un-fucking-believable," Wood fell silent, giving Dr. Lap a moment to comprehend the scope of No Hope's torment. He then capped it. "Would you believe he still hears that baby cry?"

Dr. Lap leaned back against the booth. The look on his face disclosed his bewilderment. "If you had not told me, I would have never guessed."

"Yea, I guess not, but," Wood asked, "would you trade your suicide for his, would you?"

Dr. Lap, momentarily speechless, shook his head in awe. Didn't he just witness No Hope battle with Buffalo, falling over in a drunken stupor? No, Dr. Lap couldn't imagine him in combat. "Wait a minute," he exclaimed, rising up from his seat. "He's a hero. If he did this stuff, wouldn't you think?"

"You're kidding me, right? Do you really think he's a hero? Do you think he believes that he's a hero?" Wood snickered. "No, he's a killer, a murderer, and I believe that's what he thinks."

"You do?"

"Listen, do you really want to know what I think?" Leaning back, Wood picked up his beer and slowly emptied the bottle. Turning his attention back to Dr. Lap, he continued. "I knew Eddie, No Hope, when I was a kid. He was vicious, a mean son of a bitch. I mean there were stories. Anyway, I don't believe that shit about he doing it for the mission. That's okay for Hollywood, but its bull shit. He has no heart. I don't think he had a second thought about killing that kid, you know, to save his own ass, if he really did it."

"What about the ghosts and all that stuff?"

"Yea I know, seeing the faces, hearing the baby cry. I kinda think something happened to him. You know, being left for dead, something like that, got to him. Like, he came face to face with the devil and he finally saw his own darkness. I think that's what got to him. I think that's what he's trying to drown."

"So he's not a hero."

Leaning forward on the table, Wood calmly spoke. "Yea, I mean, if he was a hero, he would have written a book, or he'll be in some government position, backed by some corrupted political machine. Instead, he's a drunk, slowing killing himself, escaping his demons." Briefly pausing, Wood added. "You know what? Fuck it, there's nothing we can do about it. Just fuck it."

"Yea, you're right, fuck it." Dr. Lap replied, sensing Wood's agitation. "Let's get out of here and go for some Chinese. I'm starving."

"Sounds good" Wood rejoined. "Let's do it."

—

China One was just down the block from Paci's. Wood and Dr. Lap entered the small storefront and quickly ordered a take out. Dr. Lap turned and sat in one of the booths that lined the left wall under a row of mirrors. Wood, grabbing two cokes from the refrigerator on the right, joined him. Wood, picking up a community newsletter from the table, quietly read while Dr. Lap studied the ceiling.

"You know, I have always liked these old tin ceilings." Dr. Lap said, breaking the silence. "They give a place character."

"Yea, I agree."

Dr. Lap, surveying the store, asked. "Wasn't this place an Italian deli when we were in school? I kinda remember coming in here, when we would come up to visit your family."

In a previous incarnation, China One had been Greco's Market. Looking around, Wood tried to visualize the old store. Where now hung pictures of various Chinese quickie meals, once hung balls of Italian cheeses and lengths of salami and pepperoni. Instead of tables, there were aisles of imported pastas of different shapes and sizes, canned Italian delicacies, canned sauces, breads, cookies and candies. The counter, a glass encased refrigerator, displayed different cuts of beef, pork, lamb and chicken. A sign sat above, reminding shoppers that tripe and goat was also available. In another freezer, one would find various homemade dishes and sauces including ravioli, lasagna, and manicotti. And of course, the store was not complete without the wood barrels of olives and dried slabs of *baccala*.

"I remember coming here to buy provolone and mozzarella cheeses, as well as, sticks of pepperoni, to take back with us. Man, you couldn't get that stuff down south." Dr. Lap reminisced.

"You know, I use to come here with my grandfather to get lunch for our fishing trips." Wood said, smiling. "Back in those days we would get these great sandwiches, you know a half loaf of Italian bread with cold cuts and cheese for less than a dollar. My grandfather would get his *mortadella,* and I would get my provolone with roast beef. Gramps would make sure I had a couple bottles of cream soda for the trip."

"Those were the days." Dr. Lap reflected.

Wood continued, "I remember, the old man and I would walk in, he'd start flirting with the women in the store, or bullshit with one of the old timers about the old country. Just like he owned the place, Gramps would grab a wedge of parmesan. With his pocketknife, he'd cut a piece and flip it to me. I would suck on that chunk, savoring every bit of its salty flavor. I could almost taste it now."

"I never met your grandfather," Dr. Lap said, "but you did talk about him a lot. I also remember on several trips up from school, you would go to his grave."

"Yea, you know I still go." Slowly sipping from his drink, Wood continued. "Not as much as when I was younger, but I still visit his grave. I still talk to him. Sometimes, I think Gramps is the only one that understands me."

Wood, adjusting his seating in the booth, turned with his back against the wall. With his feet propped up on the bench, he was able to look out the store window and maintain eye contact with Dr. Lap. Casually, Wood observed the people passing by outside the storefront. Undeterred, he continued his conversation with Dr. Lap.

"You know I really miss that old man. I miss those fishing trips we used to take. He would take me down to Belmar and Shark's River Inlet. We fished for blowfish and fluke. I remember sitting on that concrete wall at the inlet. He would frequently joke with me about catching the big one. More often than not, we would just go up to the Hudson to fish for eels."

Distracted by a young Hispanic women, walking pass the decorated front window, Wood momentarily hesitated. Her smile caught his attention. She appeared to be quite happy and full of life, not a care in the world. For reasons only known to Wood, he was saddened.

Returning to the conversation with Dr. Lap, Wood continued, "That man really liked his eels. We would drive home from the Hudson in his old fifty-one Chevy. I would sit there watching him bang gears, opera blasting out of the old car radio. Once home, Gramps would clean and cut up the catch. He'd have me set the iron skillet on the stove with a little olive oil. I'll get that thing smoking and he would throw in some garlic and onion. On top of that went the eels. Man, that house would stink. My grandmother would come in, yelling at him in her Italian. In the end, Grandma would be at that table with us laughing and eating like no tomorrow."

"Do you still fish?" Dr. Lap asked.

"Nah, it has been a long time since I have. Besides would you eat anything caught out of the Hudson?"

"I guess not."

Waiting on their take-out, they sat quietly. Wood watched Dr. Lap anxiously fidget, obviously preoccupied. He knew his friend Chris didn't come up from his campus in Virginia just to talk about college days, or to hear Wood reminisce about growing up. It had to be serious. It was the beginning of the term. Wood understood Dr. Lap should be at school attending to his classes. Dr. Lap was known to be a little eccentric, but was also a dedicated educator. Not being at school just wasn't him. Wood needed to know what was troubling him. More importantly, he needed to know when Dr. Lap planned to leave.

Repositioned in the booth to faced Dr. Lap, Wood decided to chance questioning him about his visit. "So tell me." Wood whispered, "What's going on?"

Dr. Lap looked up, making eye contact with Wood. "Nothing, I'm just sitting here with my best friend waiting on an exquisite Chinese meal."

"No, seriously," Wood firmly asked, "why are you here? I mean classes are not over. They're just starting. You are not even close to a midterm break."

Dr. Lap sat back in his seat. "Is that's what's bothering you. I got Jimmy Shines, one of the teaching assistants, to cover for me." He lied. Dr. Lap didn't want to think about, never mind talk about, the charges against him. He wasn't sure how Wood would respond, nor was he ready to explain himself. "I just wanted to take a break."

Wood did not believe him. He knew that you just don't walk away from your classes without a reason. "No seriously, what's going on?"

Dr. Lap remained evasive. "Nah, nothing serious, just a little disagreement I have with Dean Trudy." He lied again.

"You know that is bull. You and Trudy never agreed on anything."

"Look," Dr. Lap said firmly, "I just needed some time off. Like I said, there's nothing serious, nothing to be concerned about."

Wood, knowing that Dr. Lap was lying to him, conceded. He also knew Dr. Lap wasn't going to give him an answer. He had to let it go, at least for the moment. He had to be patient.

—

"Number forty-seven you food ready," the cashier announced in a thick Chinese accent.

"That's us." Wood said, sliding out of the booth. Dr. Lap followed closely behind.

At the counter a young Chinese woman waited. Her smile exposed a gap to the right where a tooth once was. "You pay fourteen ninety-two," she said.

Wood, reaching into his pocket, pulled out a twenty dollar bill. As he was about to hand it over to the cashier, a bug slithered out from under the bag of food. "Look, a fuckin' roach just came from that bag," he said, withdrawing his cash offering.

"No roachie, no roachie," surprised by the insect, the woman lost her smile.

Standing at the counter, the three stared at each other until a second bug tried to escape from under the bag. Dr. Lap immediately slammed the side of his fist on the roach, crushing it. On the counter a small pool of gooey bug guts was left. Wiping his fist across the young woman's apron, he smeared the remains of the mangled creature on her shoulder. "Yes, roachie," was all he said as he and Wood turned to leave.

Once outside, they both broke out into laughter. "I bet you never found one of those in your *mortadella*."

"No," Wood responded. "But one of these days remind me to tell you the story about maggots in lamb heads."

"Yea, I can't wait to hear that one." Dr. Lap replied. "But, as the saying goes don't hold your breath."

Chapter 12

Paci's was unusually busy for a Wednesday evening. Buffalo and No Hope, immune to the crowd around them, manned their usual station at the end of the mahogany and marble bar. Luscious, who was usually found shooting pool with her lover Lady Cakes, kept herself busy helping Jake, the bartender, serve drinks. Meanwhile, Lady Cakes remained in the back, challenging all comers to a game of eight ball.

At a far booth sat Four-Thirty, speaking with a young woman with longish brown hair and dressed in a tan jacket. Wood recognized her as from the neighborhood and, most recently, soliciting at Paci's. Seeing Dr. Lap and Wood enter, Four-Thirty waved them over to her table. As the two men approached, the younger woman got up from her seat. Whispering "thanks" to Four-Thirty, she brushed pass Wood, giving him a shy smile. Both men, eyes fixated on the shimmy of her skirt, watched as she walked past the bar. The sensual rhythm of her high heels, clicking across the worn wooden floor, soon diminished in the midst of the music of the street.

"She didn't have to leave on my part." Dr. Lap said.

"Hmm, I not sure about that," Wood responded. Turning to Four-Thirty he added, "Would you trust him around any woman?"

"Well, lucky for him she's gone." Four-Thirty replied, looking toward the closing door. "I don't think he could afford her these days."

"And that's cheap my friend. I mean," Wood said, pointing at the bar. "Most of her johns are up there. You really don't want to be counted among that crew." To Wood's dismay, she had never approached him. Intrigued by her dark eyes and how her chestnut color hair set against her near ivory skin, he was often left observing, as she propositioned others in the pub. It was quite obvious she was uncomfortable, shy, often with her head down, not making eye contact as though she was subservient, doing them a favor. Unbeknownst to Wood, his watchful glances made her feel even more apprehensive, as she mingled among the men of Paci's.

"Not anymore. Soon she will be taking over my guys and, you know, I don't come cheap."

"And?"

"Oh, that's a conversation you and I can have, will have, at another time. Other than that, I have decided it was time to get out." Not wanting to pursue the discussion in front of Wood's friend, she turned to Dr. Lap. "And what brings you back to our corner of the universe?"

Before he could answer Luscious, dressed in jeans and a faded blue work shirt, appeared at the table. With hands in her pockets and rocking on the balls of her feet, she turned first to Four-Thirty, "I know you're good for another wine," then addressing Wood, "and you the usual, but what about your friend here?"

"Still drinking vodka with a chaser?"

"Yea," Dr. Lap answered. "But make it a double."

"Kinda busy tonight, isn't it." Four-Thirty asked Luscious.

Looking over the crowd, Luscious reached up with the sleeve of her cotton work shirt and swiped a bead of sweat off her forehead. "Yea, seems like the whole freakin' neighborhood is here. Hope it will thin out soon. I would like to get back to my table."

"It is kinda strange, coming in here and seeing you without a cue stick." Wood added.

"Yea, I do feel a little naked. Besides," nodding toward the pool table in the back where, surrounded by several out-of-town bikers, Lady Cakes just sunk the last shot taking another game, "I don't like those guys hitting on Lady back there."

"Hell, they're no competition," Four-Thirty replied, watching Lady Cakes take her winnings off the table's railing as another mark set the rack, "nor can they compete with her on that table."

"You're right there. She sure can kick ass with that stick of hers." Luscious acknowledged. "Anyway, you guys hungry? We got some good specials."

All three indicated that they would wait, until the dinner crowd thinned out, before ordering. "Not now, we'll wait a little while." Wood advised Luscious.

"Yea, I'll go with that." Dr. Lap added. "But, bring us a plate of your famous mussels, just to hold us over."

"Okay, you got it. Funny," Luscious contemplated, turning away to get their drinks, "to think this dump might be famous for something."

—

At a booth across from their table sat Kitty, in deep conversation with a man several years her senior. He was new to the neighborhood, having moved into the old Corso home. Talk at the corner deli described him as a medical doctor from Saudi Arabia. Waiting on being licensed to practice medicine in the United States, he took a job working part time as a guard for a security firm. It was obvious Kitty was sinking in her claws, not feeling any loss with Jose in jail. There she sat, in a pink halter top, her sagging breast slipping out, nearly exposing her nipple. With an arm draped around the doctor's neck, she playfully fingered the badge pinned to his chest. He was hooked. The doc had no idea as to what was in store for him. All he wanted was to get laid. Kitty kept that promise dangling, as long as he kept buying the drinks.

"Poor guy," Wood mumbled.

"What?"

Pointing across toward Kitty, Wood answered. "Look, she's got him so suckered he's about ready to blow his paycheck."

"Damn, she's really has let herself go since Jose got busted." Four-Thirty replied. "That's not to say, she wasn't a mess before, but I hear she's in here most nights, getting drunk and hitting on whomever. I mean, just a few weeks ago she was all over this guy Ritchie, you know from the Hess station, when his ole' lady walked in."

"Yea, I know him. He's the mechanic there." Wood answered. "I know both him and his wife. I bet that was a scene."

"Yea, that's the guy. And you're right, it was a scene. Jake nearly called the cops, I mean, if it wasn't for Luscious."

The incident involving Ritchie and Kitty unfolded on a drab Tuesday afternoon. It had been drizzling most of the morning. Although the rain had stopped, there were still overcast skies with infrequent teasing rays of sunshine. Ritchie had just finished a brake job on old man Petrie's Ford when he decided to grab lunch at Paci's. Ritchie entered the pub to the drone of the TV, broadcasting the midday news. Luscious was in the back sweeping the floor in the dining area, while Jake, having served a couple their lunch, stepped back behind the bar. Ritchie, taking a seat near the beer taps with a direct view of the TV, quickly ordered a medium well cheeseburger and a cold mug of ale.

The heavy wood and glass door swung open as Kitty entered the pub. Seeing Ritchie having lunch at the bar alone, she took a stool next to him. Undeterred, he continued watching the news and eating his burger. Kitty ordered a scotch and water. She quickly downed it, ordering another. It was after her third when Kitty, draping one arm around Ritchie's neck, began to rub the inside of his thigh. As her fingers rode up the seam of his overalls, Ritchie called for another round of drinks. Underneath her hand, Ritchie could feel his erection swell. Sensing this, Kitty tightened her grip and leaned over to whisper in his ear. Apparently, liking what was offered, Ritchie slipped off his stool and headed toward the restroom with Kitty close behind him.

"Man, I can't believe he would go for her. I know his family, you know, his kids and wife." Wood said. "I mean, he and his wife are tight. Didn't think he'll ever go for some strange, especially someone like Kitty."

"Yea, I thought so too but, who knows nowadays." Four-Thirty added.

"So, what happened?" Dr. Lap questioned.

"Well," Four-Thirty explained how Lisa, Ritchie's wife, had called the station with the idea of bringing him lunch. Being informed that he had just left for Paci's, she decided to join him and perhaps, talk him into taking the afternoon off. Walking in, Lisa caught a glimpse of first Ritchie, then Kitty, entering the men's room. Initially, she thought nothing of it, considering that in fifteen years of marriage Ritchie never gave her a reason not to trust him. Yet, seeing Jake standing speechless behind the bar, and Luscious frozen with her broom in mid stroke, she knew something was wrong.

Luscious made no attempts to block Lisa as she rushed past her. Swinging open the men's room door, Lisa felt the knot in the pit of her stomach burst into the flames of anger. There, in front of her, stood Kitty, bent over the bathroom sink and Ritchie, overalls down below his knees, about to enter her from behind. Seeing Lisa's reflection in the mirror, Kitty swiftly pulled up her undergarments and screamed "rape". Sensing his wife's rage, Ritchie stepped back with his erection diminishing into his groin. Knocking Ritchie into a stall pushing past him, Lisa grabbed Kitty by her hair, slamming her face onto her knee.

"Damn," exclaimed Dr. Lap.

"Yea," Four-Thirty continued. "Luscious said there was blood everywhere. I mean she broke Kitty's nose and shit. Anyway, Jake was about to call the cops when Luscious stepped in, breaking up the fight before Lisa caused anymore damage to Kitty."

"I can see that, I would never mess with her. That Luscious is one tough bitch." Wood replied.

"I heard Kitty was banned from the bar. But, look at her, sitting there like nothing ever happened."

"Well. You know Jake," Wood said. "He's easy, you know what I mean. If she doesn't cause any more shit, he'll let her slide."

"What happened with the guy Ritchie?" Dr Lap asked.

"I think he and his ole' lady are okay." Four-Thirty responded. "You know, he's still in the doghouse. But you know, he's really a good guy and, I think, really cares about Lisa."

"It surprises me 'cause I never thought he was one to stray." Wood added.

"Yea and I think Lisa knows that, otherwise she would have cut him loose. Still, I'll bet she'll keep him on a short lease and give him some shit for a while."

A large platter of mussels, steaming in a red sauce, and a basket of semolina bread were placed on the table. The aroma of tomatoes and peppers, rising from the sauce, spiked their appetite. Teased by the appetizer, the three decided to order dinner. From the breast pocket of his shirt, Jake withdrew a pencil and notepad, carefully writing down their order. All three decided to forgo the specials, with Wood and Dr. Lap ordering deluxe half pound cheeseburger platters. Four-Thirty, conscious of her weight, requested a large chef salad with chicken. The three then quietly indulged in the appetizer.

"Hey Wood, remember that Volkswagen we had in college?" Dr. Lap asked, eventually breaking the silence.

"Yea, I do." Wood answered. "Didn't we get that out of a junkyard?

"I think so. Yea, I think we did."

They were nearing the end of their junior year in college, when Wood and Dr. Lap agreed to spend the summer on a cross country trip. Deciding against hitchhiking, they picked up a relic of a VW bug from a salvage yard, not far from the campus. In spite of the need of extensive repair, they were elated as they drove it back to the dorm, concurring that twenty-five dollars could not have been better spent.

Once back on campus, they quickly began to address the needed repairs, a cracked rear axle and a leaky master cylinder. Although Wood has had the experience of getting his hands greasy building a hot rod as a teen, he soon realized that a Volkswagen was nothing like a Ford. Dr. Lap, for his part, had little experience with auto mechanics beyond the simple tune-up and maintenance. Yet, they were determined. Through the recruitment of fellow students for their expertise, quizzing local auto mechanics, and the borrowing of shop tools, Greenie, as it was affectionately known, was soon up and running. Satisfied with their accomplishment, Dr. Lap was anxious to assume his role of Neal Cassidy to Wood's Jack Kerouac.

"Wait a minute," Four-Thirty interjected. "No way, not the guy I know."

Dr. Lap, fairly amused by her comment, laughed, "Why's that?"

"You see, when we were growing up, this guy was into hot rods. You know old Fords, Chevys, you know." Four-Thirty added, "I mean he even built these plastic models of hot rods. A Volkswagen, no not Wood, I just can't see it."

Wood slowly slurped down a mussel from its shell. With the back of his hand, he wiped off the little sauce that dripped onto his lip. He then placed the empty shell on a plate in front of him. Smiling, he turned toward Four-Thirty and replied, "Well you know, sometimes shit happens."

"Un-fuckin'-believable, so what happened with this fancy sports car you never told me about?" Four-Thirty joked.

"Wait, stop," Dr. Lap exclaimed, leaning forward and reaching for his beer. "You mean to tell me, that after all these fuckin' years, you had me thinking you were some intellectual freakin' hippie, I now come to find out you built hot rods? That you were a greaser?"

"Well, not really," Wood replied, after downing another mussel. "I kinda fooled around with a flathead eight, nothing serious. If that's what you mean by building hot rods, I guess you can say I did."

"Man, that's a side of you I never knew. I mean, after a lifetime, and all the shit we been through, it might have come up. You think?" Turning to Four-Thirty, Dr. Lap continued, "I guess we both learned something new about our friend tonight. You think he's got other secrets he's keeping from us?"

"You'll never know." Four-Thirty giggled. "Just when you think you know a man, you know what I mean?"

"Do you remember that trip to Atlanta? Or should I say," Dr. Lap, broadly smiling, continued, "the trip to Atlanta that we almost made?"

Picking up a napkin, Wood began to laugh, wiping tomato sauce off his fingers. "Boy, do I remember."

"Yea, that trip was freakin' doomed before it even started."

—

It was just before final exams, the two were lounging in their dormitory room getting high. Joining them was Dr. Lap's cousin Groovy, a New York City hippie, who had come down for a weekend visit. Standing over the stereo, Wood gently held a newly purchased album, between the palms of his hands, as he carefully placed it on the turntable. The stylus, when prompted, floated onto the disk. Hitting its groove, the aching sounds of a blues harmonica began to filter through twin speakers. It was Charlie Mussellwhite and his Southside Blues Band.

At his desk, Dr. Lap sat busily packing the last of his marijuana into a soapstone bong. Carved into the shape of a nude, its bowl was firmly planted between the woman's legs. "It's your hit," he directed, passing the bong and a lighter to Groovy.

Groovy placed the pipe against his mouth. As he lit the weed, he began to inhale, drawing smoke into the bong's chamber. At the point where he could no longer breathe in, he released his index finger from the hole carved into the nude's navel. A rush of air shot through the opening, forcing the smoke deeply into his lungs. With his respiratory organs fully expanded, Groovy began to cough violently as they began to push back. "Boy that is good shit." He declared, brushing a tear from the corner of his eye.

"So," Dr Lap asked, grabbing the bong from Groovy and reloading it for Wood, "anything going on in town tonight?"

"Don't know." Wood answered, picking up the newspaper from the desk. "Let's see." He began to survey the pages, occasionally pausing to read a headline. Reaching the last page of the entertainment section, he jumped from his seat. "Whoa, whoa, whoa," handing the paper to Dr. Lap, "look at this. Butterfield is playing in Atlanta this weekend." Paul Butterfield, a Chicago bluesman, had been a favorite of both Dr. Lap and Wood. There was no doubt, if this famous blues harp player was to be in Atlanta, so were they.

Ordinarily, a trip to Atlanta would have been a six hour drive. The Volkswagen, not an ordinary car, would take longer. Thus, they needed supplies. Specifically, they needed marijuana. All agreed a jaunt to their trusted dealer was in order. Without hesitation, Wood and Dr. Lap, with Groovy tagging along, headed into town.

Decker, their dealer, lived in a small apartment above The Punch Bowl, a Main Street sandwich shop, a favorite of the college crowd. Parking the bug just around the corner from the deli, they were quickly up the steps, knocking at Decker's door. The three had agreed, they were just going to buy a bag of marijuana and leave. While they were striking a deal for an ounce in Decker's living room, unbeknownst to them, a policewoman was writing down the tag number off the Volkswagen. As Wood was beginning to roll a joint to sample their purchase, the officer was on her radio calling for assistance. It was when they decided to leave, after smoking a second joint, the bug was being pulled from the curb and towed to the impoundment lot.

"What the fuck?"Dr. Lap stood, with arms outstretched, in the space where the car was once parked. "Where the fuck is Greenie?"

"Greenie," Groovy questioned.

"Yea, the Volkswagen," turning to Dr. Lap, Wood sighed. "I don't know."

"Greenie?"

"Shut the fuck up."

"We did park it legally, didn't we?"

"Yea, I'm sure of it." Wood answered.

"Then, where the fuck is it?"

"It been towed." A voice came from the doorway of the bakery, not far from where they were standing."

"Yea," the baker, a young woman in a peasant dress and a flour covered black apron, stepped out to join them, "this lady cop, she come up after ya'll parked here."

"I don't understand." Dr. Lap directed to Wood.

"I come out when Chester's Tow come up fo' it. Tried lookin' fo' ya'll but didn't see ya'll in any of them shops. I guess ya'll gone up to see Decker." She said, smiling knowingly. "Anyhow, I did hear the cop say sumthin' about them tags being no good."

"That can't be right, we just," Dr. Lap stopped midsentence and turned to Wood. "Don't you, don't you fucking tell me."

—

Hesitating, Dr. Lap took a suspenseful break from the telling of his tale. Waving to Jake, he signaled an order for another round of drinks.

"They're on the house." Jake announced, placing the drinks on the table. "You guys doing okay?"

"Yea, yea thanks," Wood answered for the others. I think we're doing fine."

"Your meals should be here shortly. If you need anything else, give a holler." Jake cleared the table of the empty glasses and the plates of mussel shells before heading back to the bar.

The three sat quietly to the opening lines of Billy Stewart's *I Do Love You* seeping from the jukebox. Subconsciously, Four-Thirty began to gently sway to the slow tempo of the music. Carefully balancing a tray of food in one hand, Luscious approached the booth. Bending at the knee, she cautiously placed each of their meals on the table. "Thanks," Wood offered to Luscious as she turned to leave.

"Would you believe," Dr. Lap returned to the story, "he never registered the Volkswagen."

"You're kidding."

"No, not at all," Dr. Lap smiled. "I mean, we had this car for weeks, driving it everywhere, and he never registered it. The expired plates, well, they were these ancient used plates that were on the bug when we bought it."

"So you just left those on?" Four-Thirty asked Wood.

"Yea," Dr. Lap answered for him. "Not that we really cared at the time, but could you imagine, what would have happened if we were stopped after scoring from Decker?"

"That would have been bad but," Wood hesitated, "not as bad if we were caught busting out old Greenie."

"You mean you stole…"

"Yea, exactly," Dr. Lap interrupted Four-Thirty, "right out of the freakin' county impoundment lot."

—

Misty Breeze, the baker girl, had offer to take the three back to campus, with the hope of getting high. Besides, she was fascinated by Groovy. He was the real deal, a New York hippie, unlike the local breed, with their high water bell bottom jeans and white socks. "Just let me tell my ma I'm goin'." Then, flipping her keys to Wood, "Ya can drive. It's out back, ya ain't gonna miss it, a white Corvair with the peace symbol painted on top."

Later that evening, around nine, Dr. Lap, Groovy, and Misty Breeze were back in the dorm room sharing bong hits, listening to the Rolling Stones' *Beggar's Banquet*. Groovy had stationed himself on the designated reading chair, an old recliner Wood had stolen from an English professor's back porch. Nestled on Groovy's lap, Misty Breeze sat, with arms wrapped around his neck, and his hand up the front of her blouse.

Sitting at his desk with a matchbook and album cover, Dr. Lap was separating seeds from the marijuana they had purchased earlier during the day. Nearly done, he was dumping the seeds into a jar when the door sprung open, startling the three. Misty Breeze leaped off Groovy's lap, hastily straightening her blouse while Groovy, grabbing a magazine, tried to hide the visible lump in the front of his jeans.

"Whoa," it was Wood, "am I interrupting something?"

"What the fuck?" Dr. Lap, having overturned the jar, started to scrap the seeds off the floor. "Damn, look at what you made me do. Next fuckin' time knock or something."

"Hey, let's go." Wood said, directing the others. "Get your shit together. You too Groovy, don't forget the pot."

"Where the fuck are we going?" Dr. Lap asked, carefully dumping the last of the seeds back in the jar.

"Do you really think we're passing up Paul Butterfield?" Wood began a little dance to the Stones' *Factory Girl*, letting his enthusiasm get the best of him. "We're going to Atlanta!"

"How?" quizzed Dr. Lap.

"I got a plan." Facing Misty Breeze, Wood asked. "Can you do something for us?"

"I ain't takin' ya'll to Atlanta. Much as I would like it," turning to Groovy, she reached up her blouse to adjust the cup of her bra, "my ma would give me one hell of a whipping."

"No, no just give us a ride back into town."

"Well yea, that's sumthin' I can do fo' ya."

Located on the west side of town was a small industrial park, bordering on an abandoned railroad line. The once prosperous manufacturing sector fell into disarray after a suspicious fire broke out in a garment factory, quickly spreading to several other buildings. Nearly one half of the district was destroyed. Among the survivors were several small machine shops, a warehouse, and a scrap yard. At the far end, amongst the ghostly shells of the few remaining fire scared buildings, sat the county impoundment lot.

Just a few blocks to the north of the industrial park was a Greyhound Bus Terminal where, as instructed, Misty Breeze transported the three adventurers. Although the station was closed for the night, Wood easily convinced Misty Breeze that a bus to Atlanta was soon to arrive and sent her off smiling, with two firmly rolled joints in the palm of her hand. Once she was out of sight, he walked toward the rear of the building, motioning for Dr. Lap to follow him.

"Groovy," Wood directed, "stay here and don't wander from that bench. We will be right back."

"Where the hell are we going?" Dr. Lap asked, trotting to catch up with Wood.

"There," pointing to the industrial park, "we're rescuing Greenie."

"You're serious?"

"Listen," Wood stopped, facing Dr. Lap. "I've checked it out, earlier and yea, I'm serious. We can do it."

The impoundment yard was situated on what was once the main parking lot for the industrial complex. Covering an area slightly less than an acre, a ten foot high chain linked fence, topped by spiraling barbwire, served as its perimeter. Just inside its front gate a lone security guard, engrossed in the most recent issue of *Playboy*, manned a small office trailer.

Approaching from the rear, Wood and Dr. Lap crept quietly along the fence, avoiding detection by the guard. Reaching the end they stopped. On the opposite side of the fence, two long rows of cars stretched out before them. In the row to the left, the third car from the far end, sat the Volkswagen.

"There she is," whispered Wood.

"Man," Dr. Lap looking up at the barbwire, "that looks like a *Slinky* with razors. How the fuck are we getting over that?"

"We're not." From his jacket pocket, Wood pulled out a pair of snippers. While keeping an eye on the office trailer, he started cutting through the lead wires that fastened the fence to a stretch of metal posts. Freeing a length from four posts, and satisfied that he had not attracted the guard's attention, Wood smiled. "You first," lifting the lower portion, he instructed Dr. Lap to crawl through.

"Damn," Dr. Lap whispered, slipping into Greenie and quietly closing the door. "This is crazy. Seriously," turning to Wood, "you are fuckin' crazy."

"Yea maybe," Wood answered, inserting the key into the ignition. Leaning back, he slowly let out a long sigh.

"What's next?"

"Getting the fuck out of Dodge, but first," plucking a joint from his shirt pocket Wood added, "a toast."

The interior of the bug rapidly filled up with the heavy blue smoke from the marijuana. Anxiously, Dr. Lap took deep and frequent drags off the joint, hoping to finish it as quickly as possible. Meanwhile, Wood, closely monitoring any movement by the guard in the trailer, remained visibly calm.

"Isn't this a felony?"

"What?"

"I mean," Dr. Lap questioned Wood, "stealing a car. Isn't it a felony?"

"Are you nuts? It's my fuckin' car."

Dr. Lap began to nervously chuckle, "Your car, you really are out of your freakin' mind. You never registered the damn thing. That's how we got into this mess in the first place."

"That's just a technicality. Besides…" Wood was distracted. The guard rose from his chair and briefly looked out a window. Then, with the magazine in his hand, he turned and walked toward the back of the trailer.

"What's he doing?"

"I think we're in luck." Wood inferred. "I think he's going to the bathroom."

"Hope he's taking a shit."

"Yea," Throwing the nearly finished joint out his window, Wood turned the ignition key. The engine quickly started, releasing a deep throated hum from it broken muffler. Inching Greenie into the lane between the rows of cars, Wood called out to Dr. Lap, "Hold on!"

Wood prematurely popped the clutch, causing the Volkswagen to initially sputter, the bug then surged forward, as the gears engaged. Dropping into second, Wood pushed the car up to thirty-five miles per hour before slamming it into third gear. The car barely reached forty when it hit a section of fence, between two of the posts where Wood had cut the fasteners.

"Holy shit," Dr. Lap yelled upon the impact. "Go mother, go!"

Hanging tightly to the steering wheel, Wood watched as the chain link fence scrapped first across the hood, then the windshield, and finally the roof, leaving deep scratches embedded in the paint. There was a slight jolt to the left as the fence caught on the rear bumper. Quickly pulling free, Wood headed straight to the terminal.

"Mother fuck, you did it!" Dr. Lap cried out.

"Yea, we did, didn't we?"

—

Amazed, Four-Thirty sat watching the two men laugh over their college day exploits. "Damn," she exclaimed during a lull, "I know you had done some crazy shit back in the day but, nothing like this. To think you have gone off to college to get serious, man, I never was so mistaken."

"Oh, I don't know," Wood reflected. "It was just the times, I mean, I don't think anyone took it serious back then."

"At least not in college," Dr. Lap added. "Back then we had everything we needed, and not a care. So why not?"

For Four-Thirty, life was so much different. She could not imagine being so carefree. She was still a child having Deadeye's baby, one she had decided, or more realistically, had been told by her mother, to give up for adoption. She was scared and so very much alone in her cold corner of the world. Four-Thirty had no choice. She had to take it seriously.

"Whew," Dr. Lap picked up a napkin from the table, wiping a tear from the corner of his eye, "that was one strange day." Placing the napkin back, he leaned forward, resting his elbows against the edge of the table. Somberly, Dr. Lap turned to Wood, "You know Wood, there's one thing I need to ask. I mean, I've been trying to figure it out and you, you never would talk about it."

"Yea, what's that?"

"You know," Dr. Lap wavered, unsure of Wood's response, "that night when we almost crashed, on the interstate to Atlanta, What happened?"

—

They had been driving for a little over an hour and had just crossed the Tennessee state line. At the Tri-Cities exist a pit stop was made for gas, a couple of six-packs, and a much needed visit to the men's room. Back on the road, Wood once again took the wheel. Washing down several caffeine pills with a swig of beer, he settled in, with a joint in one hand, and the beer safely nestled between his legs.

On a stretch of highway, somewhere between the Greeneville and Morristown exits, the sky darkened and the moon slowly slipped behind the developing clouds. "Looks like rain," Dr. Lap surmised.

"Sure looks that way." Groovy answered, opening another can of beer.

Hearing the rustling behind him, Wood reached back, "Let me have one of..."

Without warning, the Volkswagen's headlights failed. Wood froze, staring straight into the darkness. Frantically, Dr. Lap began to pull switches and pound on the dashboard without success. Panicking, he yelled to Wood, begging him to stop the car. Instead, the car continued to accelerate. Groovy, bracing against the two front seats, slammed his foot against the dashboard. With a momentary flicker the light illuminated.

"Oh fuck!" Wood screamed, slamming on the brake. Yanking the wheel to the right, the VW swerved, stopping within inches of a concrete embankment.

Visually shaken, Dr. Lap unsteadily lit a joint and inhaled slowly. As he exhaled, he turned to pass it to Wood. There was no response. Instead, Wood sat, with his hands tightly on the wheel and a blank look in his eyes. Concerned, Dr. Lap reached for Wood's shoulder. "Are you alright?"

"Fuck it, I'm out of here." Pushing Dr. Lap away from him, Wood jumped out of the Volkswagen and ran across the highway. Dr. Lap charged after him. Block by oncoming traffic, he failed to reach Wood, who successfully flagged down a tractor trailer heading back north.

"That night," Wood spoke softly, "I was supposed to die."

"What?"

"Seriously, I was supposed to die. I mean, I saw my bother Phillie Wheels, I think I told you about him, anyway, he was calling out to me."

"Your brother," Dr. Lap answered, "the one you said was dead, killed by the mob?"

"Right, we kinda thought he was dead. Anyway," Wood continued, "that night, when the lights went out, I saw him, standing in the highway. I don't know, maybe it was a hallucination, you know, from all the shit we were taking. Anyway, there was Phillie Wheels, in all of this blackness, calling to me, like he wanted me to follow him."

Feeling Four-Thirty's hand on his knee, Wood paused. Looking up, he gave her a weak smile before continuing. "Anyway, he kept getting closer, and the closer he got, the more at ease I felt. But, at the same time, I was scared shitless. I mean, he was dead. I started thinking, if I went with him, it had to mean I would be dead too. I had to die. I was so fuckin' scared, I screamed out 'stop!' or something like that. I mean, I thought he was coming to take me. Anyway, when I started screaming, that's when the lights came on."

"Wait, I don't remember you screaming 'stop', 'fuck' maybe, but not 'stop'."

"You don't." Wood replied.

"No," Dr. Lap answered. "I just remember that you froze. You didn't say or do anything until the lights came on. Man, that's crazy."

"You think that's crazy." Wood gave Four-Thirty's hand a knowing squeeze. "The fucker wasn't dead, at least not then."

"You're kidding?"

"No, my brother, the junkie mafia wannabe, was still alive. Get this, he turned out to be a well respected, every day citizen, family man, you know, a wife and two kids."

"Damn! Did you get to see him, I mean, for real?"

"No," Wood answered. "It's a long story, but he did make something of himself, as I found out much later, after he really died."

"Damn," was all Dr. Lap could say.

"Yea, damn."

Chapter 13

J ordan had been out of prison for a little over three years. He was trying his best to get his life on track. Although it was only part time, his work remained steady. In addition, Jordan enrolled in the community college and was taking some classes, hoping that they would help him gain full time employment. In one of his evening classes, he met and then quickly moved in with a young woman. They married and soon became pregnant. They had a son. In spite of him still being on parole, things appeared to be going well for Jordan and his family. For the first time in a long while, he was happy.

One morning over breakfast, Jordan was reviewing the employment section of the classified ads. He was soon discouraged as there were few new listings and even fewer for which he was qualified. He, turning the page, was immediately drawn to a recognizable name under the obituaries. "Holy shit!"

"What?"

"It's my..." He failed to continue, proceeding to read the funeral notice.

"Honey," Lizzie asked again, "what's wrong?"

Without lifting his eyes from the article, Jordan said, "It's my mom. Not my real mother, but, my mom. You know the one who dumped me. She died."

Jordan hadn't thought about his mother in a long time. At first, thinking about how she left him at Jefferson House, he felt a twinge of anger. The anger melted into guilt. At times he couldn't shake the feeling that he was to blame. On the other hand, he had always known that he didn't do anything that warranted being abandoned. He couldn't find any justification for what she did. Seeing her obituary brought up all those old feelings. Internally he was torn. He knew that he had to come to terms with these split emotions.

"Look," as he pushed the newspaper toward Lizzie. "They found her body, day before yesterday. Like, she's been dead for awhile. She died alone in her home." He hesitated, "I should..."

"No, no, no," Lizzie interjected. "You haven't seen that woman in a lifetime. Besides, she didn't want anything to do with you."

"But..."

The voice of reason continued, "No buts. She didn't want you. You owe her nothing. She wasn't blood. She was nothing to you and she made sure you became nothing to her." Lizzie had a tear in her eye. She felt for the man she loved and did all she could to understand him. She was sure she wasn't going to let him beat himself up for this.

They first met at the community college, where they were taking a psychology class together. She had noticed Jordan sitting in the back and was immediately attracted to him. One evening, before class, she saw him in the school cafeteria. Taking a chance, she joined him at his table. In that brief encounter she found Jordan to be warm and friendly. Soon they began to date. He treated her with a respect that no man had done before. Lizzie quickly fell in love. Yet, she recognized a barrier built around Jordan, as though those that had lived on the outside, forced him to live within his head. Over time, the wall dissipated. With the birth of their son, she felt that Jordan's resurrection was final.

Watching Jordan reading the paper, Lizzie realized that she didn't want to lose all that they brought into being. She had never seen him like this before, frantic, a man practically falling off the edge. "Jordan, Honey, please tell me what you're thinking."

"I, um, really don't know." Jordan replied, "Maybe go to the funeral. What do you think I should do?"

Jordan seemed to settle down as he looked toward his wife. Lizzie felt a little relief, knowing that he was turning to her for some guidance. "I'm not sure either Honey, but going to the funeral may be too much. I mean, you haven't seen her for what?"

"Since I was eight" he answered quickly.

Slipping onto the chair next to him, Lizzie slowly wrapped her arm firmly around Jordan's waist. She would do anything for him. He knew this, reassured by the warmth of her body next to his. "Listen, we can do this together. I'll go to the wake with you. Let me be there for you." She quietly pleaded.

"No, no, no," pulling away from Lizzie, "I got to…"

"Please let me."

"No, I really have to do this myself." Jordan said, facing Lizzie, "You have to understand. I must do this on my own."

Lizzie was lost. She knew that he was right but she was afraid that she was going to lose him. She suspected, in some way, he would be damaged. She didn't want to encounter that wall again. It wasn't any good for him or their family. Yet, she conceded. She knew that he was strong and it was upon that strength, in spite of her fears, she hoped, she prayed, he will finally come to terms with his past.

"Okay," Lizzie whispered weakly, "but please tell me, what do you want to come from this? What do you expect to get?"

Jordan looked into Lizzie's eyes. He saw the pain she had for him and he saw the love she had to give. He didn't want to hurt her, but he did want her to understand. "I just, I, maybe someone will be there, who can tell me who I really am."

—

Andreano's Funeral Parlor was on Garrison Street, a block away from The Church of Saint Mary, where the memorial service was to be held.

Across the street on an old stonewall, sat Jordan, waiting for the courage to enter the building. He had been perched on that wall for nearly an hour. During that time, he had observed a few elderly women enter the funeral home, none of whom he had recognized. He had hoped there might be one face that would be familiar. Yet, he doubted that there would. As a child, the adults that he had met were mostly friends of his father. He met them during outings with his dad, or at the social club that they frequently visited, never at his home. Somehow, he knew they would not be there for his mother.

Stepping from the wall, Jordan finally decided to cross the street and entered the funeral home. Inside the glass doors, stood a stout gentleman, dressed in a charcoal suit, solemnly directing mourners to a side room. Outside the entrance of the room sat a long table with prayer cards, a guestbook, and several pictures of the deceased. Although Jordan recognized his mother, many of the pictures were unfamiliar. Several were of his mother at an age younger than he remembered, and the others, she as an elderly woman. Near the center of the table, he found the only picture of his father with his mother. It was taken on their wedding day. Nowhere in sight were there any pictures of her son.

Anxiously, Jordan walked into the viewing room. Ahead of him were rows of folding chairs, most of which were empty. Jordan estimated that there were five or six gray haired women, dressed in black, dotting the room. Just beyond the seats stretched the casket. On each side, large vases filled with freshly cut flowers, stood guard.

Self conscious, Jordan slowly approached the coffin, placing his knee on a cushioned kneeler. The body stretched out before him, wrinkled and harmless, in the tin and wood box. Hanging above was a rosary, made of tiny pink roses.

Jordan was astonished. The woman, with her bluish gray tinted hair, and a hint of a smile seeping from her sealed lips, could not have been his mother. She looked peaceful, fulfilled. His mother, contentious, always wore a frown. This spectacle, Jordan concluded, was a facade, a mortician's piece of art. Stepping back, he fought the urge to tear open her eyes, wanting to look into her hell.

Turning away from the casket, Jordan faced the mourners. Absence of family members, the front row remained empty. Walking past the abandoned chairs, he quietly stepped into the third row, taking a seat behind a woman in a black dress and a white hankie covering her gray hair.

In the far corner an elderly priest sat, fingering his beads. The low hum of an air conditioner drowned out his mumbling prayer. Other mourners quietly sat alone, staring at the coffin. Feeling ill at ease, Jordan realized that he did not belong among them.

"Are you family?" the woman in front asked, turning to Jordan.

"Ah, no," Jordan hesitated. "She knew my dad."

"Oh, seems like she had no family." She spoke again. "No, no family that I know."

Leaning forward, Jordan asked, "All these women, that priest there, are any her friends?"

"Oh no," the woman sighed. "She really didn't have any friends to speak of. She, it seems, really didn't want any. These women here, and Father Sebastian, are from the church, from the Rosary Society. I don't think they're friends, no, not at all."

"Were you one of her friends? Did you know her?"

"Well," she thought for a moment, "only as much as she would allow me to know her. A friend, I don't know. A neighbor maybe, someone she would occasionally talk to yes, but a friend I don't know. I don't think she ever allowed anyone that close, so sad."

"Did you know her long?"

"No, not really, I remember her when we were children, but we were never friends back then." She continued, adjusting her seat to face Jordan again. "I use to see her walking with her mother around the neighborhood. Never did play with her. I don't think any of the other kids played with her either. I don't know why."

One of the mourners got up from her seat. The woman and Jordan quietly watched as she approached the casket, knelt down and said a prayer before leaving. Jordan looked around and noticed that others were preparing to leave as well. Jordan knew that the viewing will soon be over. Yet, he was anxious, wanting to hear more of what the woman had to say. She sensed this.

"Then," the woman continued "about ten years ago we started talking. She seemed to be so alone. One day, she invited me to sit on her porch for some coffee. I guess that she had seen me at the church. Perhaps, she thought we had something in common. Other than that, I don't know why I was invited."

"Did she ever mention her family?"

"She did mention her husband." The woman paused. Opening her purse, she reached in withdrawing a tin of mints. Offering a candy to Jordan, she continued. "She never really talked about him. She was so secretive. You know, she would say she did this with him, or did that, but nothing about him. I can't remember if she even told me his name. No, I don't think she ever did."

"It was Gerry." Jordan offered without elaboration.

"Oh, I didn't know that. No, I didn't, seems to me that she never called him by name."

Jordan didn't respond. He was afraid that he had misspoken, and she would begin to question him. Instead, the woman led him into another direction.

"You know, there was one thing that she did get excited about."

"What was that?" Jordan quickly asked.

"Her garden it was her garden. She had the most beautiful garden, and she was so proud of it. If you would just mention flowers to her, she would just talk your ear off about her garden. Yea, it was something that made her smile. Why, I would see her in that garden almost every day cutting, pruning, taking care of her flowers like they were her children. Those plants were her family. Yes sir, they were her family. Yea, she sure did like her garden."

Jordan was taken aback by the thought of his mother in a garden.

He had no memory of her ever working with plants. His father would grow some vegetables, and cared for a fig tree but, he had absolutely no memory of his mother working in the yard.

"Oh my Lord," she said, beginning to recollect memories of the deceased. "Several years ago, we were sitting on her porch, and there was a group of children playing out in front of her house. She seemed to be so annoyed by them. Yea, she acted that it pained her to see them happy."

"Oh."

First, looking at the casket, then Jordan, she continued, "We began to talk about children and I asked her if she had any. That woman said right out, 'no', said that her husband didn't want any."

Jordan's eyes opened wide. He began to feel his body begin to rumble. He just could not believe what he had just heard. He knew it wasn't true. It was his father who wanted children, not her. It pained him, thinking that she would lie about his father.

"I've been told, my neighbors," she continued, looking into Jordan's eyes, "they told me that she had a child. She had a boy. People say that she gave him up. I believe he was just about school age, when his daddy died, and she just gave up on her boy."

"Eight years old," Jordan thought to himself. Curiously he asked, "Do you know anything about her son?"

"Of course she would never say anything. How could she, after denying she ever had children?"

"The neighbors?" Jordan asked if they had known about the child.

"They didn't say much. Just that he was a quiet boy." She continued, "Yea, not much. I did hear that he was about school age. Never a problem, she just didn't want him. Now tell me, how can you do that to your own blood?"

Jordan felt a rush of anxiety. He wanted to scream, "I'm not blood," but held back. He shivered, beads of sweat formed along his forehead. Fighting panic, he turned to move toward the exit door.

The woman look at him strangely, "Boy, you don't look too good. Are you all right?"

Jordan, rising from his seat, could not hold it in any longer. "That was me," his voice quivering.

She looked up into Jordan's face. That's when he realized, seeing it in her eyes, she suspected he was that child. "Oh my boy, I am so sorry. I really am."

"That was me she threw away. That bitch, I was only eight," crying softly as he pointed to the casket, "that, that fuckin' bitch should fry in hell!"

Jordan, turning away, quickly walked into the bathroom, bawling like a child. Although he heard several voices outside in the hall, no one followed him in. Jordan was fine with this. Alone with his sorrow, the solitude gave him a cushion of comfort. Eventually, he was able to regain his composure and, when he no longer heard any sounds from outside the door, he turned to leave.

Looking around he saw that all the mourners, including the woman he spoke with, were gone. In the viewing room, the gentleman he met earlier, was closing the casket. Jordan walked over to the table and picked up the picture of his mother and father. Slipping it from the frame, he tore his father away from his mother, put his father's picture in his pocket, throwing the rest to the floor as he walk out the front door.

—

Leaving Andreano's, Jordan stepped into a steady drizzle. Its mist, hitting his face, was cooling. Existing the building, he turned left, roaming aimlessly, unsure of where to go, unsure of what to do. He couldn't go home, not yet. He wasn't ready to face Lizzie, afraid to admit she was right. Going to the funeral home was a mistake.

His anxiety escalated, he didn't understand the emptiness churning inside him. The words were not within him. So he wandered in the soft rain, gathering his thoughts, building the courage to face his wife with his failure. As Jordan walked, the rain's intensity grew, nurturing the numbness inside him.

Jordan ambled aimlessly for what seem like hours. Disenchanted in his quest to find his identity, he hoped that at least for the moment, it was over. Still, he rambled, allowing the steady rainfall to lead him to streets, which suddenly became familiar. With clothing thoroughly soaked and his body shivering, Jordan finally stopped, standing outside his childhood home.

Behind its disarray, the home was barely recognizable. Unkempt bushes adorned the front porch. Like adolescents with bad haircuts branches of various lengths spiked in all directions. A dim light, barely illuminating the front door, left on, perhaps to trick unwelcome visitors into thinking that someone was home. Yet, several days of the daily newspaper were scattered on the steps.

Jordan moved into the shadows on the right side of the house, looking for an unlocked entrance. Walking past the garbage pails, he tried the side door. It was locked. So too were the kitchen windows and the one for the basement. He continued around the house to the rear door, the entrance to the cellar, and all other windows within his reach. They too were locked.

Not to be deterred, Jordan returned to the kitchen side of the house. Under cover of the darkest shadows, he removed his jacket, wrapping it around his fist. First, taking a deep breath, he then quickly jabbed a windowpane close to the lock on the door. Sounds of glass shattering echoed through the alley and the surrounding backyards. Pausing for a moment, he listened. The only sound heard was the barking of a distant dog. Feeling safe, he reached through the broken window, unlocking the door.

Stepping over the threshold, Jordan crossed into his past. He felt eight again, standing in the kitchen of his childhood home. The home he grew up in, so many years ago. With minimal light filtering in from the outside, he surveyed the room. It was all too familiar to him. The toaster, coffee pot, and various kitchen appliances, sat on the counter, just like he pictured from his childhood. As he remembered, the table still had place settings for four. He was home. Yes, he was finally home.

It was so surrealistic. Upon his father's death he was removed, by his mother, from his home. It was upon her death he returned.

Jordan was hungry. His hunger went beyond the emptiness in his stomach, but it was for the pains for sustenance he moved to satisfy first. Comfortable in the familiarity of the kitchen, Jordan rummaged in the refrigerator, looking for something to eat. As expected, he found packages of white American cheese and spice ham. Putting his nose to the meat, he decided that it was edible. Then, grabbing a loaf of bread from the counter, he sat in his place at the table, making his favorite sandwich.

Sitting in the kitchen was like being a child again. Often, he had sat at that same table, eating his sandwich of ham and cheese, waiting for his father to come home. He waited with his stories of the day in school, or he restlessly waited for his father to come home, anticipating his tales of work.

As he sat, Jordan was overcome with the need to tell his father about being abandoned at Jefferson House by his mother. He yearned to explain to his father about his time in prison, the mistakes he had made, longing to ask for his father's understanding and forgiveness. Most of all, Jordan wanted to tell him about his family, and the grandson who had been named after him. Enjoying his meal, Jordan fantasized about the walks in the park the three of them should be taking, the trips to the shore, and fishing in the mountains.

The thought of the mountains triggered something in Jordan's memory. One of his happiest moments was during an outing with his father, fishing on a mountain lake. Jordan was only six. At dawn, they rented a small rowboat, to fish for bass. No sooner had Jordan dropped his line, he had a hit. With his father's arms around him, steadying his rod, Jordan pulled in the first, and biggest fish, he had ever caught. Jordan was elated. Not only had he caught the first fish, but also the largest of the day, a four pound largemouth bass. His father, expressing his pride, bragged to anyone on the dock who would listen, about how his son had caught the big one. Someone took a picture of the two of them. In it, there was a smiling Jordan, his father's arms wrapped around his shoulder, struggling to hold the bass. That picture sat on the mantle in the living room.

Dropping the partially eaten sandwich, Jordan rushed into the darkened living room to liberate his memories. The room had not changed much since he was a child. His dad's recliner stood in the far corner, next to a small table with a lamp and several books, waiting to be read. A small braided oval rug covered the wood flooring between the couch and fireplace.

Jordan proceeded straight to the mantle. The picture was gone. So were all the other photos of his childhood. In their place, sat several inexpensive dime store frames. Although some of these held pictures of his mother and father, most framed images were of people he had never seen. Upon closer examination, he realized, they were the stock paper photos that came with the frames. It pained Jordan to think he was replaced, not by another child, but by a make believe family.

The pounding Jordan heard in his head, as he rushed to what was once his bedroom, was not that of a heavy rain beating on the old tin roof. That downpour had stopped. It was his heart, drumming his anxiety. Without a glance, he quickly passed both his parent's room and the bathroom. Behind the first door, just pass the stairs to the basement, was his bedroom. Standing before the door, he took a deep breath, attempting to slow the rhythm of his heart. With his eyes closed, Jordan gently pushed the door open.

The room beyond the entrance was dark and unfamiliar. With a flick of a switch, an overhead light illuminated the area, further erasing Jordan's childhood existence. Nothing remained. Instead, a cheap bedroom suite and some more dime store photos lay before Jordan's eyes. Gone was his bed with the Superman bedspread. Gone were his toys, posters of baseball and football heroes, the model airplanes that he and his father so painfully pieced together, his train set with its little plastic village that sat in the corner across from his bed. Gone was all evidence that the child Jordan, once lived and played within the walls that surrounded him.

Jordan retreated into his parent's bedroom. The pounding intensified, as if two marching bands were simultaneously competing within his chest. Questioning his own memories, he ripped through dresser drawers, looking for anything to confirm his being. A photograph, school papers, birth certificate, anything with his image or name would do. Boxes were pulled from closet shelves and dumped on the bed. Proof of his existence was absent. Missing were those pictures taken at the beach, his school play, those taken in the back yard grilling with his father. He didn't imagine these. He was there, flesh and blood. His search continued, fruitlessly, unable to find anything among the boxes of old bills, canceled checks, yellowed pages of newspaper clippings, and hand written recipes. He did not exist.

Frustrated and angry, Jordan looked around for any other possible places that the desired documents would be stored. There were none. Although he was not satisfied, Jordan refused exposure to any additional disappointments. He gave up, deciding that the search was futile.

This was his home and it had been taken from him. Now, it belonged to no one. Jordan took from the top of a dresser, one of his mother's kerosene lamps, pouring the fluid onto the pile of papers stretching across the bed. A second lantern was found. Its contents dumped on the dresser and the carpeted floor. Striking a match, Jordan, without hesitation, dropped it on the bed. With the first flicker of flames, the drumming began to cease.

—

The light show surpassed all of Jordan's expectations. Flashes of colors, initially visible through the first floor windows, soon built into a crescendo, bursting into the attic and through the roof. Within a matter of minutes, the fire roared through the old wood frame house. Enhanced by the mist of previously fallen rain and the spray from fire hoses, the sky erupted into warn shades of red, yellow, and orange. Puddles lining the street mirrored the evening's spectacle. Jordan stood by, watching as the roof over his parents' bedroom collapsed, sending sparks skyward, like the Fourth of July fireworks.

Entrenched with the fire, Jordan failed to notice the crowd gathering around to witness the demise of his childhood home. Not far from his right, an elderly woman, dressed in a pink housecoat, talking with two police officers, occasionally pointed in the direction of Jordan. As the home wilted into smothering embers, Jordan looked around at the spectators. Among those that remained, he recognized the woman from the funeral home. It was she who had been talking to the officers, now walking toward Jordan, with hands on their holsters.

Hastily turning away, Jordan began his retreat. In the debris, a familiar object caught his attention, causing him to hesitate. It was a trunk, an old tin steamer, bought for him by his father. It once sat at the foot of his bed. In the trunk, Jordan stored his toys and other childhood memories. "That's funny," he thought. He didn't remember seeing it before setting the fire.

"Fuck, the attic," he whispered. "It had to be in the attic." He soon realized that was the one place he did not look.

"I fucked up." Jordan said as the officers approached him.

"You sure did." The older one said, grabbing Jordan by the arm and cuffing him.

"No, No, you don't understand," Jordan continued without resisting. "That trunk, my life..."

"What, your wife?" the younger, heavier officer misunderstood. He turned, seeing the steamer protruding out of the ashes.

"No," Jordan said, trying to explain but the policemen ignored him.

Wrestling Jordan to the ground, the officer signaled to the other policemen mingling with the onlookers. "We got a body!" He yelled.

"There, in the trunk." The other pointed.

Several ran into the ruins, dragging the chest across the front lawn to the curb. A crowbar was pulled from the back of a police cruiser. An officer, wearing sergeant stripes, frantically worked on the lock, as the spectators stood around, anticipating the worse.

"You don't understand," Jordan again tried to explain. "I didn't say my wife, damn it. I said my life, my life is in there."

"Shut up." Commanded the older officer kneeling on the small of Jordan's back.

"Please, you..."

"I said shut the fuck up you sick bastard." The officer snarled, slamming Jordan's face into the concrete roadway. "How could you?"

The last blow stunned Jordan. Pressed against the pavement, his face began to hurt. Unable to breathe he remained still, in a pool of rainwater, turning red from the blood dripping down his nose.

Beyond Jordan's field of vision, the sergeant continued to work at the lock, with images of a charred body imprisoned in the trunk. He thought that this could not be happening. Not in his small town. This only happens in the big cities. Neither had he, with his twenty years of experience, nor any of his men, had to pull a body from the aftermath of a fire. Adrenaline fueled his apprehension, when finally, the latch pulled away from the trunk. Teary eyed, the sergeant yelled to his men, directing them to stand back as he hurriedly opened the lid. With a visible sigh of relief, he reached in, pulling out a child's toy truck, its tires melted from the heat.

"We're alright here." He called out.

"What?"

"We're alright here." The sergeant repeated. "There ain't no body here. Just some old toys, ya know, kid's stuff."

"My life," Jordan whispered, whimpering softly into the puddle of blood and rain.

Chapter 14

D r. Lap sat alone in a booth, nursing his third vodka and beer chaser, when Four-Thirty walked into Paci's. He decided, he was returning south, to surrender to the authorities and to face his consequences. The decision to plead guilty was made knowing that he may serve some jail time. Skipping out on his initial hearing and violating the conditions of his bail, Dr. Lap suspected that the judge would not be lenient. His crime was serious, and his actions only made his situation worse. He held a little hope that Dean Trudy, and perhaps a few others at the college, may speak up for him, that they may be able to sway the judge. Yet, as each day passed without Dr. Lap returning, his optimism diminished. He had to leave soon but not without an explanation, and perhaps an apology, to his friend Wood.

Seeing Dr. Lap in the corner booth, Four-Thirty was deflated. Distressed over a recent conflict with her daughter Oria, she needed to talk with Wood. Wishing that Dr. Lap had left, returned to his college, she hoped to find Wood alone in Paci's. At first she considered avoiding Dr. Lap, and sit at the bar alone. Yet, needing to see Wood, she had to talk to Dr. Lap to find out where he was. Besides, Dr. Lap saw her enter the pub, making her feel obligated to join him.

"Where's our boy?" Four-Thirty asked, sliding into the seat across from Dr. Lap. She noticed that he was still wearing the same reddish brown flannel shirt and wrinkled kaki jeans from the day before. His hair was disheveled, as though he had just gotten out of bed, failing to comb it. He looked tired, preoccupied and overwhelmed.

"That guy up there," Dr. Lap replied pointing to No Hope, "his buddy."

"Yea, Buffalo."

"Yea, I guess that's his name, Buffalo," Dr. Lap continued. "Anyway he asked Wood to help him, help him move some stuff. Wood said it wouldn't take long. They should be back soon."

Signaling to Jake, leaning against the back of the bar with a dishtowel slung over his shoulder, Four-Thirty ordered her usual glass of red wine. Luscious, taking a break from the pool table promptly brought it over, offering to the two copies of the menu. Both Four-Thirty and Dr. Lap declined, indicating that they would wait for Wood to return.

The two, sat sipping their drinks in a pregnant silence. Four-Thirty quietly observed Dr. Lap as he nervously toyed with his glass. Wood had confided in her about his concerns of Dr. Lap being in serious trouble. Watching him, she was convinced, Wood was right. He was in trouble and it was serious. Lines of nervous perspiration coated his forehead. His eyes, unable to remain focus, darted from point to point. What she was seeing, Four-Thirty concluded, was not a man of confidence but one whose world was crumbling. Deciding that the silence was becoming unbearable, Four-Thirty broke the ice, "So how is our guy doing?"

"Wood?" Dr. Lap said, startled out of his deep thought, "I guess he's doing okay. I mean, he's not the happiest man out there."

"Yea, I know what you mean." Four-Thirty replied. "I remember when we were growing up he was always the upbeat one, carefree, happy-go-lucky. People liked being around him, he made you feel good. You know, always saw the positive."

"He was like that when we were in college together." Dr. Lap added.

"College," Four-Thirty reminisced. "I remember when he left. We were so proud of him. The first, and only I might add, who really got to go. Unlike the others, you know, OD's and what not, he did good.

The whole neighborhood was proud." Four-Thirty, placing her glass on the table, eased back in her seat. A sigh was heard, softly escaping from between her lips. "Yea, we all thought he was doing so well. Then, out of nowhere he's back here, a different person. Would you believe he was back for several years without me knowing? Yea, without me knowing, ain't that a bitch."

"I didn't know that."

"Yea," Four-Thirty continued. "Like, he didn't look up any of his old friend or anything. Then one day, I heard through the grapevine, he was hanging out here almost on a daily basis. Sure enough, I came looking for him and here he was. I've been checking up on him ever since."

A round of shots was brought to the table. Luscious lazily pointed to a customer dressed in a light tan suit and olive green tie. "They're on him. He hit for a few thousand on the lottery, *Pick-Five*." Both lifted up their drinks, offering a toast to the lucky one. "*Saluti*," Four-Thirty called out before she and Dr. Lap downed their whiskey.

"I guess you guys are close." Dr. Lap spoke.

"Yea, we are." Four-Thirty thought back to her childhood, how she first met Wood, and how they became friends. "Not at first, when I was little he picked on me a lot, teased me. Gradually we got close and he was like a big brother. Hell, when Deadeye, you know my first boyfriend, beat the shit out of me, darn near killed me and my baby, it was Wood who came to the hospital. His was the first face I saw when I came to. You can say, he had been my guardian."

"I don't know if you know this but, at one time, that guy really had it made." Dr. Lap exclaimed. "I'm sure you know about his writings, you know, textbooks and such."

"Textbooks?!" Four-Thirty had copies of his literary writings, but she knew nothing of his academic work. Once, when he appeared at the local community college, she sat through his reading from one of his novels. Hearing that he had written textbooks took her by surprise.

"Yea, textbooks, he wrote several in a very short span. A few are still being used. Hell, I still use them." Dr. Lap continued. "I mean, he was well respected. His writings were just small change compared to his other achievements. For example, he was the force behind a student run community outreach program. That was so successful it served as a model for centers in other communities throughout the state's southern region. At the college it was widely rumored that he was being considered for a dean position."

It was difficult for Four-Thirty to imagine, someone from the old neighborhood reaching high levels of success in the academic environment. Attending her daughter Oria's graduation was the closest Four-Thirty had gotten to the world of higher education. Barely making it through high school, the concepts of degree programs, deans, and departmental chairmanships were foreign to her. Yet, her chest swelled with a sense of pride, knowing that one of her own kind had, at one time, found success in that arena. On the other hand, it hurt knowing, for whatever reason, he gave it all away.

"So," Four-Thirty quietly asked. "What happened? What changed him?"

Dr. Lap downed the last of his beer. Placing the bottle back on the table, he hesitated. He knew how secretive Wood could be, and had no idea how much he had told Four-Thirty about his past. Dr. Lap decided that it really didn't matter. He did not think he was betraying his old friend. Wood had been living in a state of depression for too long. Perhaps, Dr. Lap thought, by revealing what he knew might be beneficial. It couldn't get much worse. "I guess," Dr. Lap answered. "He started losing it when Becca died."

"Becca?"

"Yea, she was an instructor at the college. They had met in her first year, then lived together for three, maybe four years, something like that."

"Hmm, I remember seeing him with someone at his sister's wedding, but he never spoke about her. I assumed that she was just a date. I mean, Wood has never been known to be serious about anyone." It was a small wedding Four-Thirty recalled. The ceremony was held at the Church of the Virgin Mother with a simple reception in the local hall.

It was at the reception, when Four-Thirty had caught her first glimpse of Wood's companion. With her brother Casey, Four-Thirty, and a few of Lucia's friends, were sitting at a rear table, when Wood and his date entered the hall. She was gorgeous, Four-Thirty remembered, in a soft pastel cotton dress, accenting her thin frame. A single lily, from which a lone braid cascaded to her shoulder, highlighted her hair. At the time she would not have admitted to it, but Four-Thirty was jealous. Being with Wood had always been her fantasy.

"Well," Dr. Lap continued. "That was Becca. And I'll tell you what, he was serious about her."

—

It was a Wednesday afternoon when Dr. Lap, standing outside his office door, flipping through the morning mail, encountered an overly excited Becca. Turning to enter his office, he spotted Becca stepping out of the elevator, hurriedly walking toward him. Dressed in a yellow tank top and jeans, she was barely discernable from the students mingling around her. Making eye contact, Becca waved, quickening her pace. She was on a mission from Wood she announced, as she hugged Dr. Lap, pressing her braless breast against his chest. Feeling a twinge of arousal, he quickly pulled back, avoiding embarrassment. They had news for him and, would he join them for dinner?

"Sure," He readily agreed.

"Don't forget six o'clock," Becca called to him, briskly walking back down the corridor. "We'll see you at the hotel."

Reservations were made for three by Wood, at the Evergreen Lounge, in the historic General Alexander Hotel. Built in 1827, the hotel was the centerpiece in the restoration of Olde City, in the downtown district. Shortly before the end of the Civil War, the building was briefly occupied by the Confederate Army. According to local legend, a decimated rebel unit set up in the hotel to wait on orders for a final assault. In the midst of rumors that General Lee was about to surrender, and fearing further devastation by advancing Union forces, the militia disbanded. The occupation lasted a mere three days.

Entering from the lobby, Dr. Lap walked through the display of Civil War artifacts to the restaurant doorway. Waiting for the maître d' to seat him, Dr. Lap observed Becca and Wood at a corner table in quiet conversation. Becca, in her elegance, wore a simple black dress and a single strand of pearls. Seeing Wood in a jacket and tie, Dr. Lap feared being underdressed, standing there in a short sleeve shirt and brown corduroy slacks. Slight panic set in as he imagined a more formal dress requirement. Surveying the room, as he was being escorted to the table, he felt a sigh of relief, seeing others dressed even less formal than he. Among them a diner, wearing a Mack truck tee-shirt and John Deere cap. "Hum, a tractor jockey," Dr. Lap surmised.

Becca, spotting Dr. Lap walking toward the table, smiled, waving to him from her seat. As he approached, Wood stood up and reached out to shake his hand. "Chris, we're so glad you could make it."

"You had to know," Dr. Lap responded, bending forward to gently kiss Becca on the cheek. "I could never turn down an invitation from such a beautiful woman."

"Oh stop it." Becca blushed.

Once seated, a waitress briskly walked over, placing a menu in front of Dr. Lap. She introduced herself as Amy. Dr. Lap recognized her. She was a student in one of his classes, from a previous term. She was quite interested, he recalled, in child welfare and had done some volunteer work in a pre-school breakfast program. "Social Service major, am I right?" He asked.

"Yes," Her eyes widened, amazed that he remembered. "Graduate this term."

"That's great." Becca added. "Have any plans as to what you might do?"

Placing her hand on her hip, Amy contemplated for a moment. "Well, I had thought about going for my masters but, you know, I don't think I'm ready. I might just hang out around here for a while and think things out."

"Well good luck, whatever you do."

"Thanks." Turning to Dr. Lap she asked, "So can I get you something to drink?"

"Yea, I guess so. What are you guys having?"

Looking up from his menu Wood responded. "I think we'll have a bottle of white wine, a chardonnay perhaps."

"Yea, I can go for that." Dr. Lap replied. Pointing to a selection on the wine list, he turned to the waitress, "Amy, I think this California chardonnay will do. And it's on me."

"Okay, I'll go get the wine. And three glasses, right?" Without waiting for an answer, she continued, "When I get back, I'll take your order."

The wine was promptly brought to the table, all agreeing that it was a good choice. After serving the wine, Amy placed the bottle on ice and began to take their orders.

Dr. Lap couldn't keep his eyes off the waitress, as she attentively wrote down their dinner requests. Although he was currently involved with another student, he knew that relationship would end, once the spring semester was over. With eyes fixed on Amy's breast, he began to feel aroused. Fantasizing about taking her into his bed, he realized that he too was being watched. His pleasure shriveled knowing that Becca caught him, ogling the young woman.

"So," Wood said as the waitress walked away from the table. "It's time for a toast. This one is for friends, may we always be."

"Yes," Becca added, touching her glass to theirs.

Still unable to make eye contact with Becca Dr. Lap turned, facing Wood. "I agree the three of us, forever."

Soon after the toast, a young ponytailed Mexican, in a red jacket and black slacks, brought to the table three plates of salad. All, but Becca, declined his offering of freshly ground black pepper. Once he was finished dusting Becca's salad, the busboy politely nodded to the party and quickly retreated back into the kitchen.

The three ate quietly. Midway through their first course, Becca reached over and gently grabbed Wood by the hand. Looking up, he realized she was attempting to direct his attention toward Dr. Lap. Wood immediately knew, by her smile, she was overly anxious to tell Dr. Lap of their intentions.

"Hey Chris, aren't you curious?" Wood asked.

Placing his fork on his plate, Dr. Lap sat back in his chair. "You mean about this, you know, fancy restaurant and all?"

"Yea, about this, aren't you just a little bit curious?"

Across from him Becca sat, clutching Wood's arm, with a captivating smile and a twinkle in her eye. Noticing that her dress sleeve was beginning to slip over her shoulder, about to expose her breast, he quickly made eye contact, avoiding a second embarrassment of being caught. Becca, perhaps sensing his uneasiness, made the necessary adjustments to her sleeve.

"To be honest, I thought you guys were planning on announcing a new book. But, seeing the two of you like this, I'm not so sure."

Becca, overcome by her anxiety, blurted out, "We're getting married!"

Taken by surprise, Dr. Lap was unable to respond. He sat there motionless, unsure of what he heard. Then, shaking off his initial shock, Dr. Lap jumped up from the table, rushed to the other side, giving both a hug. "I just can't believe it! Married, you two, that is so wonderful. I can't believe it." Realizing that several of the other diners were watching, he quickly returned to his chair. To whomever was listening, he announced, "My two friends, they're getting married."

Acknowledging the impromptu pronouncement, several guests from the surrounding tables, offered a polite applause.

"Geez, hope ya'll know what ya'll are doing." The tractor jockey asserted, lifting his bottle of beer in a toast. His wife feigned a frown, as she playfully punched him on his tattooed arm.

Slightly embarrassed by the unsolicited attention, Becca blushed, pulling closer to Wood. Responding to the applause, both graciously waved.

"So, when did this all come about?" Dr. Lap asked. "I mean, I know you guys are in love. It's so freakin' obvious. But marriage, hell, I guess I can see it. You two are perfect together."

The busboy quietly retrieved their salad plates and, as before, he quickly retreated back into the kitchen. Amy, with the assistance of a second busboy, began to serve the main course. Dr. Lap, visibly excited for his friends, shared the news of the upcoming union. Mechanically serving the meal, the busboy ignored Dr. Lap. Amy respectfully smiled, nodding in affirmation to Becca and Wood. "Enjoy your meal." She softly conveyed, "And best wishes to both of you."

"Thanks," Wood replied.

"We had just gotten back from a trip up north, you know, for Lucia's wedding, Wood's sister." It was Becca, describing the events surrounding Wood's clumsy proposal. After the wedding, she reported, they decided to take a day off before returning home. The intent was to relax, make it a lazy day, with no plans and no commitments. For Wood, it became one for nostalgia and reflection. Becca was given the grand tour of his childhood and adolescent years. They started in his old neighborhood, driving past his schools, pointing out the teenage hangouts, eventually visiting the abandoned factory and the nearby park. "Can you imagine, the man assumed that I would marry him."

"So, he didn't get down on one knee." Dr. Lap laughed. Turning to Wood, he said, "To think, I really thought you were the romantic one."

"We", I, you know…" Wood stumbled.

"He's my sweetheart." Becca said, giving Wood a hug. "He's my one and only."

"We're going up north again." Wood regained his composure. "We need to go to Ohio this time, to meet up with Becca's parents. We haven't told them yet. Besides, Becca has always dreamed of getting married in her family garden, so we need to go and start making some of the preparations."

Dr. Lap cut into the breast of his roasted duck. The meat was a little dry and tough to chew. Pointing with his fork at Wood, he began to speak, "So," pausing to swallow. "Excuse me, it's a little tough. So, when are you guys planning on doing this?"

"Well, with meeting with my parents and the preparation, we're looking at six to seven weeks. You know right after we finish this semester." Becca replied.

"Yea, we'll be back for the spring semester, and plan on taking our honeymoon during the midterm break." Wood added.

Amy made a brief appearance to check on the diners. Although he was dissatisfied with his meal, Dr. Lap did not make mention of it. Instead, he acknowledged the quality of the wine and requested a second bottle. Once Amy left, Becca commented that she had considered ordering the duck, before deciding on the grilled swordfish. Both she and Wood, who had stuck with his usual diet of steak and potatoes, were quite satisfied with their meals.

Nearly devouring his sirloin, Wood placed his knife and fork on his plate. Giving up on the overcooked duck, Dr. Lap pushed his plate from him, as Becca continued to pick at her fish. Pausing before taking another bite, she asked Wood. "Do you think we should tell him the rest?"

"Rest," Dr. Lap quizzed, "you mean there's more? Don't tell me. You took another position, where?"

"No, no, not at all," Wood hesitated before he continued. He could see in Dr. Lap's eyes some apprehension. Although Dr. Lap had several people he called friends, Wood knew he and Becca were his true allies. Rumors were afloat about Dr. Lap's antics with several coeds, as well as, possible drug use with students. Because of his relationship with Wood, the college often turned a blind eye. They were his security blanket. It was on Wood's coattails he rode "No, we're not leaving."

"Then, what is it?" Dr. Lap, sighing with relief, questioned.

The second bottle of wine was brought to the table by the ponytailed busboy. With a shy smile and downcast eyes, he opened the bottle topping, off each of the three glasses. Becca, the first to pick up her drink, offered a silent toast to the others. Placing her glass down, she announced, "We're having a baby."

The wine caught in Dr. Lap's throat. With his glass still against his lips, he stared over its rim toward Wood. A broad smile covered Wood's face. His eyes gleamed with happiness. A wedding was predictable. That had been obvious for a while. Dr. Lap had just been waiting for the announcement. On the other hand, he never had thought of his friend fathering a child. Over the years, he had assumed that Wood and he were of the same opinion, they didn't want the commitment. Yet, he now could see, he was wrong. Wood most welcomed a stab at parenthood. That look, those eyes, that smile, could not tell a different story.

"Well, what do you think?" Wood asked.

Able to move his drink from his mouth, "I'm shocked. I would have never thought, you, a father." Reaching over the table, Dr. Lap shook Wood's hand. "Wow, I'm so happy for you. For both of you, I am."

"Well we're hoping…" Wood stopped mid-sentence. Watching Dr. Lap's eyes fill with horror, he felt Becca jerk away from his side. Wood turned, seeing her drop to the floor, her hands grasping her head. The room fell silent. The only sound heard was a low painful moan, seeping from Becca's slightly closed lips. A thin stream of foam oozed from the edge of her mouth.

—

As he did on that tragic evening, Dr. Lap froze. The image of Becca convulsing on the floor still haunted him. Struggling to speak, he described to Four-Thirty how he, paralyzed, just sat helplessly watching Becca slam to the floor, her body seized by violent tremors. He remembered her legs jerking uncontrollably, pushing her dress over her thighs. He watched, as her white panties turned semitransparent, exposing her neatly trimmed pubic hairs. Beneath Becca, the coffee color carpet darkened. Dr. Lap tracked the transformation as it flowed, spreading toward the tips of his shoes. It was then he realized that Becca, losing bladder control, had urinated. Still, he was unable to move. Wood fell next to Becca, reaching down he lifted her into his arms. He held and rocked Becca until she fell into unconsciousness.

Wood looked up at Dr. Lap sitting at the table, a wine glass still in his hand. "Why?" Wood hopelessly whispered.

"Oh no, it's so sad." Four-Thirty exclaimed.

Dr. Lap, signaling to Jake for another round of drinks, mumbled. "I didn't know what to do. I was useless, just useless."

"I'm not sure there was anything you could have done."

A glass of red wine and a shot with a beer chaser was brought to the table. The whiskey was downed quickly by Dr. Lap. Soothing the flowing heat in his throat, he took a long swallow of beer.

A tee-shirt and leather clad biker stepped from the bar to drop a few quarters in the jukebox. His first selection *Sweet Baby James* by James Taylor began to play. It took Dr. Lap by surprise. "That's strange," Dr. Lap commented.

"Strange?"

"Yea, seems like James Taylor and bikers somehow don't fit."

Four-Thirty nodded in agreement. "I kinda expected Steppenwolf or Megadeath when I saw him at the box." Redirecting Dr. Lap back to the conversation on Becca, "I'm kinda surprise that Wood never spoke to me about all this. Yet, I think I can understand how it had to be painful for him. To relive it, I mean."

"He never speaks to me about it either, and I was there." Dr Lap added.

"It seems to me Becca had something like an epileptic seizure. But that's not how she died, was it?"

"No, no it was sometime later," Dr. Lap answered.

One of the restaurant's guests, a gentleman in a gray suit and dark green tie, rushed over shouting that he was a doctor. He knelt on the floor next to Wood. Taking off his jacket, the doctor placed it under Becca's head. Directing the maître d' to call 911, he pulled a tablecloth off a nearby table and covered Becca's exposed torso. "Let's keep her comfortable and warm until an ambulance gets here." He instructed Wood.

An emergency medical unit arrived, within a short period of time, to transport Becca to the hospital. Wood rode in the ambulance with her. Dr. Lap followed in his car. Still unconscious, she was taken into an examination room, where several nurses hooked Becca up to various monitoring machines.

"You two need to go outside, in the waiting room." A tall, gray haired nurse instructed Wood and Dr. Lap. "There's not much either of you can do for her in here. Beside, one of you needs to do some paperwork. You know insurance, medical history, any other helpful information."

"Fuck," Wood exclaimed in frustration. "I know nothing about her medical history."

"That's okay. Whatever you can give to us will be fine, I'm sure."

"She's pregnant. Oh my God," he began, tears swelling in his eyes. "The baby, will it be okay?"

Wood and Dr. Lap were led into a windowless room, situated between the patient's entrance to the emergency room and that of the walk-in clinic. The room was disquieting. Its mustard yellow walls were haunting, the air heavy, permeated with moans of the injured and the whimpering of a small child, ill with fever. Taking seats along a far wall, Dr. Lap and Wood positioned themselves away from several patients and their companions.

The nurse handed Wood a number of admission forms, attached to a clipboard. Anxiously, he started the paperwork, providing what little information he had. "I'll make sure that the doctor knows about the baby," the nurse said, turning to walk away.

Completing the documentation, Wood left the clipboard at the reception's desk. Wood, returning to his seat, withdrew, burying his face in his hands. To any observer it would appear that he had fallen asleep, but Dr. Lap knew better. He tried engaging him in a conversation. Wood ignored him, drawing deeper into himself.

What seemed to be an eternity was a mere fifteen minutes, when the nurse reentered the waiting room. Hearing the door close behind her, Wood snapped to attention.

"She's conscious." The nurse, reaching up and pinning a loose strand of hair beneath her cap, said coldly. "We're keeping her overnight. There are more tests that need to be run, and we want to keep her under observation for a day or two."

"Can you tell me what happened? What about the baby?"

"You really need to speak with the doctor, but the baby seems to be okay." She flatly replied.

"Can I see her?"

"In a few minutes, once she's settled in her room I'll come for you." The nurse answered as she walked away.

Releasing a sigh of relief, Wood leaned back in his chair resting his head against the wall. Watching the nurse disappear through the door, near the receptionist's desk, Wood began to giggle. "Do you remember in college that book we read? *Cuckoo's Nest*, you know, *One Flew over the Cuckoo's Nest?*"

"Yea, I remember, Kesey's book."

"Yea," Wood continued to laugh. "What was that nurse's name? Hatchet, or was it Ratchet, you know, the frigid bitch? Anyway, she just walked out that door. She needs to get laid."

Dr. Lap chuckled, thinking of the scene in which Kesey's protagonist McMurphy, a psychiatric patient, ripped open the blouse of the ward's head nurse, blaming her for the suicide of another patient. For his deed, he was rewarded with a lobotomy. Seeing similarities between the two women, Dr. Lap readily agreed.

It was nearly an hour before the nurse returned to escort Wood and Dr. Lap to Becca's room. She had been taken from the ER to the intensive care unit.

The ICU was housed on the second floor of the main hospital building. In its center sat, back to back, two nurse's stations. Situated along the walls were glass enclosed rooms for the patients. Becca's bed was in the second cubicle, to the right of the ward's entrance.

Wood was visibly shaken by Becca's appearance. She looked prematurely aged. Her eyes, embedded in dark circles, had lost their sheen. Her skin paled against the crisp white sheets of the hospital bed. The tubes, wires, and beeping machines surrounding her, created an eerie image. Lifting her frail arm, she waved as Wood and Dr. Lap entered the room. Wood, attempting to hide his shock, forced a smile. It didn't work.

"I'm alright," Becca said weakly. She tried to sit up. Unable to do so, Becca fell back onto the propped up pillows.

Taking a stool next to the bed, Wood sat in silence as he held Becca's hand. It felt cold and lifeless. Becca feebly squeezed his fingers, as if to tell him not to worry. Holding back a tear, Wood watched Becca, drift back into sleep, her hand slowly loosening its grip. Her breathing was shallow. Occasionally, Wood found a need to check the monitors, with their flowing graphs and ever changing numbers, for reassurance that she was still alive.

Becca stirred, briefly opening her eyes, when the doctor entered the room. "Good, I see that our little lady is getting some rest." He quickly looked over her chart and adjusted the flow of one of the IV's before he asked, "Are we family?"

Reaching out to shake the doctor's hand Wood replied, "Well yes, I'm her fiancé." Then after a slight hesitation he added, "And the baby's father. This here is a family friend. Chris Lap, he's from the college and hopefully the godfather."

"What?" Dr. Lap was caught off guard by the announcement.

"Obviously, Wood continued, pointing to Becca with and opened palm. "We didn't have time to ask."

"Congratulations," sensing Wood's frustration, the doctor directed his attention to Becca. "Let's see where our patient is at."

"Is she, the baby, are they going to be alright?" Wood asked.

"I'm going to be cautious, but I think both will be just fine." The doctor explained that the hospital had run a number of tests, all of which appeared to be negative. The vital signs, for both Becca and the baby, seemed to be stable and within the normal range. Yet, the seizure was highly traumatic, especially for the fetus. Wood was advised that a neurologist was being brought in, and other test have been scheduled. "What we do know is that she had a seizure. What we don't know is what caused it. That is what we need to find out. Hopefully, we can get some answers by morning. In the meantime, she needs to get some rest. She needs to sleep."

"Doc, I think I'm going to stay here with Becca." Wood said, addressing the doctor, "You think that will be alright?"

"No, I don't think that's a good idea." The doctor replied. "She really needs her rest. You're too edgy, restless. I can't have you here pacing the floor. Go home, do it there. I promise you, she'll be fine."

Wood looked over to Dr. Lap who nodded in agreement. "Okay, I'll go. But call me if anything, you know."

"I'll leave a note on the chart. You'll be called."

In his gut, Wood wasn't convinced leaving was the right thing to do. Yet, he conceded after seeing Becca sleeping peacefully and breathing steadily. Standing next to the bed, he lightly brushed her hair from her eyes and leaned over, kissing her softly on the forehead. "See you first thing in the morning, I promise." He whispered, turning to leave, with Dr. Lap following closely behind.

Dr. Lap agreed to help Wood retrieve his car in the morning. In the meantime, he was to stay at Dr. Lap's home, where a couch was available for Wood to sleep on. Once there, Dr. Lap offered a marijuana joint, to help ease the anxiety, to take off the edge. In the process, they downed a six pack of beer and smoked several more joints. It was just before dawn when they finally decided to get some sleep.

Rays of sun split through the slats of the blinds behind the couch, where Wood restlessly slept. Falling like prison stripes on his aching body, the lines slowly crept up toward the bridge of his nose. There, the light gently caressed his eyes opened. Reaching up, he tried to close the blinds. As he turned, he felt a stabbing pain in his hip, where a spring had poked its way through a cushion. Heightening his discomfort, the stench of stale beer and marijuana aggravated the impending hangover.

He was late. Seeing it was almost noon, he realized he had broken his promise to Becca. He was to be there, at her side, first thing in the morning. His car was still at the restaurant, forcing him to depend on Dr. Lap to get to the hospital. Fortunately, Dr. Lap, nursing his own version of a hangover, understood. Agreeing to slapping some cold water on the face to freshen up, and to grabbing hot coffee at the local deli, the two rushed out the door, still dressed in their clothes from the night before.

With a large coffee in one hand, and a bouquet of wild flowers, purchased from the deli, in the other, Wood hurried into the hospital. Too impatient to wait for the elevator, he anxiously ran up the stairs to the ICU. Pushing past the nurse's station, Wood entered Becca's room.

"What the fa…?" He exclaimed. An eerie feeling overcame him. The room was uncomfortably dark, with its shades drawn and the lights off. The bed was tightly made as though no one had slept in it, the surrounding machinery gone. Turning to the on duty nurse, he was speechless. Fearing the worse, all he managed to do was point to bed with flowers in hand.

"Oh, my," the nurse nervously spoke. "We tried, we tried calling you. Wait here," she added, hurrying to the other side of the ward. "I'll get the doctor. We did try, but no one answered." She was heard muttering as she turned the corner.

"Where is she?" Wood yelled to no one, the flowers slipping from his hands, scattering on the floor.

Having taken the elevator, Dr. Lap entered the ICU in time to see Wood, led by staff to a small office behind the nurse's desk. Stepping through the flowers blanketing the floor, he sensed something wrong and followed the entourage into the cubicle. As he walked in, a nurse brushed past him, returning to her desk. Across from the entrance Wood sat, cupping his coffee in both hands. A veil of confusion shrouded his face. Dr. Lap stepped to Wood's side, listening to the doctor as he began to speak, "I'm sorry to inform you…"

"No, no it can't be. I was supposed to be here." Wood cried. "How, what happened?"

Placing his hand on Wood's shoulder, the doctor talked softly and steadily. "She was sleeping peacefully. There were no signs of anything wrong when, why we don't know, her heart stopped beating. Then, shortly after, less than a minute I think, the fetus, his heart stopped."

"His?" Wood looked up questioning.

"Yes," the doctor continued. "The fetus was a male. We tried, but we couldn't revive them. I'm so sorry."

"If I was here, when you called if…" Wood mumbled with tears streaming.

"No, there was nothing you could have done. She had slept peacefully, from the time you left until, you know. It was painless for both."

"Thank you doctor," Wood whispered as he rose from the chair. "Thank you? Fuck," Wood's voice tinged with anger, "I don't know why I'm fuckin' thanking you. I just don't know."

Feeling helpless, Dr. Lap reached down and hugged Wood. In hindsight, he knew that the doctor was wrong. He should have let Wood stay in the room with Becca. If anything, he thought, Wood would not feel as though he had abandoned Becca and their child. Dr. Lap wanted to reassure him that he had not, but he remained speechless. Quietly he stood, with Wood trembling in his arms, for what seemed to be an eternity.

—

Reliving the night Becca died was most difficult for Dr. Lap. Sensing this, Four-Thirty reached across the table, gently stroking his hand.

Feeling the comfort, he did not withdraw. He was taken by the smoothness of her hands, much like a woman many years younger than she. "You know," looking into Four-Thirty's eyes. "He didn't go to Becca's funeral."

"You're kidding me," Four-Thirty exclaimed, pulling back from Dr. Lap. "Why?"

"Her parents," Dr Lap continued. "They were so different from her. Where she was warm and caring, they were cold as ice, snobbish. They were from money, and made Wood really know he wasn't. Even after Beeca died, they made sure he knew he was not good enough for their daughter."

"But, they were going to marry, have a child together."

"That didn't matter. They blamed Wood for Becca's death. And, as for the fetus, they denied the child. Kinda like saying, their daughter was too good to get pregnant by someone like Wood."

Four-Thirty was amazed. "Obviously they didn't know him. Wood is such a…"

"I know, I know." Dr. Lap cut her off. "Anyway, they banned him from the funeral, threatened to have him arrested if he showed up. He tried anyway and, sure enough, he was arrested. They had the police waiting for him outside the funeral home."

"Bastards," Four-Thirty exclaimed.

"From there it all went downhill." Dr. Lap went on and explained how Wood started to drink heavily, avoiding his closest friends. As for his classes, he began to arrive late, often reeking of alcohol. On several occasions, he did not show up at all. "One day, he decided he had enough. He was in a class and, as I had been told, in the middle of a discussion, he just walked out." Picking up his empty bottle, Dr. Lap waved to Jake for another round of drinks before he continued. "I mean, he just disappeared. I was supposed to have lunch with him that day. Instead, he went missing."

The entrance to Paci's opened with a burst of sunlight. Startled, Four-Thirty looked up. In the doorway a frail silhouette stood. It was Wood. With shoulders hunched forward, he slowly began to shuffle across the barroom floor. Taking a seat next to Four-Thirty, he wiped the perspiration from his forehead with the back of his sleeve. The top two buttons of his flannel work shirt were opened. A bead of sweat gently flowed along his Adam's apple, down onto his chest.

Suddenly, his pain became quite obvious. Four-Thirty saw it clearly for the first time. She wanted to hold him, cradle him like an injured child. The mother in her wanted to heal his hurt. "Kiss it up to God," as her mother would say. Instead, she, placing her hand on his leg, rested her head softly on his shoulder.

Wood ordered a beer and asked Jake to bring a menu. Four-Thirty continued to lean against Wood, watching Dr. Lap as he quietly rolled his finger along the rim of his empty shot glass. No one spoke. Wood, feeling uncomfortable, took a drink from his beer and began to read the menu. The silence was too much. "What the fuck," he questioned, dropping the menu onto the table. "Did someone die? I feel like I'm at a fuckin' wake."

Four-Thirty pulled back from him. "No, no, we were just talking. And, you know, it's just been a long day." Shaken by his reference to dying and a wake, she wondered if he knew that they had been talking about Becca's death. There was no way he could have, she concluded. Breathing a little easier, Four-Thirty once again rested her head on Wood's shoulder.

Conversely Dr. Lap, preoccupied with his own state of affairs, continued in his restlessness. Wood did not fail to notice, making Dr. Lap even more uncomfortable. Avoiding eye contact, Dr. Lap leaned his back against the wall and swung his legs onto the bench seat. Yet, he still felt Wood staring at him.

"So…" Dr. Lap was about to ask about Buffalo. Instead, the silence was broken by Luscious. Dressed in a dark green tee-shirt and cut off jeans, she approached the booth. A pack of *Camel* cigarettes were rolled up in her right sleeve. Across her braless chest the words "Fuck Men" was written in white. From underneath the cloth, the nipple of her left breast pushed through, accenting the period after the word Men. Brushing Dr. Lap's legs aside, she took the seat next to him.

"Nice shirt," Dr. Lap smiled. "Bet that could be an interesting debate."

"Not sure you would want to get into that ring with me." Luscious flatly responded.

"Yea, you might be right on that one."

"Thanks," she said, turning to Wood. "Thanks for helping my big brother."

"It was nothing."

Luscious, leaning back against the seat, rested her head on the top of the bench. "Thanks anyway. If he could only hold his life together, ya know. I try to keep an eye on him. Do the best I can but," Expressionless, she turned to Dr. Lap. "That war really fucked him up, No Hope too."

She remembered the day Buffalo was shipped out. He was proud, chest out, duffel bag swung over his shoulder, ready to serve his country. She also remembered when he returned, limping from his wounds. The physical ones were the least damaging. She never got to know what was happening in his head. Buffalo wouldn't let her in. Instead, he withdrew into his room, numbing his pain with alcohol and drugs.

"At least Buffalo has some family." Four-Thirty interjected.

Pointing to Wood, Luscious added, "Yea, and friends like this guy."

Wood, embarrassed, smiled. Not one who could take a compliment, he blushed. "Like I said, it was nothing."

"So, how did you like his place?" Failing to adjust to living with family, Buffalo moved from shelter to shelter. Unable to control his drinking and drug use, his welcome at these facilities were short lived. Eventually, he hooked up with several other homeless veterans, establishing a camp near the river. Over time, shanties were built which the men, and a few women, shared, along with communal meals. Among his peers, Buffalo finally felt at home.

"Well," Wood hesitated thinking he would upset Luscious. "I'll tell you this, I couldn't live there. But for Buffalo, I guess it works, unfortunately."

"Yea, I guess it does." Luscious sadly surrendered. "Like I said, thanks for helping with his couch."

"Must tell you," Wood rejoined, laughing. "If I knew we were to carry that thing along the tracks and the river, I might have not done it. I mean, we had to carry that thing for more than two miles."

Grinning, Luscious replied. "Yea, but once you knew you didn't quit on him. No, you didn't."

Pushing up from the booth, Luscious stepped next to Wood. Leaning over, she softly kissed him on top of his balding head. He felt her warm lips against the skin, under his thinning hair. As her breast brushed against the side of face, he turned a darker shade of red. "Thanks again, to me it was something. Ya know he's my brother." She whispered before walking away.

Dr. Lap watched as Luscious returned to the pool table, resuming her game with Lady Cakes. Her walk was steady, calf muscles bulged with each step, her shoulders firm, exposing her dedication to the weight room. Dr. Lap quietly admired her. She came across as being tough, hard. Yet, she was just as comfortable showing her soft side. Picking up her cue stick, she gently chalked its tip. Seeing Dr. Lap watching, she gave him a smile before bending over the table to take her shot.

"Wait a minute," Four-Thirty interrupted. "There aren't any houses along the river, at least not on that stretch."

"Yea, I know, I didn't think so either. Anyway, we get to this wooded area and we start walking into the woods through some heavy brush. And you know, there it was, in the freakin' middle of nowhere." Wood hesitated. Picking up his glass, he slowly took a drink to prolong the suspense. "Well, you know what they say about seeing is believing. I mean, these guys, squatters, built a settlement of about ten people, maybe more. And our friend Buffalo, he's living among them. Like, he's got this, this house made of scrap wood, cardboard and whatever. You really got to see it."

"How can people live like that?" Dr. Lap wondered out loud.

"I don't know." Wood shivered, thinking that it wasn't really that long ago, it could have been him. He was almost there or someplace like it. He continued to shiver, knowing that he's not that far from sinking that low again.

Chapter 15

It was just before noon. Dr. Lap, standing at Wood's living room window, watched the morning rain steadily fall. Somewhere in the distance, the eerie sounds of a bank building's chimes played The Beatles' *Here Comes the Sun*.

"Fuck," Lap mumbled inaudibly, turning away from the view, "something is wrong here."

"What's that, Chris?" Wood asked, entering the room from the kitchen, carrying two cups of coffee and the daily newspaper.

"Oh, it was nothing, just an observation."

Dropping the paper on a chair, Wood handed one of the coffees to Dr. Lap. "You okay? Seem a little preoccupied."

"Yea, I'm okay. Maybe a little tired, but I'm okay, really."

Joining Dr. Lap at the window, both quietly stared out at the drab weather. Conceding to the dreariness, Wood, raising his coffee to Dr. Lap, said, "This could use a little boost."

Dr. Lap smiled. "Yea, maybe some anisette, you know that will do me some good."

"Yea, something like that," Wood agreed.

"You think this rain might ease up?"Dr. Lap asked. "I really don't like driving in crappy weather like this."

"I don't know, maybe." Wood said, turning toward Dr. Lap. "Chris, you know, you really don't have to leave yet. Who knows, it might clear up later this afternoon, and if not, you got tomorrow. Besides, you've been gone this long, what's another day?"

"It's like," Dr. Lap said, looking through the rain into a void, "I don't know. I really need to get back. I mean, there's stuff I need to take care of, you know."

Wood watched his friend nervously pace in front of the window. He was lost in thought, tight lip and edgy, a distant look in his eyes. It was obvious, something was bothering him, and something engrossed him. Throughout Dr. Lap's visit, Wood was concerned as Dr. Lap often appeared anxious. Even the talk of suicide scared Wood.

"Chris, I know there is something wrong. I know, I mean, look at you you're a wreck." Wood pointed to Dr. Lap's hands, both wrapped around the coffee cup. "Look, you can't even hold that cup steady. You need two hands."

Turning toward Wood, Dr. Lap uneasily looked into his eyes. Trying to speak, his lips quivered unable to form a word. Slowly he walked toward the couch. Moving a pile of books off the cushion, he cleared a spot and sat. Holding his head down, Dr. Lap forced a whisper. "I think you need to sit for this one."

Without speaking, Wood moved from the window to a chair across from Dr. Lap. He sat watching patiently, as Dr. Lap quietly fidgeted with his cup. After a few moments, he placed the cup on the end table, leaned back, draping an arm across the back of the couch. Dr. Lap broke the charged silence, uncomfortably declaring, "I think I'm going to jail. No, no that's not right. I know I'm going to jail."

"Chris, don't bullshit me. I..."

"No, listen. I'm sure, I fucked up."

"What happened? Did you get busted?" Wood anxiously moved to the edge of his seat, "That was fuckin' stupid. Of course you got busted. Why else..."

"Stop, please." Dr. Lap pleaded. "Just listen for a minute."

"Alright," Wood sank back into the chair.

Restlessly, Dr. Lap lifted his cup, taking a sip. Placing the coffee back on the table, he said. "You know, I, well, shit."

Wood started to speak, "If you..."

Nervously raising his hand, Dr. Lap stopped him. "You know how you were always on my case about dating students? You always warned me but, you know, I just laughed it off. But you know me, had to be the campus stud. Anyway..."

"What the fuck," Wood exclaimed. "What happened? Did someone..."

"Stop, just listen, please." Dr. Lap said firmly. "I really need you to just listen, please."

"Okay." Wood reluctantly conceded.

"Do you remember Legree, Jerry Legree?" Dr. Lap began. "And all those end of the term parties he threw?"

"Yea, I remember him. His parties were legendary."

"You know," Dr. Lap said. "I never really liked going to those things. But, with Katie gone..."

"You miss her?" Wood interjected.

"Yea, I do." Dr. Lap answered softly. "I guess I really fooled myself. I thought, this time it would really be different. I didn't think she would leave. I mean, oh, I don't know. Like, she left a void."

"I don't understand. You know the routine. You've been playing this game forever. They're students, school is over and they go." Wood firmly expressed his frustration. He never thought Dr. Lap would stop dating students. Wood had not agreed with it, but the dating was expected, a part of the college culture. Becoming emotionally involved was not necessarily a part of it. "What happened, you fall in love?"

"Well I, I just don't know." Dr. Lap nervously responded. "Maybe, I really don't know."

"So, you, feeling sorry for yourself, went to the party."

"Yea, I went to Dr. Legree's place."

Long before Wood and Dr. Lap were hired by the college, Dr. Legree was a fixture on the campus. An established author of academic and literary writings, Dr. Legree brought both notoriety and prestige to the school. Having one of his novels made into a moderately successful movie, and he being a spokesman for the bohemian fringe, was not lost on the student population. He was the local celebrity, relishing in the attention it brought him. Whether he was on campus, or in town, Dr. Legree was rarely seen without an entourage, of admirers and aspiring writers, following him.

As it has become a tradition, Dr. Legree's celebration of the end of the summer term, was a Saturday evening barbeque and bonfire at his farm. Rumors had been floating for months that another of his novels was being considered for a screenplay. That fueled speculations of various Hollywood types, attending the gathering. One such tale, allegedly from a reliable source, insinuated that the deal for the movie had been made, with scenes for the film to be shot at the party. With the stage set, so to speak, high attendance was guaranteed.

Dr. Lap had no intention of going. Desiring not to be labeled as just another one of Legree's groupie, Dr. Lap avoided the Legree party circuit. Having submitted his final grades to the dean, his plan was to have a quiet weekend at home, sipping wine and vegetating in front of a TV screen.

At first, all went well. Having stocked up for the weekend with food and wine, Dr. Lap changed into his favorite lounging shorts and ripped tee-shirt. With bottle in one hand and the remote in the other, he melted into his favorite chair, a self imposed isolation.

This lasted until the evening news, when Dr. Lap began to feel the anxiety of being alone. His thoughts turned to Katie, a senior he had dated, and with whom he had spent most of his weekends. They had met during the fall term and, in violation of school policy, openly displayed their relationship. Then, upon graduation, she had abruptly ended her involvement with Dr. Lap, announcing that she was returning home with plans to marry her high school sweetheart.

At first, Dr. Lap shrugged it off. He rationalized that the relationship with Katie had been no different than those he had in previous years. As usual, he would become involved with a student and, for whatever reason that was convenient, they part at the end of the academic year. Yet, Dr. Lap, feeling every bit the senior professor that he was, didn't cherish the incoming competition of the newer and younger instructors. Thus, he decided to attend the barbeque. Dr. Lap knew that many of the students, who were planning on remaining on campus until the new term started, were at the party. Perhaps, Dr. Lap thought, he could survey his options and get a jump on the new instructors.

By the time Dr. Lap arrived at Legree's farm, the party was well underway. The driveway to the house was lined with cars, forcing him to park along a dirt road, leading away from the home. Following the sounds of live music, he wandered toward the back.

A group of students met up with Dr. Lap as he walked up the drive. It was obvious they had started drinking earlier in the day and were already drunk. Dr. Lap recognized one of the students from his *Social Problems* course. Pulling a can of beer from the plastic ring of the six-pack he carried under his arm, the student turned, offering it to his professor. "Have one on me Doc. Think it'll buy me an 'A'?"

Taking the beer, Dr. Lap pulled the tap, taking several long gulps, he answered. "I don't know, maybe a small deposit on one."

"Well, it really doesn't matter. You gave a good class and I think I got a lot out of it."

"Thanks," Dr. Lap replied. "But, if my memory serves me well, you don't need to worry about your grade."

"Sounds like the place is jumpin'." Another student from the group said.

"Yea, man I'm ready to par-tee!" A third said as he threw his empty beer can across the front yard.

"Seem like you already have started." Dr. Lap replied.

"Yes sir, school is fuckin' out and I'm rearing to go."

Approaching the end of the driveway, Dr. Lap turned toward the rear of the house, while the group headed toward a large gathering near the bonfire.

"Hey Doc, enjoy the night." The *Social Problems* student called to Dr. Lap.

"Yea, you too."

Set up on the rear patio was Cheyenne, a local band, hired by Dr. Legree for the day's entertainment. Several students and faculty were dancing, as the band played an acceptable cover of the Doors' *Light My Fire*. To the left of the patio sat a beer keg, in a large tub of ice. Next to it, a table was covered with various bottles of alcohol, cups, plates and an assortment of appetizers. Behind the table, Dr. Legree, dressed in jeans and a dark blue tee-shirt, stood bent over a second beer keg, attempting to tap into it.

"*Pinot Noir*," Dr. Lap said, approaching Dr. Legree, handed him a bottle of wine. "A local wine, I think the vineyard is a neighbor of yours."

Dr. Legree, taking the bottle from Dr. Lap, looked at the label. "Yea, *Cedar Pond Vineyard*, it's my friend Jim's place. In fact he's here, somewhere."

"He does make a good wine."

"Yea, we drink it all the time." Dr. Legree answered.

A young woman, with short blonde hair and wearing a soiled apron, took the wine from Dr. Legree, placing it on the table. As she brushed past Dr. Lap, she gave him a short innocent smile. Nodding his head, he reluctantly acknowledged her gesture.

"Want me to open this for you?" She, directing her question to Dr. Lap.

"No Chris, take this instead. It's good and cold." Dr. Legree said, taking the empty can from Dr. Lap and handing him a paper cup, filled with foaming beer, from the freshly tapped keg. Pointing to several tables loaded with food, he continued. "Get yourself something to eat. We barbecued a whole hog in a pit we dug down by the barn. There should be a lot of choice meat left."

"Yea, I might just go ahead and do that."

"Hey Jonesy," Dr. Legree called out to one of his protégés. "Fix up a plate for Chris, won't 'cha."

"That's okay," Dr. Lap interjected. "I can get it."

"No, no let Jonesy do it." Dr. Legree insisted. "He'll get it for you. Jonesy will take care of you."

Dr. Lap reluctantly agreed, walking toward the tables and barbeque pit. There, he was handed a plate with freshly cut pork, baked beans, and brown rice. Jonesy directed him to a smaller table where, a variety of salads and breads were available. From the assortments, Dr. Lap added a scoop of potato salad to his plate.

The remainder of the evening proved to be uneventful. After indulging on the roasted pig, Dr. Lap settled in, listening to the music. Living up to his anti-intellectual reputation, he was quite successful in his attempts to maintain contacts with his colleagues on a superficial level. With students, he avoided engagement in intellectual banter, noting that school was out, and they no longer needed to compete for grades. Soon, he was left alone to his musings, as he strolled around the bonfire.

It wasn't long before Dr. Lap concluded that the party justified every reason why he avoided Dr. Legree's previous gatherings. Having witness too many of his fellow faculty drunkenly making fools of themselves on the dance floor, and these colleagues, along with several of the male students, drooling over any female that crossed their path, Dr. Lap decided it was time to make his exit. Besides, he could not bear another drunken discourse unrelated to reality.

Approaching his car, Dr. Lap began to feel a sense of relief. In a minute way, he met a social obligation with his fellow staff, and he eased his sense of loneliness, brought on by Katie's departure.

As he reached into his pocket, searching for his keys, Dr. Lap was startled by a soft female voice. "Hi, leaving already?"

Turning, Dr. Lap faced a petite coed with cropped dark hair, dressed in a tee-shirt and Daisy Duke shorts. It was Susanne, a student from one of his introductory courses. She, a little intoxicated, anxiously rocked on her feet, standing across from him. Dr. Lap couldn't help noticed that she was braless. The front of her white shirt was wet. The damp material embraced her right breast, outlining the nipple.

"Oh," Susanne giggled, catching Dr. Lap staring. "One of the jock bumped into me, dumped a whole mug of beer." Looking down at her shirt, she added, "Do you think, maybe, he did it in purpose?"

"Sorry." Dr. Lap mumbled, unlocking his car door.

"No, that's okay, I mean it's, oh never mind." Susanne stumbled, trying to speak.

"So, ah..."

"Oh, yes." Susanne spoke again, trying to regain her composure. "I saw you earlier and wanted to say hello but, you know. Anyway, then you were leaving and I, well, just want to say hi."

"Hi."

"Yea, hi. So," Susanne responded, pointing toward the opened door of Dr. Lap's car. "I see you're leaving."

"Yea, I'm not much of a party person. Besides it's been a long week and..."

"I see," Susanne interrupted, "neither am I. I mean, you know, I'm not much into parties either."

"Yet, you got to give the man credit though," Dr, Lap continued. "He sure knows what he's doing. I mean the food was great and that band was pretty tight."

"Yea, and he had a lot of stuff to drink." She agreed as she raised her cup in a faint toast. "I guess I'm a little woozy from it all."

"Anyway, I need to get on the road. Enjoy the rest of the party."

Susanne hesitated at first. She, turning to look back toward the house and then to Dr. Lap, uttered, "Well, my ride, well I don't know. I think she left with some guy, and I..."

"Do you need a ride?" Dr. Lap reluctantly offered, hoping she turn him down. "I can give you a lift."

"Are you sure?"

"Yea," Dr. Lap answered. "Where do you want to go?"

"Great!" Throwing her half empty cup to the ground, Susanne swiftly walked to the passenger side. Climbing onto the front seat she turned, looking up to Dr. Lap, still standing outside the car. "I guess I can go back to the dorm, whatever. I mean you're the pilot and, you know, I'm here, I guess I'm the copilot."

Hindsight was all Dr. Lap had left at his disposal. He knew that he could have easily, and should have, sent her back to the party. Then later, when she offered him a joint, he could have said no, instead of taking her to his place, to smoke the marijuana. Did he think that "Just say no" wouldn't work, just like it failed Ronald Reagan as his anti-drug initiative? Dr. Lap also knew his intoxication, as well as hers, was not an excuse to take her to his bed. He did anyway, knowing he should have taken her back to the dorm. As it always is with retrospection, all the "could haves" and the "should haves" are meaningless. They don't change a damn thing.

—

Wood watched Dr. Lap struggled, reliving his tale. Yet, he had heard it, saw it, all before. With each new term there was a new face, a new name, but the same old story, faculty partying with students, then sleeping with them. Instructors carried their grade books, like Jesse James carried his six-shooter. Every naïve freshman, brought to the sack, was just another notch on the handle. They were supposed to be educators, but they literally, and figuratively, fucked people instead. His friend, Dr. Lap, was no different.

"Come on Chris, none of this is new." Wood spoke firmly. "What's going on here?"

Dr. Lap was caught off guard. He was stung by the absence of sympathy. They have been friends for an eternity. The sense of understanding was not there. "Ah, I..."

"I know you were both drunk, but," Wood continued, "wasn't it consensual?"

"I don't know." Dr. Lap answered. "It's like, she and I well, I really don't know."

"I don't understand. Either it was or..." Wood froze. In a millisecond, he understood what hiding between the lines. Rising on the edge of his seat, a finger pointed directly at Dr.Lap, Wood sharply spoke. "Don't tell me! Don't you fuckin' tell me!"

"I know. I fucked up." Dr. Lap explained. "Susanne was in the accelerated program for high school students. She was fifteen. I think she had just turned fifteen."

Wood was at a loss for words. It was unimaginable that his friend was that reckless. Or was he just careless, unconcerned about what he does to others? This time, it was a child.

"I never saw her again after that night. She had gone home. When school had started up again, she bragged to her high school friends, about getting high with her college teacher. I guess she told them about the sex." Dr. Lap hesitated, drinking the last of his coffee. "Anyway, one of her friends, I guess, told her parents, and one thing lead to another. So, there I was in class on the first day of the new term, just about to start the lecture, when the cops walked in. I had no idea. You can never imagine."

"What did they charge you with?"

"Statutory rape and endangerment of a minor," Dr. Lap replied. "I mean, it's not like I'm a pedophile."

"I think you are."

"What?"

"Yea, I think you are." Wood answered without hesitation. "I guess I always have. It's just that you usually wait until they're eighteen. I mean, your attraction to these students is that they're young and innocent. Maybe, somewhere in the back of your mind, you're still in the eighth grade chasing that elusive virgin. But, if you really look in the mirror, you're old, gray and getting fat. You're not that kid anymore. You just have to let go, but you won't. So, yea, to me that makes you a pedophile."

Chapter 16

Gerry walked into the kitchen, quietly placing his book bag on the table. From the living room, he heard the low moan of the TV. Looking in, he saw his father stretched out on a recliner, with eyes closed. On the lamp stand to the left sat a half empty beer bottle and an unfinished sandwich. The child entered the living room. Trying not to wake his father, he headed for his bedroom.

"Where's your mom, boy?" Jordan asked without stirring.

"She's coming." Gerry softly answered. "She's getting the groceries."

Jordan, picking up the beer, slowly took a sip. "Boy, you got homework?"

"Yes."

"Well then, you best get to it. I don't want to see you playing them damn video games in your room."

"Yes Daddy." Gerry turned back toward the kitchen to retrieve his bag.

Sitting up in the recliner, Jordan gulped down the rest of his beer and turned off the TV. Hearing Lizzie in the adjoining room, he got up from his chair, following Gerry into the kitchen. His wife, standing across from the entrance, placed a carton of milk into the refrigerator. He slowly walked up behind her. With one hand, Jordan reached into the refrigerator, clutching a beer. The other, he slipped under Lizzie's sweater cupping her breast.

"No." She said, pushing him away from her side. "Can't you see I'm busy?"

"Fuck, you're always busy." Rejected, Jordan mumbled incoherently, walking back toward the living room.

It has been a little over six months since Jordan had been released from the Central State Correctional Facility, where he was incarcerated for arson, having burned down his childhood home. Although his time in prison was easier than his previous stretches, being released wasn't, at least not this time around. He was having difficulties making adjustments to the outside world.

Employment was hard to come by. At first, Jordan tried finding work. Wanting to help support his family, he was willing to do anything to earn a few dollars. Yet, after several promising interviews, Jordan, mentioning being a two time felon, soon found out these jobs were no longer available, having been mysteriously offered to someone else.

Relating to people, he found, was even harder. Jordan had nothing in common with people in the outside world. With Lizzie's friends, he had even less. All that Jordan owned were stories of prison life. Current affairs, music, and politics seemed foreign to him. Conversations with others often regressed with him insipidly listening, anxious to escape into solitude.

This disconnection from the outside was most evident at home. His wife, after his first week home, began sleeping in their son's room. She was afraid of Jordan. Not accustomed to sleeping with another, he tossed and turned throughout the night. Any attempts by Lizzie to comfort him often failed. One night, in a light sleep, he grabbed Lizzie by the throat, when she brushed against him. It was at that moment, she realized how violent her husband really was.

The distance between Jordan and Lizzie went beyond the bedroom. They no longer lived as a couple. Instead, they coexisted. Conversation was at its minimum, often escalating into arguments. Lizzie hoped, prayed, that Jordan would find employment, thinking that it would help him ease back into civilian life. She would also push him to spend more time with their son, who sorely needed his father. Instead, with each day, Jordan became more distant, more withdrawn. His little boy, who was yet two when Jordan was incarcerated for the arson, had grown further from his father since he's was released from prison, than he had in the five years that Jordan was behind bars.

There was no question that Jordan wanted to be a father to Gerry. Nights in his cell at Central State were spent dreaming of all the fatherly things he would do with his son. Unfortunately, like most men, Jordan didn't know how to be a parent. Unlike most of them, he knew even less.

As a father, Jordan thought of himself a failure. It was at the most basic level, he was least successful. He didn't know how to communicate, talk to his son. Whenever they spoke, Jordan would talk at Gerry, talk down to him, and tell him what to do and how to do it. He never had a conversation with Gerry. He didn't know his son.

Not long after being released, Jordan took Gerry to a hobby shop and bought a model airplane kit, a father and son project. Gerry, quite anxious to build the craft with his father, rushed through his dinner the night they planned to start the build. The table was quickly cleaned as the little boy covered the work area with newspaper. Gerry, sitting patiently, watched as Jordan opened the box from which he spread out the various plastic parts, miniature bottles of paint, glue and printed directions.

It didn't take long for the child's excitement to dissipate. Jordan rolling up his sleeves, turned to Gerry, "O.K. son, let's get this going." And Jordan did. He began by reading the instructions out loud. After which, he looked through the array of plastic, fitting the pieces together. Gerry sat unwearyingly, waiting for his turn. It never came. Jordan, reading the directions and gluing the plane together, monopolized the evening, forgetting to include his son. Soon, to Jordan's dismay, Gerry, feeling lost, stepped away from the table to go into his room and play a video game.

"Daddy," Gerry said to his father, sleeping on the recliner. "Wake up."

"Huh?"

"Wake up," Gerri repeated, shaking his father cautiously. "Mommy says it's time to eat."

"O.K. boy, I'm coming." Jordan grunted as he woke.

Getting up from the lounge chair, Jordan slowly walked into the kitchen. Opening the refrigerator he reached in, grabbing another beer. Lizzie watched him emotionlessly, as he turned toward the table, taking his seat across from their son.

Feeling uncomfortable, Jordan had never sat at the head of the table. Coming from prison he felt that this was Lizzie's home, not his, not theirs. He, not feeling like a part of the family, quickly resigned to playing the role of a subordinate, kind of like an older child. Thus, he left that seat opened for Lizzie to which she never objected. He made a promise, that one day, this will all change. They will have a home where he belonged, a home where they would be a family. Only then, would he take on the role of the head of household, and take what he assumed to be his place at the head of the table.

Lizzie placed a basket of sliced bread in the center of the table before taking her seat. Bowing her head, she quietly said a prayer, asking that her family be blessed. Filling a plate with rice and black beans, and a generous helping of roasted vegetables, she passed it to Gerry. Making his own plate, Jordan watched his son, without hesitation, eat.

"How was work today?" Jordan asked to break the silence.

"Oh, just the usual," she answered, without looking up. Lizzie worked in a medical center as a receptionist. She was primarily responsible for coordinating appointments and billing. "Nothing special, I'm just glad that the day is done."

"I guess it's nice that it's Friday. You could sleep late tomorrow."

Lizzie forced a giggle, "That will be the day. Not with you two early birds and Saturday morning kiddy shows."

"Yea, Dad likes those cartoons too." Gerry interjected with a laugh.

Jordan, turning his attention toward Gerry, smiled. After the model plane fiasco, he discovered that TV was something he could share with his son, something nonthreatening to either. On Saturday mornings, like he had done in prison, Jordan would sit in front of the small screen. He and Gerry would eat cold cereal, while cheering on various animated characters. They each had their favorites, which invited playful banter between them.

So, how was your day?" Lizzie asked Jordan.

"Oh," Jordan responded nervously. "You know nothing out of the ordinary."

Lizzie did not answer. She looked coldly at Jordan. In her eyes, he could see the anger beginning to burn. Sensing an argument brewing, he added, "Well, I looked in the paper but," he hesitated, "you know, its Friday. There was nothing new. Nothing I haven't seen before."

"Did you go anywhere?"

"Yea, yea," Jordan lied. He knew he agreed to go out looking for work. The last thing he promised Lizzie, before she left in the morning, was that he would go out to the factories and spend the day filling out employment applications. Instead, he watched TV, and drank beer, most of the day. He knew he was caught, but he tried to weasel out anyway.

"Yea," he continued. "I went into Clifton, to the warehouses along the river. I got a couple maybes but nothing promising."

Lizzie, sitting up straight in her chair, angrily placed her fork on the table. Trying to control her fury, she started to speak softly, only to be cut off by Jordan.

"You know, maybe Monday," he continued, avoiding her stare. "Yea, maybe Monday I'll stop at a few of the other warehouses, you know, something might come up. I think something will. I'm sure of it."

Reluctant to listen to any more of his lies and excuses, Lizzie pulled away from the table. She, walking to the sink, poured herself a glass of water. Turning to address Jordan, Her voice echoed with disappointment. "I don't understand you. I really don't."

"But..."

"No, no, no," she continued, feeling herself losing control. "No buts. Just tell me. How can you sit there and lie to me? How can you? You didn't go anywhere."

"I, you know..."

"Look at you," Lizzie pointed at Jordan, raising her voice. "You didn't even dress. You got on the same clothes you slept in. Hell, from what I see around here, all you did was drink a freakin' twelve pack of beer. Am I right?"

"What do you want from me?" Jordan said loudly.

"Oh Jordan, Jordan, it's not what I want from you. It's what you need to do for yourself."

"Damn it," he got up from the table, throwing his plate, dinner and all, into the sink. "Can't you see? I'm a felon, a fuckin' big time loser. No one will hire me, no one wants me."

"How would you know?" Lizzie snapped back. "You haven't even tried."

"It's just useless," Jordan yelled. "Just useless, I..."

"Oh Jordan, please stop it. You know, I feel like you're not the man I married. I don't know you anymore. Seems like the man I love walked out. And then you, just a shell of that man, five years later, walked in to take his place."

Fearing Jordan, Lizzie backed away from him. The tension between the two escalated as Jordan's voice grew louder. "Fuck, you just don't know. You don't know what it's like to..."

"Stop, stop it!" Gerry yelled from the table. Both parents froze, watching their child with his hands over his ears, crying for them to end the fighting.

Lizzie was the first to move. She, wrapping her arms around Gerry, snuggled him to her breast. "It's all right baby. It's over. It's all right."

Gerry pulled tighter to his mother. He looked up to his father for reassurance. But, unable to make eye contact, Jordan turned away. Rejected, Gerry buried his face against his mother's side sobbing.

"Can't you see what you're doing to us?" Lizzie asked softly. "Can't you see what you're doing to him? You're so full of self pity that you just can't let us in."

Jordan turned, watching his wife cradle their son. He couldn't speak. Instead, he grabbed his coat and walked out the door. The silence in the hall was deafening. In his heart he knew, he had lost his family.

Inside, at the kitchen table, Lizzie held Gerry rocking him gently in her arms. As tears slowly streamed down her face, she whispered "I don't know him. I just don't know him anymore."

—

Stepping out of his apartment building, Jordan walked to the corner, taking a bus to Paterson. Feeling uncomfortable among the rush hour commuters, returning home from their office jobs in the city, he sat close to the rear door, anticipating a quick exit. At the Market and Main intersection, Jordan got off and headed toward Ellison Street. Turning left, he walked several blocks before making a right, onto a narrow side street.

A group of young Latinos gathered outside an old brownstone. Guarding its stoop, a boy of about fifteen years old, sat. Seeing Jordan approach the entrance, the teenager rose up from the steps, blocking the doorway.

"Need to see Chi Chi." Jordan mumbled.

The young soldier looked toward another, leaning against the lamppost, smoking a slim cigar. Jordan knew him. They had been in the Central State Correctional Facility together. Recognizing Jordan, he nodded approval. "Okay, man," the teen replied, turning to Jordan, "second floor, rear door."

Reaching the second floor, Jordan quickly entered the apartment. It, blanketed in a haze of marijuana smoke, was ill lit. Across from the entrance, Chi Chi sat on a worn leather couch with two women, playing a video game. To his left, another male, in a brown overstuffed chair, was rolling a joint. Seeing Jordan entering the room, Chi Chi got up with a smile and hugged his visitor. "Hey man, so good to see you."

"Likewise."

"Pleez, *mi amigo*, sit," Chi Chi directed Jordan to the couch.

One of the women quitting the game, moved to another chair in the room. Jordan eased uncomfortably onto the cushion, were she had been sitting. On the coffee table, parallel to the couch sat a mirror with traces of white powder. "Cocaine" Jordan thought.

"Wanna taste?" Chi Chi asked, catching Jordan looking at the mirror.

"Na, not now. Maybe another time."

"This gringo, his balls, *mucho grande*," Chi Chi addressed the others in the room. Then, with a swishing motion in the air, as if he was swinging a sword, he continued, "Swoosh, swoosh just like Zorro he take down the baddest motha' fuck in the prison. That was sumptin' man. You crazy man."

It had been a long time since Jordan last thought about the incident with Eric. The killing, brought up by Chi Chi embarrassed him. Unwilling to reminisce, Jordan lowered his head as Chi Chi sat next to him.

A joint was passed to Chi Chi. Putting the marijuana to his lips, he deeply inhaled the smoke. He slowly let out a blue stream, passing the joint to Jordan. He took a deep drag. As the smoke built up in his lungs, a burning sensation rose up into his throat. Unable to suppress a cough, Jordan began to gag violently.

"Easy man," Chi Chi instructed.

"It's just been a long time. Ya know, too long a time since I smoked." Jordan answered. With that, he took a second drag, holding the coughing to a minimum.

Jordan, passing the joint to his left, noticed a little table near the door. On it, sat a shrine, with a statute and various religious artifacts. He saw that someone had carefully placed dried flowers on the table and lit a candle. It reminded him of his mother's altar to the Virgin Mary.

"Nice touch," he said, pointing to the shrine. "*Santeria?*"

"Well you know man, if it helps. Why not man?"

"Yea, why not," Jordan sighed. "I sure in hell could use some help. Maybe you can cast a spell for me. You know, some of that Voodoo shit."

"Sure man, maybe." Chi Chi laughed.

The room remained relatively calm, while the joint was passed around. Turning off the video game, the second woman turned on the TV to a Spanish talk show. Meanwhile, the men sat back quietly enjoying the effects of the marijuana.

For Jordan, the experience was initially pleasurable. It had been several years since he had last used the drug. Slowly, he began to recognize its symptoms. He was taken by surprise by the depth of the euphoria he felt, and pleased by the tingling, or rushes, running through his limbs. It wasn't long before the sensation of paranoia began to take over his senses. With every knock on the door, or person entering the apartment, Jordan expected the police to soon follow. His discomfort became obvious.

Observing his friend's uneasiness, Chi Chi asked. "So tell me, what is it man. Why ya here?"

Jordan, trying to focus on what he needed to say, replied. "It's kinda, a..."

"I mean man," Chi Chi interrupted. "This is no social visit. Ya not like that. Ya want somethin', *si?*"

"Well," Jordan continued, wishing that he did not get high. It would have been easier to explain his needs. "It's, like, I just can't make it out there. I can't make it as a civilian."

Jordan and Chi Chi freely discussed the difficulties adjusting to life outside of prison. Both recognized that parole had placed high expectations on them. Both thought theses were unrealistic. It was accepted, that by being felons, they couldn't get a fair shake in society. Jordan talked about the distrust of those close to him, and his failure to provide for them.

"Ya see man," Chi Chi spoke. "You and me, we're different. You, it's the good life, ya know. Family, kids, two cars, ya know. But they won't let ya have it. You can't get it. You want dreams. Me man, I no dream. I know I'm goin' die in there, in a cell. So I do my drugs, ya know man. I have my girls and I do this an' a little of that, and maybe they come get me. So maybe man, the next time, you know, is the last time, maybe not. Tomorrow I might be dead man, maybe, maybe not."

Jordan sat quietly. He knew that Chi Chi was right. Throughout his life he had reached for the dream, only to have it snatched away. What the use, he thought. He was losing his family. He tried playing it straight, but soon gave up. He no longer had the desire within him. He no longer felt that spark, the one that embraced him when he first met Lizzie, the one that warmed him to the bone when he first saw his son. It was gone and, as he felt so many times before, he was alone.

"So man, what can I do? What ya want?"

"I," Jordan hesitated. "I need a piece but..."

"But ya have no money."

"Right, I don't have any money."

Chi Chi motioned to one of his soldiers, who quickly went into another room. He returned, with a small handgun and some shells. Chi Chi took these from him and passed it onto Jordan. Jordan, putting the shells in his shirt pocket, began to rock in his seat, cradling the pistol in his hands.

"How much?" Jordan asked. "How can I pay you?"

"*Nada.*" Chi Chi answered. "So ya givin' up dreamin'?"

"I don't know. It's like, right now, I need to feed my family."

"Be careful, *mi amigo*." With that, the two got up and hugged. Chi Chi watched as Jordan walked away. At the door, he turned and nodded as to say thanks. Jordan wasn't sure why he was being so grateful. Having never handled a gun before, he was afraid that this would be his undoing. Yet, that was a chance he was willing to take.

Chapter 17

Wood had just begun reading *The Barfly Boys*, a novel he recently purchased for ten cents at a used bookstore. The book by John D. Wells, a fairly unknown writer, was about a rock group's struggles in the music business, complicated by one of its member's decline into mental illness. The drummer Todd's adventures with drugs and schizophrenia convinced him that MTV was sending out messages to him from the *Book of Revelations*.

Wood particularly liked how Wells drew from the movie *Barfly*. Starring Mickey Rourke, the movie was based on the life of another writer, although much more famous than Wells, Charles Bukowski. In the book, as well in the movie, the characters never wanted to do real work in any sense. Parodying Bukowski's litany of jobs he had no desire to do, the band members would pick an occupation they didn't want to be for the day. Thus, in their game, the question "Who are you not going to be today?" was heard across the barroom floor. It was often answered by the likes of "I'm not going to be a fireman today" or "Today I'm not going to be an accountant". In a salute to both authors Wood, a barfly in his own right, decided not to be a child welfare worker for the day, on second thought, ever.

Well into the second chapter, Wood was interrupted by his phone ringing. Finishing the paragraph he was reading, he allowed the phone to ring several times, before he reluctantly answered. "Hello."

"Oh yes, hello," A faint, but familiar voice, replied. It was one he heard almost daily when he taught at the college. Most calls were quite insignificant, such as the dean requesting copies of his class handouts. He last heard the voice the day before he abruptly walked out of his classroom, never to return again. But that was years ago. Recently, the calls have resurfaced around the unpleasant exploits of Dr. Lap. "This is Michelle from Dean Trudy's office. Is this..."

"Yes, yea it's, I mean, yea it's me." It had been several weeks since Dr. Lap left. He had intended to turn himself in, and attend his court hearing. Wood knew that Dr. Lap's bond would be revoked. Thus, he did not expect to hear from him, believing Dr. Lap would be jailed until his trial. He had hoped that someone, preferably Dean Trudy, would call with an update on Dr. Lap's status. Yet, in his gut, he knew that the news wouldn't be pleasant.

"I have Dean Trudy here. He would like to speak with you. Please hold." Michelle instructed.

There was a frozen pause before the voice of Dean Trudy broke through. "Hey Wood, hello, how are you doing?"

"Well, I'm doing. Guess you can say I'm doing just fine."

"Good, good, glad to hear that." Dean Trudy hesitated, attempting to keep the conversation light. Yet, there was urgency in his voice. Wood sensed the dean straining as he continued. "Haven't changed your mind about wanting to come back, have you?"

"No, no, not the slightest, haven't even given it a thought." Wood had been at the college for several years teaching in the Sociology Department. While there, he was making a name for himself, not only among the professionals within his discipline, but also in the community. One of his achievements was receiving grant money and developing an Associate Arts Program for inmates at the regional state prison. It was widely rumored that he would be appointed chair of his department, as a primer for him to eventually become Dean of the Faculty. Then Becca died. All mechanisms for coping failed. Wood fell into a deep depression, resorting to drug and alcohol binges. Often hung over, he began going to his classes late, if, or when, he decided to show up at all. Finally in the midst of a lecture he, without reason, walked out of his classroom never to return again.

"Well," Dean Trudy again hesitated. "If, you know, reconsider, there's a place for you here. You were a good teacher, got a lot of respect."

"Well, that's in retrospect. But you know, back then, in the heat of it, ya'll were glad to get rid of me. We both knew I was a mess."

"Yea, that's true to a certain extent." Dean Trudy continued. "But you were a fighter. I liked that. It's, well, the circumstances around your leaving were so tragic. I was willing to stick with you. I'm sure we would have worked it out."

"Thanks." Wood responded, not wanting to justify his past.

"So, how's the weather up there?" Dean Trudy continued in his avoidance. "Down here we've been having a lot of rain. And you can imagine how dreary that makes..."

"Dean," Wood impatiently cut him short. Rainfall and Wood's ancient history weren't Dean Trudy's intended topics of discussion. Whatever the dean was avoiding was most disquieting. Wood, fearing that Dr. Lap may have disappeared again, or worse, he was hurt, was impatient. "Dean please, we both know neither the weather, nor my teaching again, is the reason for your call. I mean, is he alright? Did something happen?"

"Oh my, this is really difficult." Dean Trudy softly replied. "Well, you know he did come back and turned himself in. Although they initially revoked his bond, well, I spoke up for him, you know, to get him out of jail. And the judge, well, reluctantly released him to me. Read to both of us the riot act, you know what I mean. But, anyway, at the hearing he admitted to it, you know, pled guilty."

"I'm surprised by that," Wood replied. "I mean, when he was here, I didn't think he would admit to doing anything wrong. He actually tried to justify it to me, but I wasn't buying. I don't know if he said anything to you, but when he left here, I was really pissed off and let him know it."

"Jesus no, he didn't. When I saw him he was really despondent and we didn't have much time to talk." Dean Trudy continued. "But you know, He did say something strange at the hearing. It was something like, I guess, he was admitting to being a pedophile. Then he mumbled something about not waiting or he should have waited for her to be legal. It didn't make sense, at least not to me. So, anyway, they set a date for sentencing. I think he was hoping for probation but I think he knew he was going to prison."

"I kinda know what he was talking about." Wood answered, remembering the rainy morning conversation he had with Dr. Lap. "So, is he in jail?"

"No, no, they did let him back out on bond, you know house arrest, and he was being fitted for an ankle monitor. But," Dean Trudy was obvious struggling. His voice quivered as he was having difficulties conveying his thoughts. "Oh my, this is so disheartening, and you know he did name you as next of kin and..."

—

Dean Trudy shuddered, thinking of the call from the police, requesting he meet with them at Dr. Lap's home. He was in his office, finalizing the schedule of class offerings for the new term, when his phone rang. It was Detective Vonadore, the police officer whom had initially investigated Dr. Lap's involvement with the student Susanne. Dean Trudy was advised that Dr. Lap had been scheduled to meet with a probation officer. He failed to do so. Detective Vanadore explained that, in addition, Dr. Lap failed to respond to phone calls made over a period of two days. The officer, having no choice but to arrest Dr. Lap, asked Dean Trudy to meet him at Dr. Lap's home. Dean Trudy agreed to be there within the hour.

Unsure of what the police expected of him, Dean Trudy quickly drove to Dr. Lap's home, hoping to meet with him before Detective Vonadore arrived. Turning onto Dr. Lap's street, Dean Trudy was taken aback by the sheer number of police cars outside of the house. Most disconcerting was the ambulance, parked on the front lawn, it rear door swung open and two attendants unloading a stretcher. At first, he speculated that Dr. Lap resisted and got hurt, perhaps shot in the process. Yet, he feared the worst, Dr. Lap harming himself.

Dean Trudy quickly parked behind one of the police cars. Exiting from his car, he swiftly walked toward the house, leaving the car door opened. As he approached the front porch, a uniformed officer blocked his path. Although Dean Trudy had advised him of the call from Detective Vonadore, the officer was reluctant in allowing the dean to enter the home until another detective, recognizing Dean Trudy from the court hearing, waved him in.

Passing through the foyer, Dean Trudy entered the living room. He was quickly overwhelmed by the brightness of the lights, and the number of officers going through Dr. Lap's personal items. One officer, slightly overweight with thinning grey hair, flipped through a collection of phonographs, occasionally commenting to a fellow officer. A younger one, perhaps in his early twenties, standing by the bay window, leafed through a stack of mail.

To the right of the living room, was the entrance to Dr. Lap's home office. Inside, along the far wall stood Detective Vonadore, and another officer, next to an oak and glass trophy case. Approaching the officers, Dean Trudy, peering into the case, was startled but what he saw. Dr. Lap had lined the shelves with photographs of himself, each with a different coed. "Oh my God!" he exclaimed, taking a step back.

"Fuckin' predator," replied the officer standing with Detective Vonadore. "There must be over twenty pictures in there."

Ignoring the comment, Dean Trudy turned toward Detective Vonadore. "Where is he?"

"You really don't want to see this."

Why, what's wrong?"

"It's not a pretty sight."

Dean Trudy hesitated before answering. "Yes I do," speaking firmly. "Besides, it was you who called me here."

"Yea, I did but when I called, ya know, this wasn't what I expected, damn." Detective Vonadore acquiesced to the dean. "But, like I said, it ain't pretty."

Detective Vonadore led Dean Trudy down a short hallway lined with shelves of books. Stepping around a stretcher, left outside the bathroom door, the dean observed several flashes coming from inside the room. As they approached, an officer, holding a camera, stepped out and to the side, allowing the dean and the detective to enter the room. Dean Trudy's stomach began to tighten as he turned into the room. Seeing the scene laid out before him, vomit, like a rising flame, crept up his throat. Briefly closing his eyes, he controlled the gagging and refocused.

The bathroom was dim, illuminated solely by candles, one place at each corner of the tub. Soft jazz emanated from a radio, sitting on the floor below the tub. In a pool of blood tinted water, rested Dr. Lap, facing the doorway, both wrists slashed, hanging at his sides. On his face, a calm smile radiated a sense of relief, perhaps a release from his burdens. The shiver in Dean Trudy's spine began to recede. For a split second, he empathized with Dr. Lap, momentarily absorbing his calmness.

"We found a bottle of pills near the tub." Detective Vonadore said, breaking the silence. "Pain pills, seems like he didn't take enough to cause his death, but perhaps just enough to ease the pain of cutting himself."

"Did you find a note, anything?" Dean Trudy solemnly asked.

"No not yet." Detective Vonadore replied. "I'm sure there is one. In these cases rarely is there not one. But ya know, I think we all know why he did it."

"Yea, maybe," Dean Trudy answered. Feeling the sickness in his stomach again, Dean Trudy started to turn away. "I need to get out of here."

Placing his hand on the dean's shoulder Detective Vonadore offered his condolences. "Sorry Dean, I didn't expect all this. I mean, I called ya because I thought ya help getting him to give up. I never thought he'd kill himself, never thought we'd walk into this. I'm really sorry."

"That's okay." Dean Trudy mumbled, walking out the door.

—

"What in hell, Dean," Wood said, breaking into Dean Trudy's hesitation. "You were telling me something. What is it?!"

"Oh, I'm so sorry but Dr. Lap is dead. He..."

"Fuck, no, he can't be. What, how?"

Dean Trudy continued. "I'm so sorry. I know you two were so close. But, oh my, he killed himself. He committed suicide."

Tightness grew in Wood's chest, seizing his breath. Losing his balance, he fell back onto his chair. In spite of all of his failings, Dr. Lap was his best friend. That one fact he could not let go. Sure, Dr. Lap had his problems. Wood had been confident he would serve his time and get the help needed. Suicide was not part of that plan. At least, that's how Wood saw it. Tears slowly rolled down his cheek. It frightened him, not knowing if he was crying for his dead friend, or for his own sense of emptiness.

"Wood, are you still with me?" Dean Trudy's voice broke through the phone line.

"Yea, I'm here." Wood answered, choking back his tears.

"I'm so sorry. I know the two of you go back a long way." Speaking sympathetically, Dean Trudy described how he was called to the home by the investigating officer. Dr. Lap, failing to report to his probation officer and failing to follow the conditions of his release, was to be arrested. He gave the details on how Dr. Lap was found, his use of pain medication, and the slicing of his wrist. Although he omitted seeing the trophy case filled with photographs of coeds, he did detail how impersonal the officers were as they rifled through Dr. Lap's personal belongings. Finally, he spoke about how physically upset he became.

"You know, when I last saw him, he talked about suicide." Wood said, thinking of the afternoon they spent in Paci's. "Although he denied wanting to kill himself, he did say if he were to do it, he would do it right, whatever that was supposed to mean. I guess we now know. I mean, he did it. He succeeded."

"It's so sad. I had never expected this." Dean Trudy replied. "Well, the police let me have his address book, so I guess I should contact his family, unless you want to."

"No, that's okay. I really can't do it. Besides shouldn't the police call them?"

"You may be right, but, oh I don't know. I'll call Detective Vonadore, get his thoughts. But I still need to send my condolences."

"I think you should, talk with the police that is, as well as offer your condolences. Anyway, thanks for calling." Wood sighed. "It's difficult, for me it is, and I know it's difficult for you as well."

"Thanks Wood, I never had one of my people commit suicide before. After a lifetime in education, this is a first. Anyway, I need to take care of some business. Let's talk again. And, if there's anything I can do please let me know."

"Dean," Wood spoke.

"Yes?"

"Maybe there is something."

"Sure anything," Dean Trudy responded inquisitively.

"Well, I'm thinking about relocating. Nothing firm at this time, but my brother had owned a farm in Missouri. On it, there's this old farmhouse my sister-in-law offered to me. You know, fix it up and live there. I think my brother wanted me to move up there before he died but, you know, too much history between us. Anyway, I'm considering it."

"That sounds like a good idea." The dean replied, and then jokingly added, "I'm not sure how I can help. I mean, a fix 'er upper, I'm not even sure of what end I'm to hold a hammer."

Thanks Dean, I needed that." Wood laughed. "Anyway, financially I'm okay, but I do want to keep myself busy, aside of working on the house. So, I thought that I might want to teach a class or two. You know, try to do some adjunct work. Well, there's this small religious school just outside St. Joseph, Missouri."

"Why yes, you mean the Presbyterian school, Tacoma College." Dean Trudy exclaimed. "That is such beautiful country, tornado country, but very pretty."

"Yes, that's the school." Wood replied. "Do you know it?"

"Talking about six degrees of separation," Dean Trudy exclaimed. "I have a connection there. Actually, he's the one who replaced you when you left." Wood, leaving the college in the way he had, placed the dean in a very difficult position. Getting a replacement, several weeks into the semester, was no easy task. Luckily, Dean Trudy was able to get a doctorial student to step in. After completing his graduate work, Bobby Sessions continued teaching at the college, until the position at Tacoma opened. It was upon Dean Trudy's recommendation, he was hired.

"You're kidding me."

"No, no, I wouldn't do that. I don't know if you know Bobby Sessions, but he's the Chairperson for the Social Science Department there. He's a good man."

"Yea, I have heard of him. We never met, but Dr. Lap mentioned him a few times." Wood was hesitant. He did leave his classes in a mess with tests ungraded, grade book incomplete, and no resemblance of completed lesson plans. Anyone taking over would be angry. "Do you think, maybe...?"

Dean Trudy, interrupting Wood, said, "Look, there won't be a problem. Bobby knows what happened, and he won't hold it against you. Whenever you're ready, just let me know. I'm sure we can set you up."

"Thanks Dean, I'm sure it will be appreciated. I need just a little time. I need to talk with my sister-in-law about the farm. Then this friend of mine, haven't talked to her yet. But, I would like for her to come with me."

"Don't tell me, you're getting married?"

"Oh no," Wood quickly responded. "I don't think there will be a marriage, living together, I hope. That's if she is willing."

"Well, good luck. Hope to hear from you soon."

"I'll be in touch." Wood softly said, hanging up the phone.

Chapter 18

Several spectators gathered at Belmont Lake to watch the city's Parks and Recreation Department remove the remains of the fallen weeping willow tree. The tree, standing alone on a tiny island, had been adorned by many generations of visitors. It was the park's identity. Poems were written about it, and the tree served as a backdrop for numerous wedding photographs. It was a sad day felt by all, when a violent storm uprooted the ancient soldier. Stripped of its pride, the willow laid on its side, its branches bleeding memories into the water.

Wood, perched on the back of a bench, sat scrutinizing the tree's removal. Across from him, on the island, two men in their early twenties were busy slicing through the branches with chainsaws. Three others, older, were standing around, hands in pockets, supervising the work. One of them, dressed in a tan suit and chomping on a stogie, was Chas Bueno. Following in his father's political footsteps Chas, supported by the Garibaldi Avenue Social Club, had been elected mayor. To show his appreciation for the club's endorsement, several of its members were awarded with political appointments and no show jobs.

Across the lake, in a beach chair, sat Carlo "Fingers" DeMarco, one of the recipients, chatting with several other city employees. Fingers, an ex-cop, had an affliction for the horses. It was rumored he was fired from the Police Department, for stealing from its petty cash to support his gambling addiction. He owed a lot of money, most of it to the bookies out of Garibaldi Avenue. Not wanting to lose his account, the club had Chas appoint him to head the Parks and Recreation Department. It was widely believed that a large cut of his salary goes directly to the club.

Growing tired of the demolition, and speculating on the inner workings of city politics, Wood decided to leave. As he stepped from the bench, Wood spotted Four-Thirty, dressed in faded jeans and an oversized yellow tee shirt, walking up the gravel pathway. Printed across the front of her shirt, the words "Forever Young", gently dance to the rhythm of her uneven gait. Retreating back to his seat, Wood watched as she approached.

"Hey," Four-Thirty said, pulling herself up next to Wood. Reaching down, Wood gently grasped Four-Thirty's elbow, assisting her onto the bench. He gave her a warm smile as she positioned herself on the top rail next to him. Lifting her face toward the sun, she continued. "Boy, those rays sure feel good today."

"Yea, it has turned out to be a nice day."

"So," Four-Thirty, placing her hand on Wood's, asked, "What you been up too?"

"Not much," Wood replied, continuing to stare across the lake. "You know just thinking, and watching the action." A bead of perspiration across Wood's forehead eased along the bridge of his nose. With the tail of his shirt he reached up, wiping it dry. "Must say, I'm gonna miss that old tree."

Four-Thirty laughed, pointing across the lake. "Look at Fingers over there." Getting up from his beach chair, Fingers walked over to one of the city's dump trucks. On the tailgate sat a cooler. Reaching in, Fingers pulled out two cans of beer. One he flipped to a coworker, the other he opened, taking a long gulp from it. Stepping back to his chair, he eased down in it, reclining with his shirt opened to the sun.

"Yea," Wood said, shaking his head in disbelief. "I guess that's your tax dollars well spent. And Chas, he ain't much better. Look at him out there, throwing his freaking weight around. Just like his dad."

On the island, the two workers, finished with the cutting of the dead tree, were stacking the wood onto a small barge, attached to a motorboat. Chas, sitting in the boat, demanded that the workers hurry and return to the shoreline. One of the men, in his rush, fell off the craft splashing water on Chas. Furiously he threw his stogie at the worker. As the fallen laborer desperately tried to get back onto the boat, Chas stepped on the worker's shoulder, pushing him back into the water. His voice, in its usual bravado, floated loudly across the lake. "You can fuckin' swim, you guinea bastard."

"Asshole," Wood whispered.

"Yea," answered Four-Thirty.

Reaching shore, Chas was helped out of the boat by Fingers. Several of the others assisted in securing the load of wood to the land, while the second laborer disconnected the boat from the barge. Turning the craft around, he headed back to pick up his companion.

"Where the fuck ya goin'?" Chas yelled out. "He could fuckin' swim, I said."

Chas was ignored. The boat continued to the island. Having taken off his wet shirt, the young worker stood waiting, the garment draped around his neck and tanned chest.

Becoming more agitated, Chas called out again, "Get back here. If, if you don't. I mean it, you're fuckin' fired."

From the boat, the worker turned to Chas, quietly giving him his middle finger. Joining in his friend's defiance toward their boss, the mayor, the other yelled out to Chas, "Fucka you."

"Oh no," Wood said to Four-Thirty. "I think those two are headed for some real trouble."

"I don't know about that. I've seen them around." Four-Thirty responded. "I've seen them with Streaky Latonia, you know, at the club. I understand he's their uncle. It might be that Chas is the one asking for trouble."

It was Streaky's father and grandfather, who established the Garibaldi Avenue Social Club. In doing so, they organized the community, bringing to it political muscle. Eventually, the club's influence spread throughout the town. As it had been from its beginnings, all town business, political or otherwise, passed through the club, and it was always a Latonia who had the last word.

"Yea, I guess you are right on that one." Wood conceded.

—

Wood and Four-Thirty sat quietly as the commotion from across the lake began to recede. Wood slipped his hand over Four-Thirty's. Smiling, she leaned her head on his shoulder as the warmth of affection flowed through her. There was a pleasurable stillness in the air, occasionally punctured by the chirping of a bird, or a child laughing at play.

"Look!" Wood instructed Four-Thirty. To their left, a toddler, with short blonde curls and in a pale blue dress, began to scream, calling for her father. Fishing with a toy rod, she hooked a fish. In her excitement the child, her father rushing to assist her, dropped her line into the water. Retrieving it he, with his daughter bouncing on his knee, reeled in her catch.

"Me hold Daddy, me hold Daddy." She squealed as he unhooked the small blue gill. Unable to clutch it in her tiny hands, the fish fell. Trying to snatch it off the ground, the fish again slipped from her grasp, flipping into the water. Not to be deterred, she reached for the rod, taking it from her father's hands, "More Daddy, me fish more."

"Girls are so cute when they're little." Four-Thirty softly said. "I remember when Oria was that age. But, boy do they grow up fast."

"Did you bring her here a lot?"

"Yea, some," Four-Thirty quietly answered. "But, back in those days being a single mom, people frowned upon it, you know. So I took her to a park up in Montclair for awhile. People didn't know us there. But then, as she got older, you know, starting school and such, she wanted to be near her friends. So, I sucked up to all those evil eyes and brought her here."

"Times have changed about single mothers. Unfortunately for you, it just wasn't soon enough."

"Well," Four-Thirty reflected. "I did the best I could. I know, when she was young, I did her right. I'm not so sure I can say that about the two of us now."

"Still butting heads over that Dennis fiasco?"

"You know," Four-Thirty's body stiffened. She pulled away from Wood. The anger in her voice rattled Wood. "He could have just, shit, I just don't know."

—

Dennis Slovinski had gone to school with both Wood and Four-Thirty. Although they knew of each other, often crossing paths at school and The Hut, they were never close. Living in another part of town, Dennis ran with a different crowd. It wasn't until several years later, when Dennis and Four-Thirty began a relationship. Having grown tired of his wife, he sought out Four-Thirty for her services.

When first employed as a county supervisor, Dennis occasionally met with Four-Thirty for lunch and oral sex. As his job responsibilities expanded he frequently had to leave town to attend business meetings and conferences. Four-Thirty often accompanied him on these excursions. He made it easy for her. His only expectation, she was to be in his hotel suite, ready for him, after he spent the night in the hotel bar, drinking with the boys. During these trysts, Dennis would often brag about his influence within county government, promising Four-Thirty that he could use this influence to help her, if need be.

It was a mistake. Four-Thirty should have known not to trust Dennis. She should have known not to involve her family with her business associates. But she didn't. She tried to help Oria, who had recently finished graduate school, and desperately needed to find work. With its salary and benefits, county employment was highly attractive. Counting on what she thought was a promise made, she turned to Dennis who agreed to meet with Oria.

The sun was shining brightly, as it had all day, when Oria entered the county court building, for her five-fifteen appointment with Dennis Slovinski. An aura of confidence radiated from her. Dressed in a light grey suit and white blouse, Oria loosely fitted a wine red scarf around her neck to serve as an accent. Reaching the fourth floor office suite, she paused for a moment. Oria, lightly tugging at the front of her jacket, took a measured breath before opening the door.

To the right of the entrance an older woman, dressed in a dark green polyester suit, was standing behind a metal desk, locking a file cabinet. Placing the key in a small plastic handbag, she turned toward the door. Seeing Oria she stopped.

Politely, Oria reach out her hand, "Good afternoon, I'm Oria Visconti."

Ignoring the gesture, the woman gave Oria a look of disdain. Picking up a manila envelope off the top of the desk, the secretary once again turned toward the door.

"But, I have an appointment."

"Have a seat over there," pointing to several chairs along the wall on the left. "Mr. Slovinski will be with you in a moment." She added, loudly closing the door behind her.

Oria waited for a little over twenty minutes, before Dennis emerged from his inner office. "You must be Oreo." mispronouncing her name, he directed her into his office. "Have a seat."

She sat in a black leather chair, across from Dennis' massive mahogany desk. "It's Oria, Oria Visconti."

Once seated behind his desk, Dennis rolled up the sleeves of his heavily starched shirt. His tie, adorned with a picture of Marilyn Monroe, hung below the opened top button. "So it is Ms. Visconti. I see your mom gave you your father's name."

"Yes."

"I knew your dad." Dennis leaned back in his chair, peering out his window. The descending sun, streaking through half opened blinds, fell like zebra stripes across his dark blue shirt. "Yea, I knew him. Remember when he died. Sure in hell left your mom in a pickle. Well, what could you expect, you know, fuckin' junkie, still had the needle in his arm."

What the…" Oria was shocked. A frozen stare spread in the air between them, like ice on the Arctic plain. She knew her father had his problems. Her mom was very opened about his drug addiction and eventual overdose. No one had the right to speak about her father like this. She was angry. Controlling that fury, she bit hard, nearly causing her tongue to bleed. She needed a job. For the time being, she decided it was best to play the game his way.

"Your mom," Dennis leaned further back on the chair, placing his feet on top of the desk. "She did what she had to do, know what I mean. Yea, being crippled and all that, she did what she had to do." He said in a condescending tone that didn't sit well with Oria.

"My mom, I know she worked hard. There were times I wished she was home more, but she did her best by me."

"She was good at it." Dennis hesitated, a smile spreading across his face. "Yea, she was good. Never let that twisted leg stop her."

Oria's back stiffened, she was unsure of Dennis' insinuation. "Am I missing something here?"

Dennis ignored the question. He slowly lifted from his chair, walking around the desk he sat on its edge, facing Oria. "So your mom sent you thinking I can help you find a job. Am I right?"

"Well," Oria said, shifting uncomfortably in her seat. "Yes, she thought that you might be able to give me some advice, or maybe refer me to someone." Detailing her educational resume, Oria continued. "Well you know my mom made sure I had a good start by sending me to the local Catholic high school, Saint Mary's. As you know, it has a great reputation. After high school, I received some scholarship money and enrolled in…"

"You know your mom use to work for me." Dennis, disinterested, cut her off. He walked toward the window, briefly looking out, before closing the blinds. "Yea, I think you can say that, part time." He, hesitating momentarily, removed his tie before continuing. "Maybe you can say we had a contract."

Turning to face Dennis, "I don't understand. She never spoke…"

"Let's put it this way." Oria was interrupted again. "She working for me, it was not in the conventional sense. Catch my drift? Well that doesn't matter anymore." Stepping away from the window, Dennis stepped toward Oria, still sitting across from his desk. "You see, the bitch quit on me. No one quits on me. That was her first mistake. Her fuckin' second, thinking that I would now help you out."

Threatened, Oria rose quickly from the chair, only to be pushed back. Holding her down with one hand, Dennis slowly unzipped his pants with the other. "You know, maybe, yea maybe I can do something for you. Or, you can do something for me, like your mom did."

"What the fuck?" Oria squeezed out from under his weight, leaving Dennis, standing with his penis in his hand. "I don't know what you're thinking. But this, this is wrong."

"What, do I have to pay you, you know, like I did with that crippled bitch?" Dennis snickered.

Swinging her bag over her left shoulder, Oria turned to leave. Behind her, Dennis continued laughing. Reaching the exit, she stopped. Angry tears trickled down her cheek as she took a deep breath. She was confused. Her mother, nothing more than a prostitute, is that what he was saying? Selling her sex to trash like this, is that what she did?

Oria wanted to hide. Instead, she turned back toward Dennis. With a clinched fist, she swung, landing with a crunch just below his left ear. Intense pain rushed up her arm, her hand shattering on his jaw. "Fuck," she spat out trying to shake the pain out of her hand. "Fuck you, you squirmy bastard."

The following day, Oria read in the newspaper Dennis Slovinski had a broken jaw. His story was that he fell, tripping over a chair in his office. This she could live with, could laugh about. In the end she got the upper hand, although broken. Still, she needed time off. Angry with her mother, Oria moved out, temporarily living with her friend

Joanie. She needed the space to figure out who this woman was, that she called mom.

Although upset about being lied to throughout her life, Oria admitted she had some suspicions about her mother's lifestyle. She wasn't immune to all the whispering and innuendos made by her schoolmates and neighbors. Nor was she able to deny the comments made by her grandmother with whom, as a child, she was left for days, while Four-Thirty went on her dates. It was just that none of what she heard was so open, so direct.

—

"I'm scared," Four-Thirty confessed to Wood. "I have lost one child. I cannot survive losing another. No, I can't."

Reaching over, Wood placed his hand on the back of Four-Thirty's neck. Trying to ease her apprehension, he tenderly massaged her muscles. "I don't know. I mean, do you really think it's that bad? Aren't you guys talking?"

"Kinda," Four-Thirty answered. "She did call the other day, to see how I'm doing. But we're not speaking. You know what I mean? Everything is superficial. It's like we're both walking on glass."

"I'm sure you two will work it out." Wood gave Four-Thirty a reassuring hug as he continued, "She knows who you are and what you have been to her all these years. A child never forgets. She'll remember the warmth, the caring, the good times. She knows the real you." Wood lightly kissed Four-Thirty on her forehead. "She'll be back."

"I hope you're right." Four-Thirty sullenly replied.

Four-Thirty and Wood recoiled into silence as the sun drifted behind the tall maple trees on the far side of the lake. Although it was little more than an hour until sunset, people were beginning to vacate the park. Chas, Fingers, and their crew had long ago packed up and left. The two laborers from the island had done so as well. Finally, bored with fishing, the toddler in the pale blue dress, briefly joined a few playmates at the swing set, before her young father called it a day. Of those that remained were a few high school athletes tossing a football, a young couple sharing a bench not far from Wood and Four-Thirty, and a gentleman quietly fishing near the dam.

"Wood," Four-Thirty began, struggling with her words. It was a question she had longed to ask, but afraid of the answer. Her voice in a weak cadence, she continued. "Do you know anything about my father, like what happened to him?"

"Christ," Wood murmured, slipping his arm off Four-Thirty's shoulder. "We were so young when all that happened."

"But," Four-Thirty eased away from Wood's side. Turning, she looked into his eyes, pressing him for an answer. "You do know something, don't you? I mean, the way people treated us when he left, how they changed, how you changed. You have…"

Pressing a finger to her lips, Wood, seeing that she was agitated, tried to calm her, put her at ease. "Like I said, we were quite young. I mean, it's not like I was told about what happened, but I do remember what I overheard."

"Please, I need, want to know."

Wood remembered that evening when Lucia first spoke of the sexual abuse of Four-Thirty by her father. Frustrated with Wood teasing her while they sat at the dinner table, Lucia blurted out what she knew to be a secret, one she shared with Casey, Four-Thirty's younger brother. Lucia, in her innocence, was only trying to one-up Wood. Little did she know the impact that her little "Ha, ha I know something you don't know," would have on her closest friend.

"Wood, you knew about that, about my father, me?"

"No, not really," Wood answered. "It's more like I knew that he did something, something sexual, something bad. But what, I didn't know, never really knew."

"But," Four-Thirty questioned. "You never mentioned it, never asked. Why?"

"I'm not sure. It just wasn't my place, I guess." Letting out a deep sigh, Wood continued, "I think my father was most upset by it. You know, you and Lucia were good friends and she did spend a lot of time at your house. I don't know, maybe he was afraid that your father might be doing something to her."

Wood turned to face Four-Thirty. He saw uneasiness in her eyes. She, shaking her head as if to say "no", knew that her father had not touched Lucia. Yet, she wasn't so sure he hadn't thought about it or, if given the opportunity, he would have done so.

"You know," Wood continued. "I wish I could tell you something different. I wish that things were different. But you know…" his voice faded.

—

After dinner, Wood's father, upset by Lucia's disclosure of the sexual abuse of Four-Thirty, went to the Garibaldi Avenue Social Club. He needed to unwind, to think, and someone to talk to. It was upsetting. He couldn't comprehend how a parent could harm their child in such a vile way. It was even more upsetting, that Lucia may have been exposed to it. He knew he had to contact the police, but not yet. Thinking that they will do little to nothing, he wanted the bastard to get his due, in the old way.

When he arrived at the Garibaldi Avenue Social Club, the front door was opened, letting some of the night's cool air breeze through the clubhouse. Just past the entrance, on the left, stretched a counter. Behind it, a shelf held several bottles of liqueur and an espresso maker. Rags, a gray haired numbers runner, manned the counter.

"Hey Junior," Rags called out. "You wanna espresso?"

"Sure, anisette on the side," Wood's father answered. Looking around the room, he added, "Hey Rags is my ole' man here?"

"Yea, he'sa playin' cards, backa table."

Rags, reaching behind him, pulled a bottle of *Stock* anisette off the shelf. He first poured a shot for Junior, then one for himself. "To a you health," he said before downing the liqueur.

"And to yours," Junior followed.

Picking up a second shot and his espresso, Junior walked toward the back of the room, where his father was playing poker. Three Chins, obviously named for the fat hanging above his neck, had just finished shuffling and began to deal a game of five card draw. Next to him sat Little Paulie counting his money. Completing the table, were Sacks and Nicky No Neck, known enforcers for the Latonas.

"Hey Pops, your kid is a here." Sacks called out, seeing Junior approach the table.

Looking up, Pops gave a smile, waving to his son, "Junior, *come stai?*"

"*Buono* Pops, *Buono.*" He didn't sound convincing.

As Junior pulled up a chair next to his father, Little Paulie peeked at his hand. Not satisfied, he checked to Sacks on his left. Sacks opened with a bet of two dollars. Pops and Three Chins were in, whereas, Nicky No Neck folded. "Can't catch a break," He complained, throwing his cards on the table.

"So," Pops asked his son. "How'sa work?"

"Good, good I can't complain," Junior answered. "Should be getting a new contract soon, ya know. At least that's what the union is saying."

Holding three queens, Pops drew two cards, an ace and the deuce of clubs. Sacks, who had opened, checked to Pops. He bet two dollars. Three Chins bumped him two more, forcing Little Paulie and Sacks to fold. "I call," answered Pops, throwing a five into the pot, taking out three singles. Three Chins confidently laid down two pairs, kings and tens. Pops smiled, turning over his three queens. "No good 'nough."

Reaching over for his winnings, Pops turned toward Junior, "*La famiglia?*"

"*La famiglia è buona,*" He answered. "But *mia figlia* Lucia, I am worried."

"What'sa wrong? Is she sick?"

"No Pops." Junior took a sip from the espresso, and then placed his cup back on the table. "Actually, it's not her I'm concerned. It's her friend."

"So?"

Letting out a short sigh, Junior continued. "Ya know, she hangs a lot with that little Polish girl, at her house all the time."

"Yea, on the corner, I see'a her there."

"Yea," Little Paulie, beginning to shuffle the deck, interjected, "Seems to be a nice family, ya know, quiet, keep to themselves."

The cards were quickly dealt. Sacks opened with a bet of two dollars. Pops, disgruntled with his hand, folded. Three Chins quietly looked around the table before folding as well. Smiling, Nicky No Neck bumped Sacks another two dollars. Little Paulie picked up four bills and threw them into the pot. "Just to keep youse guys honest."

"So Pops, listen, this kid," Junior, leaning over, whispered to his father, "The old man is doing something to this kid."

"What'sa you mean?"

Sacks drew three cards, whereas, Nicky No Neck and Little Paulie each drew two. Having the bet check to him, Nicky No Neck reopened the bidding, wagering two dollars.

"Pops, I think he's doing some dirty things with her, sexual things."

Little Paulie was in. Sacks snapped his cards with his middle finger several time before bumping the bet another three dollars. Nicky No Neck called, as Little Paulie, lacking confidence in his draw, folded.

Three Chins turned to Junior and began to ask, "You mean the Pole is…"

"What the fuck," Little Paulie exclaimed, interrupting him. "He's doing her? He's sticking it to his own kid?"

Junior leaned back on his chair, "I don't know about that. But, from what I'm hearin', from my kid, he's doing something."

"Lucia, he'sa touch?" Pops anxiously asked.

"I doubt it Pops. I mean, she didn't say anything. I have no proof but, I have my doubts. Like, who's to say he won't try."

"*Mia nipote* Lucia," Pops spoke firmly. "Phew, proof I no care. He'sa, *egli è un pezzo di merda*.

"You're right old man," Sacks joined in. "He's shit."

Three Chins, pushing up from the table, looked around at each player. "Fuck this game. We can pick it up later. Right now," rubbing his fist into his hand, "we need to talk to this bastard."

"Yea," Nicky No Neck said, placing his hand face down on the table and following the others out of the club. "Let's get this sum' a bitch."

—

Like a vise, Four-Thirty's grip on Wood's arm tightened slowly. Her nails sunk steadily into his bare flesh. "Did they kill him? They did, didn't they?" Her lip began to quiver, noticeably slurring her speech, "I mean, fuck, you know I heard…"

"No," Wood interrupted, causing her to loosen her grasp. "Listen, people say things. Doesn't mean what's said is true. I've heard rumors, lots, but none of them were true. My dad, my grandfather they were there and I believe them, not the stories."

"He's alive?" Like cat claws, her nails began to retract.

Wood, gently pulling his arm free, turned to face Four-Thirty. "I don't know if he's alive. How could I, after all these years. I just know that they didn't kill him." Wood timidly exhaled. He knew what he was about to reveal would pain Four-Thirty. But he had no choice. He spoke tentatively. "He just left. I mean, he just got into his car and left."

"What?" Four-Thirty stepped off the bench. She angrily turned away from Wood. "Don't, don't give me that shit. I know he just didn't up and leave us."

Moving to her side, Wood gently placed his hand on Four-Thirty's shoulder. Pushing his hand away, she began to weep. Wood, feeling guilty, wrapped his arm s around her. As she wept, Wood softly caressed the back of her neck. "They did rough him up a little," Wood began. "At first, they were just going to talk to him, but he was so arrogant.

I mean, he was saying shit like 'she's my kid I'll do what I want with her' and 'no guinea bastard was going to tell me what to do'. You know things like that. So a couple of the guys gave him a beating."

"So, they did hurt him."

"Yea, but when they let him up, he just laughed at them. He laughed, and walked away, saying something about being tired of taking care of a family. When he got into his car he yelled back 'They're yours now' and drove off."

Looking up into Wood's eyes, Four-Thirty asked, "You mean, he just gave up on us?"

"Seems that way," Wood quickly answered. After a brief moment he added. "I guess for you it was for the best."

Pressing closer into Wood, Four-Thirty silently cried. She felt his heart beat peacefully as she put her head onto his chest. A single tear rolled down her check. Slowly, it flowed around the edge of her mouth. She licked the moisture from her lip, tasting its saltiness.

"For the longest, I felt that he left because of me," She confessed. "You know, I thought, because I wasn't right, like, because my body was so fucked up. Never did I think it was about what he was doing to me. Hell I, at least then, didn't even know what he was doing was wrong."

"So sorry," Wood whispered.

"No, no don't be sorry," she replied. "Too bad we didn't have 'good touch, bad touch' when we were in school. Maybe I've would have known. Then again, who knows? I was so caught up in blaming myself, you know, for my paralysis. I would have blamed myself for that too."

Pulling away from Wood's chest, Four-Thirty took hold of his hand leading back to the bench. She sat, drawing him to her side. "Let's just sit for a while longer, please."

"Sure," Wood replied as Four-Thirty placed her head against his shoulder.

Chapter 19

The sun had set, letting the darkness slowly creep in on a cool evening breeze. A series of lampposts, illuminating the pathway circling the lake, shed the only visible light. A lone watchman patiently strolled through the park, making his rounds. As he approached Wood and Four-Thirty, he veered from his course heading toward the bench, where they were seated. Stopping within a few feet from them he, flashing his penlight on the couple, offered a greeting, "Howdy folks."

"Hi," they both responded in unison.

"Ya'll doin' okay?"

"Yea," Wood, hand held up, shielding his eyes from the light, answered. "We just sitting here, enjoying the stillness."

"It is a nice evenin'." Turning off his light, the watchman gently kicked into the dirt with the toe of his shoe. "Don't want to be no killjoy, ya know, but the park does close at sundown."

"Sure, we'll move on." Wood pushed up from the bench, extending his hand to assist Four-Thirty.

"No, no there's no rush. Ya'll can sit a little while longer if you like. Just glad ya'll were no teenagers or some bum lookin' for a place to sleep or sumthin'."

"Thanks," Four-Thirty answered as Wood returned to the bench. "I think my bed back home is a little more comfortable." She added laughing.

"Yea I guess so. Anyway, ya'll have a good night now." Waving, the watchman walked back to the path to continue with his rounds.

"Damn," Four-Thirty exclaimed, "seems like we've been here most of the day."

"I know I have, been here since noon."

"You're kidding me. Why?"

"Don't know," Wood answered. "I guess I was taking time to think, making sure I'm making the right decision."

"I don't understand." Four-Thirty could only speculate as to what was troubling Wood. Perhaps, she thought, it had something to do with Dr. Lap's suicide. Yet, whenever she previously tried to speak to Wood about his closest friend, he acted detached, as though it didn't concern him, as if the suicide existed outside his reality.

"You know," Wood began, not making eye contact with Four-Thirty. "For the longest I've been numb, lifeless, lost. I don't know, I guess kinda, so says the poet in me, like an empty bottle floating aimlessly on the ocean."

"Anything to do with Dr. Lap?"

"Well, that's part of it but," pausing to gather his thoughts Wood took a deep breath. "You know, I really don't understand it. He was my best friend and I just turned on him. I mean, there's no question, what he did was wrong. I think he just wanted someone to listen, you know, just a little emotional support. Instead, I turned my back on him, called him a pedophile, and walked away."

Not wanting to sound callous he momentarily fell into silence. It had been less than a week since Dean Trudy had called him with the news of Dr. Lap's suicide. Despite the initial shock of hearing of his friend's death, Wood quickly reverted back into his customary state of emotional freeze. Attending the funeral, or participating in any memorial service, he would not even consider. Thinking back to how he disconnected his phone, avoiding any further intrusions concerning Dr. Lap, Wood conceded, he was callous. "It's just I simply don't have any feelings."

"I don't…"

"No, no listen," Wood interrupted Four-Thirty. "It's all my fault. Ages ago, it was my decision. When Becca and the baby died, I was in so much pain I just, I just. Oh, fuck. I just didn't want to feel any more."

Patting his leg caringly, Four-Thirty wanted to reassure him, wanted him to know that she understood. Hadn't she done the same? When she first began to sell herself, didn't she withdraw so far into herself that the dicks she sucked, the men she fucked, were so removed that they might as well not have existed? Then, there were the beatings by Deadeye, she knew of no other way she could have survived. Yes, she was able to empathize. She, for her own reasons, was no different.

"Please listen. I have to get this off my chest."

"Sure."

"After Becca died I took some time off, you know, to mourn, to try to make some sense of it all. Instead, I just isolated myself, getting drunk and taking any drug I could get my hands on. But I just couldn't kill the pain, couldn't end the agony."

—

It was a Tuesday afternoon, the day after the fall semester ended, when Dr. Lap found Wood passed out on his rear deck. Like his colleagues and their students, Dr. Lap had made plans to go on a break before the next term started. Prior to leaving, he decided to visit Wood.

Dr. Lap knew of Wood's binges, didn't think the time he had taken off was beneficial, and had decided to talk Wood into returning to teaching. He expected some resistance. What he didn't expect, was finding his friend, out cold hugging an empty wine jug, dressed only in a strap tee-shirt and torn Bermuda shorts.

"Shit," Dr. Lap exclaimed, maneuvering Wood into a sitting position on a wooden patio chair. "Man, you stink. Don't you bathe anymore?"

A low moan regurgitated from Wood, his head snapping back

against the wooden slats, and then, falling forward with his chin against his chest. In spite of Wood's resistance, Dr. Lap was able to pull the jug of wine from his tightening grip. Opening one eye slowly Wood, recognizing Dr. Lap, gave a weak smile. That was short lived. He once again fell into a stupor with mouth opened and drool creeping down the side of his chin.

It had become glaringly obvious, the time off had been utterly detrimental for Wood. It was equally obvious a return to teaching would offer the distraction he sorely needed. Yet, the crucial task at hand was restoring Wood to some level of normalcy. To do so, Dr. Lap resorted to the cliché, the proverbial pot of hot coffee and cold shower. The heavy dose of caffeine and shower proved to be of some value. Wood, having regained an acceptable level of consciousness, was ready for some solid food.

Dr. Lap took Wood to the Pathway Diner, a short drive from his home. Although it was dinner time, the diner was not crowded and the noise level was minimal. Nonetheless, the low drone was a continual attack on Wood's perpetual headache. Fighting the ongoing pressure, he periodically massaged his eyes with the heels of his hands.

"How are you doing?"

"Do you mean now or overall?" Wood dropped his hands to his side.

"I guess both." Dr. Lap replied. "Don't they go hand in hand?"

"I don't know. I mean, how am I supposed to feel? Becca, my kid, they're dead. My life, everything I ever wanted to live for is freakin' over, gone." Wood looked out the window. He watched two teenagers, walking arm in arm, approach the diner entrance. Wood, turning back to Dr. Lap, his eyes glazed over, "So you tell me. How the fuck am I suppose to feel?"

Picking up his coffee, Dr. Lap briefly stared into the mug. Without drinking, he placed it back on the table. "I don't know but…"

"But fuckin' what?" Wood angrily snapped at Dr. Lap. "You don't, you don't know. You don't know this, this," Wood pressed his palm against his forehead, desperately trying to articulate his feelings. "You don't know what it's like every fuckin' morning waking up, wishing you were dead because you can't take the emptiness. And no matter how much I drink, and how many pills I take, I just wake up again, and again." Pointing his finger at Dr. Lap, "So don't you give me any fuckin' 'buts'."

"I'm sorry." Dr. Lap feebly answered.

"Look, I have friends, family die. And my brother Phillie, he just got up and disappeared. Who the hell knows if he's dead or alive? But this is different. It's, it's like everything was sucked out of me, like a vacuum. When Becca died, and the baby, a big piece of me died with them, leaving this big fuckin' hole inside of me. And it fuckin' hurts." Picking up his fork, Wood stabbed at the fries left on his plate. "You know, I just can't do it anymore. I just can't."

At a loss, Dr. Lap mentally tried to string a series of words into a cohesive sentence. Convincing Wood to return to the college wasn't going to be easy. Yet, he had to do it out of fear of watching his friend slowly kill himself. Again, picking up his coffee, Dr. Lap took a sip and slowly savored its aroma, building up the needed courage. Instead, it was Wood who broke the silence.

"You just don't get it. It's all my fault, entirely mine."

"What?" Confusion replaced weakness. "What are you talking about?"

"That night, I shouldn't have listened to the doctor. I should've stayed." Feeling a slight trickle from his nostril, Wood brushed his right sleeve under his nose. "Instead, I was with you getting drunk and smoking fuckin' weed. I'm not blaming you. Just saying it's my fault. She needed me."

Dr. Lap, having been at the hospital with Wood, knew he was punishing himself unjustly. Becca had a seizure. Although the cause was unknown, the doctor assured Wood that there was no cause for alarm. She and the fetus were unharmed by the event, and as the doctor assured Wood, all vital signs were normal. Not to disturb Becca, who was sleeping peacefully, Wood and Dr. Lap were sent home.

"Don't do this. You know as well as I, that the chance of Becca dying, was remote. You, I, the doctor, we all knew she was fine. She was to come home that next morning. There was nothing anyone could have done."

"Maybe, maybe not. At least I could have been home when they called."

"And what?" Dr. Lap reached over, grasping Wood's hand. "She would have died before they called you. Please, don't beat yourself up."

Pulling away, Wood turned to face the window. Staring out aimlessly, he let the tears flow unchecked down his cheek. The bank clock across the street continued to count the time. Wood desolately watched, as the second hand slowly moved toward the future. A fire burned deep inside him, a desire to lunge at the timepiece, dragging it back several weeks to the time the three of them sat around, laughing over a shared bottle of wine. Dolefully, Wood looked to Dr. Lap and asked, "What am I to do?"

A door was opened and Dr. Lap crossed the threshold gingerly. Wood was vulnerable. Pushing too hard may tip him over the edge. "I think you should do what you do best, teach."

"I'm not too sure about that." Wood's inclination was to flee, to avoid contact. He feared exposing himself as emotionally naked.

"Look you can do this. I mean, in front of a classroom you are one of the best." Cautiously grinning, Dr. Lap added, "In a classroom you were the Great Communicator. Fuckin' Reagan had nothing on you. Besides, how else would you begin to reclaim who you are?"

Wood reluctantly agreed. Dr. Lap cancelled his trip, and assisted in making arrangements for Wood to teach three undergraduate courses in Sociology. In addition, and through the insistence of Dr. Lap, Wood began revisions for a second edition of a Social Psychology textbook he had previously published. Together they worked side by side, developing a syllabus for each of the classes and preparing the book's manuscript. In the few days prior to the new term, Dr. Lap observed subtle changes in Wood. It did not go unnoticed when a weak smile would crack his unrelenting frown. Yet, unbeknownst to Dr. Lap and others, his demons endured.

As if it was second nature, Wood readily recouped his position within the academic environment. He was sharp. Well prepared lectures, each a sea of knowledge, gently peppered with humorous anecdotes, maintained student interest to the final proverbial bell. Questions, challenges were easily met with unshaken confidence. He was on a roll, so it would seem. Slowly the façade was beginning to show it cracks. The balance of his yin and yang was tipping. He was falling apart.

Becca was everywhere. Whether it was a soft scent of perfume lingering in the faculty lounge, a voice rising from a distant conversation, or someone faintly familiar stepping onto a crowded elevator, she was there. No matter how hard he would try, Wood couldn't shake her. So he drank. But the vacuum kept growing, clawing at him, tearing at his soul. The pains of sorrow he could not drown nor would the images of Becca wash away.

It wasn't long before Wood began to show up for class, haggard and unshaven, nursing what had become a daily hangover. Often he would attend class dressed in clothes he had slept in, unchanged for several days. Then there were days he would not show up at all. Dr. Lap and others couldn't help but notice. He was slipping back into his depression. Hoping that he would somehow come around, Dr. Lap insisted that Wood be given some space. But his time began to run out.

It was the week before midterm exams. Dr. Lap stood waiting outside Wood's classroom door. Wood was late. Unsure that he would even show, Dr. Lap was about to dismiss the class when Wood, dressed in wrinkled khakis and an unbuttoned red flannel shirt, stepped off the elevator.

"Hey," he said, trying to walk pass Dr. Lap.

"You okay?"

"Yea, Yea, I'm okay." Wood answered, running his fingers through his uncombed hair. "What's up?"

"Meet me for lunch?"

"Sure." Wood was reluctant. "No lectures, okay."

"Yea, no lectures," Dr. Lap replied. "That's okay, just lunch."

Dr. Lap had waited in the cafeteria for a little more than an hour. Wood's class had long been over and it was becoming painfully apparent that he wasn't going to show. The lunch crowd began to thin out, when Dr. Lap, sitting over a partially eaten hamburger, noticed Dean Trudy arriving through a side entrance. Surveying the room, the dean spotted Dr. Lap and walked briskly toward him.

"Hey Chris, have you seen Wood?"

"No." Dr. Lap answered. "Actually I'm waiting for him. We were to have lunch. Is something wrong?"

"You might say that." Dean Trudy said, pulling a chair from the table, he sat across from Dr. Lap. Taking a handkerchief from his breast pocket, the dean wiped a bead of perspiration from his brow.

"Dean, what happened?"

"Well," Dean Trudy sighed. "It seems like Wood really screwed up this time. The little bastard told a student to go fuck herself."

"Damn, we should have seen this coming."

"Maybe we did." Dean Trudy replied. "We just didn't do anything to avoid it. Anyway, several students filed a complaint. Seems like they were having a discussion and Wood didn't like what he heard. I'm told he walked out after cursing out the class."

"Shit, I need to find him." Dr. Lap stepped away from the table, putting on his jacket. "Anything I can do?"

"I don't know Chris." Dean Trudy replied, standing next to Dr. Lap. "They want him fired. But I think that's moot, I think he just quit."

—

Four-Thirty tentatively listened to Wood relay his story. A slight glaze covered her eyes. She reached out for his hand. In a voice soft as a breeze, she asked him to continue. She needed to know and he needed the closure.

"Well, I guess you can say, I went on a binge." Wood continued. "Then, it must have been several weeks later, one morning, I think it was actually an afternoon, I woke up in this flea bag hotel outside of Camden. I don't know, but perhaps I was heading here. You know, home. Anyway, I had enough of teaching, and all that academic bullshit."

"So you decided to come back here?"

"Kinda," Wood answered. "But, you see there was one thing I couldn't get out of my mind, that student. You know the one I told to fuck off." Wood hesitated. "Well, I wanted to be like her."

"Why?" Four-Thirty curiously asked. "I don't understand."

"You see, that day in class, there was this other student talking about her internship in child welfare. There she was, describing the horrors she had seen, and all the shit some really screwed up parents did to their kids. And this other woman, this rich bitch, actually the wife of the county sheriff, was kinda like saying 'so what'."

"Really?"

"Yea, and she's saying things like that's their environment, you know, their culture and that's how they live. I mean, she was saying that child welfare should stay out because these people, these kids want to live that way." Wood began to scratch his head. "And you know, I'm thinking that these are just kids."

"And you wanted to be like her?"

"Yea," Wood answered. "At first, you know, it was kinda weird. I was standing there thinking that I should be angry, upset with her. I mean, these were kids she was talking about. But I didn't feel it, and I figured it was because of everything else that was going on with me. Then damn, it hit me. If I can't feel anger, then, maybe I could be just like her and not feel anything. Am I making sense?"

"Yea, I think so."

"I just wanted to feel numb. That's all. So I just said 'fuck it' and walked away." Unsure of her reaction, Wood, looking for a sign, glanced at Four-Thirty.

Four-Thirty sighed. In her little world it made perfect sense. She thought about Oria and how their relationship had fractured. It had been agonizing for both. Sure, they have recently been cordial to each other. But life has changed between them. That sacred bond between mother and daughter would forever be tarnished, and their pain will be endless. So yes Four-Thirty understood, and like Wood, she would welcome being numb, even for a fraction of a moment.

Wood stepped off the bench. With Four-Thirty's hand in his, they walked silently down the path toward the park exit. The air was still. The only sound heard, was the gravel crunching lightly under their steps. As they neared the exit, Wood paused. "Do you remember when we were talking about Phillie Wheel's family and, you know, my niece's wedding?"

"Yea," Four-Thirty answered. "Isn't it coming up soon?"

"It's at the end of the month. I decided to go." Letting out a feeble sigh, Wood hesitantly continued. "I have also decided not to come back."

Four-Thirty yanked her hand from his. "No, no you can't do this, no..."

"Wait," Wood pleaded. "Please listen. I'm not getting any younger and I can't do this anymore. I got to get out of here or I'm going to drink myself to death. Something must change." Reaching out Wood grasped Four-Thirty's shoulder and pulled her to his chest. "And you, you need to get out of here too. I mean, I want you to come with me. Leave here."

"You want me..." Taken by surprise, Four-Thirty couldn't articulate her thoughts.

"Do you remember when you, I and Dr. Lap were talking at Paci's? You know, the story about the Volkswagen and me seeing that image of Phillie Wheels?"

"Yea, yea," Four-Thirty responded. "You thought it was a sign you were suppose to die, right?"

"Well, I thought about that again, and I now believe that Phillie was calling out to me. I know it all sounds crazy, but I think he did want me to follow him. I think that he found his peace out there, you know, in Missouri. I think he wanted to share it with me. He wanted me to have my peace. That's why he appeared, and I think that's why he sent his family to me."

"Wood, I just don't understand."

"There's not much to understand. I'm just asking you to go with me. I want you to live with me, you know, as a couple. I mean, that's if you want to come."

"Yes." Four-Thirty didn't hesitate. "But first I need to talk with Oria."

Smiling, Wood described to Four-Thirty the farmhouse, and the plans he had for the two of them. He admitted that he feared being turned down. If Four-Thirty had, he confessed, he would have not gone without her.

As they began to walk again Four-Thirty said softly. "James."

Wood turned. He was taken back, hearing his name. He couldn't remember the last time someone called him by his first name. He has been called Wood so long the name James was foreign to him.

"Strange isn't it," Four-Thirty continued, "being called by your given name?"

"Yea, I guess it is," Wood thought for a moment. "You know, I've had that nickname ever since I was nine. You know the story."

"I think I do."

Making eye contact with Four-Thirty, Wood continued, "A bunch of the guys decided that we were going to build this tree house in old man Pacifico's lot. You know, in that big oak behind where he kept the junked cars. Anyway, we drew up our plans, like kids do, and started to scope out the lumber yard for materials. Not thinking that we actually had to pay for the wood, I jumped the fence and started to throw these two-by-fours to the guys on the other side. Not thinking that we were doing anything wrong, I didn't pay any attention to the workers milling around in the yard." Wood paused.

"Didn't the police come?"

"Yea, the cops were called. The salesmen in the office and the workers in the yard kept watching until they came. I was the only one caught. Not only was I shocked being thrown in the backseat of the patrol car, I was scared shitless. I spent the night in juvie hall, I guess, because I wouldn't squeal on my friends. You know something like that. Anyway, that night some guard in detention kept calling me Wood or Wood Boy. He kept harassing me and wouldn't let me sleep. When I got out all the guys treated me like some kind of hero, you know, for 'doing time'. So I told them what it was like in detention and about the guard. After that, everyone started to call me Wood, even my parents."

"It's strange how people get nicknames and how they stick," Four-Thirty grabbed Wood's hand, adding firmly, "and how they hurt."

A knot grew in Wood's stomach. He knew exactly what Four-Thirty meant about getting labels and the hurt that sometimes comes with the names. After all, it was he who first called her Four-Thirty.

It wasn't long after she moved into the neighborhood. She was hanging out in the park with Wood's little sister Lucia and her friends. They were playing with their dolls, trying to act like a group of mothers, gossiping around the bench.

Wood, fooling around with his buddies, noticed that there was something different about Four-Thirty's stance, and the way she walked. At first he teased her by calling her Duck and Waddles, all along imitating her walk. The others soon joined in with the teasing, forcing her to run away crying. Sometime after the laughter died, one of the guys in the group announced that he had to leave. He told the others he was expected to be home by Four-Thirty.

"That's it," Wood called out. "That's it, look." He drew a circle in the dirt, standing inside he set his right foot pointing straight ahead, and the other pointing to the left. "Look, she's just like a clock, Four-Thirty." All agreed laughingly.

Four-Thirty bent her head, looking into Wood's eyes. He, unable to respond, allowed her to hold his hand tightly. Finally she asked, "Do you know my name?"

Again, Wood remained silent allowing her to continue, "My name is Margaret. And from now on you're to call me Margaret."

"Okay" He answered. "Margaret it is."

Embracing Four-Thirty, Wood, looking over her shoulder, saw across the lake an image of a woman, dressed in white. She, sitting on the bench, was breastfeeding a small child. Illuminated from behind, the woman became strikingly familiar. Wood's heart stopped for a brief moment, when she, looking up, smiled. As she nodded, as if to say "yes", a single strand of braided hair fell from her shoulder. Wood whispered, "That's, no it can't be."

"What?"

Hearing Four-Thirty, he turned for a fraction of a second. Looking back, the woman was gone. Wood knew it wasn't real. It was his imagination, or the lights and shadows playing a trick on him. It didn't matter, he concluded, as a feeling of warmth overtook his body. At that instant Wood knew. "Oh nothing, just that everything will be fine."

Chapter 20

I t will be a celebration Four-Thirty had decided. She could not stop
thinking about how wonderful it felt when Wood asked her to
accompany him to his niece's wedding. Over and over again she played
in her mind, how he told her he intended to introduce her as his fiancé.
She doubted that they would have their own wedding, but she felt
warm, believing that they were a couple.

Unlike Four-Thirty, Wood was not a romantic. After Dr. Lap's
suicide, Wood decided that he had enough of the city, he had to get
away. Phillie Wheel's wife, on several occasions, spoke to him about
moving to her farm. On it was an old farmhouse he could have, and
with a little work he could make it livable. He planned to assess what
he needed to do to the farmhouse, to make it inhabitable, and then
move west. Wanting a companion, and afraid of dying alone, he had
asked Four-Thirty to go with him. Without a hint of hesitation, she
had said yes.

Having a dinner party, prior to their moving to St Joseph, Missouri,
was Four-Thirty's idea. She desperately wanted Oria to meet Wood. Her
relationship with her daughter had changed after the fiasco with Dennis
Slovinski, the county supervisor. She couldn't leave Oria believing that
her mother was nothing more than a call girl, or worse, a street tramp as
Oria called her. She never thought that her child would ever understand
what she did, or why. She wasn't sure she herself knew. Perhaps in

meeting Wood, and sharing with her their plans, seeing her mother settling down, Oria might be more receptive. Four-Thirty didn't have any delusions. Her only hope was that her child would accept her for the mother that she grew to love.

Most of the preparations for the dinner had been made. From Gerbino's Deli she put together a tray of appetizers. She decided that the meal would be a lamb roast, with Yukon Gold potatoes and broccoli in a lemon cream sauce. Dessert was to be Italian pastries, from Aloia's Bakery, and espresso. For the wine, she decided on a Riesling, a perfect complement to the lamb. Anisette was chosen as an after dinner treat.

⁓

Brownie's Home Liquors was just a short walk from Four-Thirty's apartment. She, taking her jacket off its hook, picked up her purse before heading out to the store. The sun had been shining most of the morning, making it a perfect day for a walk. Besides, Four-Thirty knew it would be good for her to catch a breath of fresh air and to exercise her legs.

The gentle heat pressed upon her face as she walked down the street. Yet, the warmth that she felt most, radiated from within. She had never felt this good before. She had never been so happy. Four-Thirty finally found a man that she truly wanted to be with, and trusted that Wood wanted to be with her. She had faith that, in Wood, she found a man who wasn't paying her for companionship and whatever that may have demanded, a man who didn't beat her, a man who wouldn't sell her to another for his next fix. Those days were far behind her, some more so than others.

Turning the corner onto Hawley Avenue, Four-Thirty slowed down as she walked past the Beltrami home. Inside of an opened window sat Mr. Beltrami, wearing a wool Henley shirt and blue suspenders, his ear pressed close to a cassette player. It was a familiar sight, one that Four-Thirty had seen when Oria was a child. Back then, he had an old phonograph from which sounds of opera floated out to the street.

"Morn' Missy," the elderly gentleman called from his window. "How are ya a doin'?"

"Good morning to you Mr. B, I'm just wonderful. You know, I really couldn't ask for better." Four-Thirty answered with a smile.

"That'sa good."

"And how are you feeling these days?"

Mr. Beltrami, lowering the volume on the cassette player, weakly pushed out of his chair and leaned out the window. "Well ya know, som' a days it'sa good an' som' a it'sa not so good."

"Well, I hope you're havin' many more good ones than bad ones."

"I hope a so too, Mr. Beltrami replied. "How'sa your little girl? She must a be fourteen, fifteen a now, huh."

When Oria was younger, she enjoyed walking with her mother, anticipating a visit with Mr. Beltrami. He, upon seeing the two coming toward his building, would get up from the record player, and greet them as they approached his window. Mr. Beltrami never missed an opportunity to tell Oria how pretty she looked. She then would give him a shy smile, as he handed her a piece of Italian candy or pastry.

"Oh, Mr. B, You're off by a few years. She's just a little older." Four-Thirty said. She didn't want to let on that Oria had just turned twenty-eight.

"Ah," he replied, waving his hand. "I'm a justa getting old."

"We all are Mr. B, we're all are." Four-Thirty said, walking away. She thought that he had to be at least ninety. It was obvious that his memory was failing him. "You have a good day."

"You a too, Missy," Mr. Beltrami replied, easing back into his seat.

Continuing down Hawley Avenue, Four-Thirty, approached the Catholic grade school she had attended when her family first moved into the neighborhood. Not much had changed since those times. Although school had been let out for the day, a number of teens were hanging out in the playground. A nun, from the convent, sat along the far wall, talking with a group of youngsters. Another played basketball with several eight graders.

Her walk then took her past the school to the corner, where the church stood. It was at this church, as a seventh grader, Four-Thirty tried to become one of the altar servers, but was turned away by the parish monsignor. "That's why they're called altar boys," he chastised her. Four-Thirty smiled to think she, as a young girl, may have been a pioneer for women's rights.

Crossing the street, she saw No Hope, sitting below the storefront window of Brownie's Home Liquors. "Hey No Hope, how are you?" She asked, approaching the figure reclining on the sidewalk.

Incoherently, No Hope babbled, pointing up toward the entrance to the store. He had been drinking. And, as usual, he was drunk.

Four-Thirty, taking his gesture as a request, asked. "Want me to get you some wine?"

"Gun," No Hope mumbled, again pointing to the doorway.

Misunderstanding what he said, Four-Thirty replied, "Hell, one is all you're getting. Don't you try to sweet talk me into getting you more than a pint."

"No," he insisted, waving his hand frantically, pointing to the door, "no, man, gun, in there."

Realizing No Hope was trying to warn her, Four-Thirty turned, looking inside the store. At that moment the door swung opened. A figure, in a black leather jacket and jeans, pushed his way around her.

"Excuse me miss," he politely said, not making eye contact.

Funny, Four-Thirty thought, Deadeye use to dress in black leather and jeans. Like this stranger, his hair also fell in curls over the upturned collar. Yet there was something else, strangely familiar, that caught her attention. There was something that she saw in his face, something in the jaw line, and his eyes that spooked Four-Thirty. Watching him, hurriedly walk away, was like watching Deadeye walk in his distinctive sway. Deadeye, her long ago lover, the man who left her penniless when she was pregnant, the man she held responsible for her giving up her baby. "No, it couldn't be," she whispered.

Pushing into Four-Thirty with the door, the store clerk momentarily knocked her off balance. "You, son of a bitch," he yelled, raising a rifle.

"Stop!" Four-Thirty screamed, as the crack of gunfire resonating in her ear. She looked toward the stranger, retreating down the street. His body jerked suddenly, when a piercing, burning sensation rip through his left side. Falling forward, he turned, unsteadily raising his right hand.

A second shot rang out. Knocked back against the storefront, Four-Thirty felt a sharp pain tear into her stomach. Clutching her abdomen, she watched her hands turn crimson red. Falling to her knees, she looked up at her slayer staring back, with a confused but welcoming gleam in his eyes. Reaching out, she softly cried, "No."

It was at the moment when Jordan pulled the trigger, at that moment when the firing pin struck the thirty-eight caliber shell, at that precise moment when the gunpowder burst into a small flame, he saw the most beautiful woman he had ever seen. In the brightness of her eyes he saw something faintly familiar. The movie reel of his life began to spin slowly in reverse and at the moment where it ended, at the moment where his life began, at that precise moment he knew. With his head softly hitting the pavement he expired, muttering two simple syllables "Mommy."

Chapter 21

Oria sat quietly on the stoop outside the empty shell of a grocery, which once served as Jennie's Market. Occasionally, someone would come up. In a handshake, money and product would be exchanged. Sometimes words would pass, sometimes not. From the corner of her eye, a familiar figure came into view. She watched, as the old man walked slowly toward her.

Wood was in no rush. His legs no longer could carry him. Approaching the corner, he reached into his pocket and, as he had countless time before, withdrew a small handful of bills. He slipped the money into the waiting hand of Oria, taking a small package in return.

"You look familiar," he said sheepishly. And she did. Wood could not put a finger on it. Yes, there was something about her eyes that he, in his stupor, knew could tell him stories. There was something reminiscent about her face, the line of her nose, the way her lips parted. Whatever it was, it stood hopelessly outside the grasp of his memory. There was something missing, something not right, he thought, as Oria stepped away, avoiding inhaling more of his stench. Without a needed spark, the triggers of his memory misfired.

"Oh man, you say that every time you buy a fuckin' bag," she replied.

She could have easily had said, "You use to fuck my mother." She knew that he was the only man her mother ever talked about. She also knew, that he was the only man she ever loved, wanting to spend her life with him. That was so long ago, in a different life. Even then, Oria didn't think he was something special. Just some guy her mother drank with and talked about. She had heard he was a writer and a teacher, but you would have never known. Here he stood, in front of her, with food and grease stains down the front of his shirt, piss stains running down the leg of his pants. Whatever her mom thought was so special was long lost.

Oria wasn't ready to stir up any memories with him. Besides, if he'd remembered her mother, she wouldn't get rid of him, knowing that he wouldn't stop talking and asking questions. It was best leaving it alone.

"Do we have a date?" a male voice called out from a beige Cadillac.

"Yea," Oria answered. Turning to Wood, she added, "Must not disappoint ya know."

Again, a misfire, something sounding so familiar, yet it remained so distant. "It couldn't be," he thought. "She's gone, she's where?" He shook his head trying to make the scattered thoughts coalesce. Behind a burning sensation, his eyes welled with tears. "I can't. I just can't," he spoke softly to no one.

Oria quickly walked away from the stoop and, just like her mother had done many times before her, jumped into the car. As it began to roll away, Oria leaned out the window, calling out to Wood, "Hey there old man, did you ever tell her you loved her?"

"What? Who?" Wood quizzed.

"Did you ever tell her you loved her?!" She exclaimed.

Wood stopped in his tracks scratching his head in confusion. "I don't, what?"

Oria gave up "Never mind. You're just like the rest of them, nothing but an old piece of shit."

"Huh?" Wood, still baffled, shuffled back to his room. His mind swiftly shifted from the verbal exchange to the package in his hand. Better things to do. Better things to think about. At least he thought so.

Once in his room, he hastily sat in the overstuffed chair. He, pulling from behind the cushion a small box containing his works, began to prepare his fix. He held a belt tightly around his left bicep, while he slowly cooked the white powder in the now blackened spoon. Through a small cotton ball, he drew the liquid into his works. He tapped slightly on the glass, causing air bubbles to rise up the syringe before injecting the warm liquid into his arm.

For a brief moment, Wood looked up, catching a glimpse of Four-Thirty, just a faint glow in the corner of the room, watching peacefully over him. "Hey Baby," he muttered. "How long has it been?" As quickly as she appeared she vanished. Refocusing his attention back on his ritual Wood's eyes fixed upon the track, riding the blue line along the length of his arm. "Yea Baby, it has been a long time."